Red Sun

Swagger, Volume 1

Matthew Waite

Published by Matthew Waite, 2022.

RED SUN

First edition. December 1, 2022.

Copyright © 2022 Matthew Waite.

ISBN: 979-8215348314

Written by Matthew Waite.

Prologue

Decapitating a man with a single stroke wasn't so hard. Though still technically an apprentice samurai, young Takagi had done exactly that on the battlefield many times. The bone was the tricky bit, but if your victim's head was bowed and you could see the vertebrae, you could aim your blow to slice through the disk, thus minimising the depth of bone the blade encountered.

Ending a man's life was simple physics. Takagi had sharpened his sword for hours the night before and when the man kneeling before him presented him with a clear shot at the neck, he'd perform his duty. And he'd enjoy it.

The man kneeling before him was General Yoshi. He was about to disembowel himself. It was a midwinter's day, and snow was falling outside. The small, dimly lit room had bamboo matting on the floor and dark-stained teak walls and rafters. Its aging thatched roof leaked in several places, leaving frozen pools on the matting, and a family of Ryukyu robins huddled against the cold in their nest above the rafters. There was one door at one end and an open balcony at the other. Takagi pondered how serene the location would be in the spring and summer, with the room affording a magnificent view of the mountains and the plains beyond. From this vantage point on Hokkaido Island, where the shoguns had retreated to make a last stand, one might even see the beautiful Uchiura Bay glistening in the west. But now, with snow swirling into the room every few minutes, the location was bleak and foreboding, and hosted the ultimate defeat of the once-powerful warrior class.

Yoshi's Seppuku was compulsory under the shogunate, as he'd failed to defeat the army sent by the Meiji emperor. Takagi held him in contempt for his military failures, and while history would regard Yoshi's ritual suicide as honourable, Takagi felt that Yoshi should have been removed months ago so that the real warriors could secure

1

victory. And if the fat German military advisor that Takagi had met recently was to be believed, victory over the Meiji, and indeed all of Asia, was very much within Japan's grasp.

Takagi was one of seven people in the room. A snow flurry blew into the room through the open balcony. The chill felt good on his tensed shoulders. Seppuku was a solemn affair that required a handful of spectators in addition to the 'second'—the role Takagi was about to fulfil. There were three lesser generals in the room and two servants, all with heads bowed. The room was silent; the only sound was the howling of the wind outside. The jasmine-scented candles had blown out and left the room suitably gloomy. A floorboard creaked loudly as Yoshi shifted his weight to lift the knife from its ceremonial case.

Through the window and the falling snow, Takagi could see distant columns of smoke from the enemy campfires. There would be generals down there patiently awaiting the news of Yoshi's death, after which they could complete their takeover of the island. But Takagi was certain he would live to defeat them and return things to the way they were before the Meiji had usurped the shoguns.

The restoration of the Meiji emperor in 1863 had ruined everything. Aging, complacent shogun warlords had let it happen. Takagi had wept when the city of Edo, the beating heart of the shogun empire, had capitulated to the emperor's forces and undergone a name change. Edo was renamed Tokyo, and its former rulers retreated to country estates and put away their swords. Proud old warriors were now tending their bonsai gardens. Not like Takagi's father, who had died gloriously in battle. He'd never have surrendered. And he might have lived had he received the reinforcements he'd needed at the Battle of Hakodate.

Ten years earlier, Takagi was there when American warships had entered Kyoto harbour, foretelling the end of Sakoku, Japan's splendid isolation. He was a boy of ten holding the hand of his father and wondered why the big-nosed, smelly, and unkempt foreign devils weren't being slaughtered as soon as they set foot on Japanese soil. His history teacher had explained how that was the usual fate of foreigners trying to enter Japan for trade. Foreigners couldn't be trusted. Whatever their stated reasons for visiting, their ultimate aim was domination. Why else would their trading ships carry such big guns?

The shoguns of old had known how to deal with foreign devils. For centuries they'd expelled them and kept Japan pure. That era was over, but Takagi could imagine the warrior class rising again. He conceded that Japan needed to trade with other, inferior countries but from a position of power.

Takagi looked at the columns of smoke in the distance and let out an audible sigh. It wouldn't be easy. He faced an uncertain future in a new world. Weapons technology had moved on, and he regarded the use of firearms as cowardly—where's the honour in killing at a distance? It's not satisfying unless you can watch the life fade from their eyes—he had to concede that such modern weaponry would have to be part of the future shogunate he envisioned, as would engagement with other countries. No, he thought, not engagement. Domination.

A loud grunt brought Takagi out of his reverie. Yoshi had plunged his knife into his abdomen and was pulling the blade from left to right across his body. Takagi didn't wait for him to finish. He swung his sword down hard on the man's neck and the severed head hit the floor with a thud. Blood dripping from his face, Takagi sheathed his sword and stormed out of the room before the head stopped rolling along the floor. He had an empire to build and no time to waste. He also had an appointment to keep with an enigmatic German, who had promised to show Takagi an easier path to dominion over not just Japan but all of the Orient.

Chapter One

B y this afternoon I could be dead, or in repose with a euphoric opium high in a comfortable chaise. It was 50/50, and I obviously hoped for the latter.

It was Summer 1894, and I found the notorious crime boss I sought at his home in the suburbs of Dongying, northern China, reclining in a cane chair in the shaded courtyard of his walled compound. He looked irritatingly relaxed. A wrong'un in repose. I'd walked from my office at Customs House as the sun rose to its zenith, through the leafy diplomatic district, down here to the disreputable quarter of town. I watched the opium dealer through a barred opening in the compound wall as sweat trickled down my neck.

This particular dealer had many irons in many fires: prostitution, protection, and all manner of contraband, including opium. My sources told me he struggled to get his hands on the good Indian opium and had to settle for the Turkish variant. This was being brought into China by American entrepreneurs who had cottoned on to Britain's genius idea that addicts made good repeat customers—if they lived long enough. Despite the well-established overland routes, the foreigners brought their drugs into China by sea. They called these seaways 'trade routes', which deftly masked the fact that they were simply drug-running rat lines.

It would normally be my duty to arrest this man, but I was out of opium, and this dealer was the only one in town with whom I still enjoyed some credit. Hopefully.

I leaned against the courtyard wall next to the gate and pondered how I'd approach the subject of extending my credit. Pathetic pleading or bluff and bluster? My job as a tariff inspector at the Imperial Maritime Customs Service, the IMCS, brought with it a modicum of status in the community, and that afforded me some leeway with the criminal classes, but it was not infinite.

Sweat dripped from my nose. In this part of northern China, the summer sun beat down like a hammer. Dongying hugged the northeast coast of China on the Yellow River delta and endured sultry summers and freezing winters.

I was alert to the fact that the dealer would have watchers stationed outside his compound. I counted six as an intoxicating spectrum of scents assailed my nostrils, from jasmine to fried noodles, from steamed buns, or bao, to raw sewage. The bao seller pushing his cart slowly along the lane was definitely one of the dealer's henchmen. The distinctive bulge of a Mauser pistol interrupted the line of his cotton tunic, which was altogether too clean for a baker. I'd been seeing the German handgun more and more lately, as the German colony in the east of the province expanded. Skirmishes were frequent, and on the rare occasions when Chinese rebels came out on top, they came away with some state-of-the-art weaponry. No doubt the crime boss I was about to accost could sell me a Mauser C96 if I asked.

Small for China, Dongying's population was around half a million, and they were all very busy. A rickshaw clattered down the road behind me carrying two giggling Western women holding brightly painted parasols. The nut-brown coolie pulling them looked about a hundred years old. His *que*, the long plait that the Han Chinese were forced to wear by the ruling Manchu, was as slate-grey as my dealer's silver front teeth. I figured the Western women were seeing how the other half lived.

They stopped giggling when they looked at me, tilting their heads like spaniels, apparently unsure as to which half I belonged. I wasn't sure myself. My mixed-race features made it difficult to slot me neatly into a known category. I was born Phillip Swageman, carrying the surname of my father, Archibald Swageman, formerly of the

British Royal Dragoons. Mother was Chinese, and they never would say how they met or how they wound up in the remote north of Australia, where they raised me. I was given the nickname 'Swagger' in high school and was thankful that my nickname hadn't been 'chink' or some such. 'Swagger' would do, and it was what all my genuine friends called me.

"You gonna loiter out there all day?" said the dealer.

Damn. He'd detected my presence, no doubt from a signal by one of the watchers. I turned the latch on the gate, strode into the courtyard and stood in front of the seated dealer. "Just enjoying the sunshine."

He grunted his way to a standing position, put his hands on his hips, where they rested on the butt of his two guns. He tilted his head to one side, less like a spaniel and more like a Doberman, and narrowed his eyes. He was only a few inches shorter than me, and though he was not short of money, he liked to sport a peasant's brown tunic and canvas shoes. A gangster of the people.

He spat on the ground and said, "I suppose you want a pound or so? And I presume you don't expect to have to pay for it. At this rate, you'll have used up all your credit by the time that shipment gets here. Where is it, by the way?"

"Oh, yes, it's well underway. Eight bales of Bengali Gold, the best quality opium out of India you've ever seen, or smelled, for that matter. Much better than your Turkish product. It'll be here any day."

My best friend, Jack, and I had hatched a plan. When we first arrived from Australia, we both got jobs with the Customs Service, and we kept our eyes peeled for opportunities for graft. When Jack was transferred to Korea, he found himself overseeing legitimate opium imports and had figured out how to skim some off the top. I was to take care of the distribution end of the scheme.

Having told the dealer about my delayed shipment, I returned his stare as benignly as I could with a grin that I hoped didn't look as idiotic as it felt. I fondled the telegram that was deep in my pants pocket. It was from Jack, who was supposed to have sent our first batch by now. Our inaugural shipment into which all our money had been invested. And his telegram, now two weeks old, told of further interminable delays. Even more ominously, he hadn't replied to the telegram I'd sent him eight days ago. I was worried, and I hoped it didn't show.

After giving me his death stare for what seemed like an eternity, his face softened into resignation. He sighed and shook his head. "You're out of your depth, posh man. You don't belong in this business." He gave me the stare for a little longer, and his silver teeth glistened in the sun. "Look, I can hook you up with someone who—"

"I don't need any help, thank you *very* much. I can handle this." I cut him off before his unwanted advice turned into a diatribe. I was *not* out of my depth. Opium smuggling was a doddle, and Jack and I could skim from the bales of the stuff in customs warehouses as easily as breathing. If we could distribute it ourselves, we wouldn't even need a dealer. What I didn't need was a lecture on my suitability for the noble trades of graft and smuggling. What's the point of having a job with access to sought-after commodities if not for the entrepreneurial opportunities for lining one's own pockets?

No one ever got filthy rich on a salary. To hear my father talk, you'd think our family belonged among the aristocracy, or would, were it not for the inconvenience of a complete absence of funds. I wasn't trying to single-handedly rebuild a mythical family fortune, but I was at least smart enough to realise that the road out of serfdom was paved with neatly stacked piles of cash. Oh yes, I knew what I was doing and needed no advice from a semiliterate, small-town crime boss.

Besides, this crime boss had only recently been the mere lieutenant of this criminal empire. The former head was killed in a fight, and the man standing before me, the second in charge, took the reins. No doubt *his* lieutenant was now pondering how to get a fight started that might hasten his own ascent to the throne.

China was like that, like Grandad's axe. He'd replaced the handle four times and the head twice but reckoned it was the best axe ever made. There were eight powerful nations vying for dominion over the Middle Kingdom, as well as factions in the Imperial Court in Beijing. There'd be a takeover of some sort soon enough. It was as inevitable as annual droughts, floods, and famine. It made little difference to the coolie in the street or the fields. Their serfdom continued under whichever oppressor had won the last fight. The next victor would be just another new handle.

Jack and I had been forced to stretch ourselves to secure this contraband opium shipment. Silver wasn't worth what it used to be. I'd read something in a newspaper about how the USA went into a depression last year and had stopped buying silver for their treasury, switching to a gold standard. Something like that. I didn't understand the economics vernacular too well, but the result was a plunge in the price of silver. This was the metal the Chinese government had borrowed against to pay reparations for imperialist wars started by Europeans that the Chinese had had the bad manners to lose. The victorious European powers were kind enough to loan them the money to pay the reparations, which was very sporting.

Silver still had the same buying power for local goods and services, but anything imported, like our precious Bengali opium, had tripled in price.

The dealer grunted, turned on his heel and went inside his house through a beaded curtain and didn't invite me in. I told myself he was fetching some opium for me and not a Samurai sword with which to separate my shoulders from my noggin. While I waited for him to get me another pouch, I turned my back on his dwelling and looked out through the gate. Despite the heat, Chinese people were bustling in the dusty streets in their usual industrious yet somehow unhurried manner. Peasants led oxen pulling carts of produce towards the market or pulling empty carts away from it and back to their allotted plot. One thing I liked about China was the respect granted to those producing food—the peasant farmers. The country seemed to experience a famine almost every single year, caused by any number of natural disasters. Sometimes even corruption. Farmers, therefore, were valuable, and well-dressed ladies gave each passing farmer a polite nod.

I wiped my brow and neck, and my handkerchief came away brown with grime and dust. I hoped that later today the traditional sea breeze would fill in and clean the air.

My dealer reappeared through the beaded curtain and handed me a one-pound bag of the pungent opium resin, which I stuffed into one of the capacious inside pockets of my woollen IMCS blazer. Why did the Brits always make uniforms suited only for their own dreary climate? The blazer constituted a uniform in the customs service. It was simply a grey jacket cut like a suit jacket but with the IMCS insignia embroidered onto the top pocket. We were free to wear whatever business-like attire suited the local climate, so long as the blazer was worn when on official business. Buying opium was definitely *not* official business. In fact, it would result in instant dismissal if discovered by my superiors. But I needed the status the IMCS bestowed upon me.

My dealer's grapevine was both extensive and effective. Formidable though it was, his willingness to give me another pouch on credit, albeit reluctantly, indicated to me that news of the delay in my shipment had not yet reached his ears. But it would, and soon. As we parted, he'd said he'd give me one more week.

The fact that I worked for the prestigious IMCS wouldn't prevent my dealer from cutting off my thumbs if I were to default on the debt. His less-than-kindly façade hid an even worse callous indifference to human life. His only reason for not killing me was the prospect of the eight bales I'd promised him. The bales that hadn't even left Korea yet, as far as I knew.

I needed to talk to Jack. Today.

Chapter Two

I thanked my dealer for the opium and turned and walked away along the footpath in the general direction of Mrs. Chow's. My mouth was already watering at the contemplation of a bowl of her legendary drunken chicken ramen noodle soup. My stomach rumbled, but I had one more appointment to keep before I would get to Mrs. Chow's.

I walked under mulberry trees that lined the road and gave welcome shade and presently arrived at the stables via the rear entrance to Customs House. Constructed of unpainted teak, the sturdy shack seemed to skulk behind the building it was attached to. The little compound smelled of manure, and the straw—used to absorb the faeces—crunched underfoot.

At the sound of my footfalls, my horse, Mistral, turned to look at me through the glassless window. Seeing her usually helped me forget my troubles and count my blessings, chief among which was my friendship with her. Coming a close second was my cushy job with Customs and the access to contraband it afforded. I was posted in a peaceful outpost and enjoyed ample amounts of opium and sex. I also got to escape the city on a thoroughbred from time to time to clear our heads. Mine and Mistral's. There, blessings counted.

When I got close to her, she snorted and shook her head. She was agitated, and I immediately saw why. There was a piece of paper attached to her ear with a hatpin. Blood from her pierced ear had trickled down the pin, staining the paper, which simply said 'No hiding place'. I started to gingerly pull out the hatpin, but Mistral shook her head violently, tearing it out herself, and leaving me holding the pin with horse blood on my sleeve. When she calmed down and stood still, I dabbed at her wound with my handkerchief and scrunched up the note.

Obviously, it was a message from the dealer to make sure I knew he could get to me and my loved ones should I cross him.

I took a brush from the shelf and brushed Mistral's flank, a meditative activity that usually calmed my mind, but the anger and worry didn't subside. My dealer wouldn't put up with my promises indefinitely. I was running out of ideas about how best to hold him off. And no matter how uncomfortable things got for me in China, I couldn't go back to Australia, not until the heat died down. If it ever would. I was still wanted for questioning about my perfectly innocent role in a labour uprising in Darwin. I'd have to go somewhere else if things went pear-shaped. But where? And would she come with me?

My co-conspirator in my fledgeling opium smuggling career was my friend Jack Spratt, head of the Opium Tariff Department of IMCS Seoul, Korea. And yes, he'd endured jokes about his name all his life. The old rhyme about not being able to eat fat had rung in his ears so long that he no longer paid it any heed. He said that it gave him an insight into the intellect of the speaker; that anyone stupid and conceited enough to imagine that he'd never heard it before, Jack could immediately write off as an intellectual pygmy.

We had become firm friends aboard the *Pearl of Malaya*, a trading steamship that plied the waters throughout the eastern Orient. He'd boarded the ship in New Zealand, fleeing from a shotgun wedding. I met him at the rail when the ship docked at Darwin. He later handed me a tattered book and told me to read the passages he'd circled in pencil. The book was by Friedrich Engels and was a weighty philosophical tome about class struggle. Much of it was self-serving claptrap, but the parts about the concept of wage slavery struck a chord with me, as Jack had intended. I was sure the book's readership was supposed to conclude that some kind of collective peasant uprising was needed to purge society of all its ills, but Jack and I had a different take. We reckoned that the real message of the book was 'If you can't beat 'em, join 'em', and we determined to team up in whatever enterprise would elevate us to the realms of the rulers, not the ruled. We would not remain proletariats. We would become entrepreneurs, by means fair or foul.

Many a fortune had been made trading opium. American traders like Forbes and Delano had started wealthy family dynasties selling the drug to the Chinese, and the proceeds funded huge infrastructure projects like America's transcontinental railway, which also used the Chinese as indentured labour. One newspaper editorial I'd read opined that America's rise would not have gotten off the ground had it not been for the exploitation of the Chinese.

Demand for the euphoric drug continued its exponential growth year on year. This was a river of cash, and we figured that dipping our buckets into the flow was our way out of serfdom.

Jack's role in our devious enterprise was to allow a modest amount of opium to 'slip through his fingers' and make its way to me and then sold on to my dealer. Jack's coded telegram two weeks ago said he'd found a suitable smuggler and that he'd send me another telegram when the shipment left the docks. The first shipment would cover my debt by a good margin. From the second shipment onwards, the proceeds would be pure gravy.

Mistral turned one eye and one ear in my direction, as if she could read my thoughts and was telling me I was a fool and I'd blown my investment. That Jack was spending up a storm five hundred miles away with my money. That I'd never see it again and will have to endure a future with no thumbs, if I remained alive at all.

"Shut up, or it's off to the glue factory for you."

She turned back to face forward again and snorted. I took a step toward her hindquarter and started brushing her tail. She didn't know Jack as I did. She wasn't there when the excrement hit the fan, and Jack and I had gone from being mere acquaintances to being comrades in arms, swearing loyalty to one another to the end. True, if my bosses at the IMCS got wind of my little sideline, I'd be out on my ear, unemployed in China and unable to return home. I'd starve, in gaol, probably.

She stamped a hind hoof when I switched to brushing the back of her leg, near her arse. That was the sweet spot I'd been working towards, and she quivered with ecstasy. I was blessed indeed to have a horse. Long rides with her through the countryside were my meditation, my sanctuary, requiring an intensity of focus that left little room in my busy mind for other concerns. After a spirited ride through challenging terrain, we'd stop for a break, and I could barely remember my own name, such was the mental cleansing I'd experience.

Though I had to pay for her stabling and care, I hesitated to say that I was her owner. We were friends and partners, and she very definitely had her own mind. Any commands I gave her while riding she regarded as mere suggestions. She'd literally go her own way, and I had to admit that her way was usually a better idea than mine.

When she became 'mine', she already had the name 'Mistral', presumably named after the strong winds that sweep down the Rhone Valley and blast southern France every winter. Old Ting, the stable master, called her JinFeng, which means 'Golden Wind' in Chinese, probably because of her blonde mane and tail.

Her previous owners were descended from the Huguenots, or so they'd said. They'd hoped to have bred a race winner, but winning races requires a capacity for following instructions. Mistral didn't have that. And as for the jockey who used a whip on her? Well, he'll be alright, so long as he has someone to mush his food for him for the rest of his life.

Luckily for me, Mistral was put up for sale rather than being sent to the knackery.

I put the bridle over her head, threw the saddle onto her back, and tightened the strap. I led her out of the stable into the yard, and then I climbed aboard. That was the end of my input into the activity; she knew what to do. She turned into the lane, and we cantered westwards. I shaded my eyes from a hazy sun, now low in the sky. A sultry and muscular man leaning against a lamppost on the other side of the lane watched us intently as we passed. *Henchman or idler?*

We turned west on the main road and as we moved further from downtown Dongying, the foot traffic diminished and the houses became smaller and spaced further apart. In no time at all we were galloping through forested foothills and cooler, cleaner air. If I'd known what tomorrow would bring, we'd have kept going until we reached Europe.

Chapter Three

At my desk the next morning in my office at Customs House, my hands still smarted from clutching Mistral's reins the evening before, while she'd galloped through the foothills on the outskirts of Dongying. My office was a little cubby-hole at the western end of the corridor on the second floor. Waist-high dark-wood panelling with water-stained plaster above painted a nauseating pale green. The end of my wonky desk was against the wall under the only window, so I could stare vacantly at the sky—sometimes visible through the oft-present mist one finds in the east—when I should have been working. Sadly, I couldn't see the sea from my window, though I could smell the canal, which is why the window was closed almost all the time. Through its grimy pane I could see the very same man I'd seen outside the stables yesterday. He stared up at me from the street, and using his thumb and index finger, he mimed firing a pistol shot at me. The period of the dealer having me watched covertly had come to an end. Now I had henchmen openly threatening me.

I stretched my fingers and started drafting yet another coded telegram to my partner-in-graft, Jack Spratt. Maybe he'd reply this time. Not knowing when the opium would arrive was shortening my lifespan.

Telegrams had revolutionised communications in the Middle Kingdom, and we ran them. The IMCS had all the most modern conveniences; it financed the laying of telegraph wires along the entire east coast of China, from Honkers to Vladivostok, and the very latest Wheatstone Morse machine had been installed in every office. Messages were written longhand, given to the operator to be translated into Morse code, then transmitted. The message was received down the wires at the other end in the form of a punched tape, again in Morse. The receiving operator translated the Morse into words and wrote them out longhand on a pad with carbon paper underneath, the top copy for the recipient, the carbon copy for the files. Truly miraculous and unimaginable only a few years ago.

When I communicated with Jack about our under-the-table matters via telegram, I had to write them in a numbered book cypher, where the numbers referred to page and line in a specific book. The book was *Crime and Punishment* by Dostoyevsky. Jack's little joke. I'd have to write a simple message on a pad and then scan through the book to find a page which contained the first word. Then on another page of the pad I'd write the page number, line number, and how many words in from the left margin the word appeared. The result was a group of three numbers that represented that word and where to find it in the book. The process was repeated until the entire message was reduced to a long string of numbers, in groupings of three. The cypher was unbreakable unless one knew the book it was based upon, and even then, one would have to know the exact edition, or else the page numbers wouldn't match up. Obviously, I'd have to burn the original message after I'd coded it.

I took out my yellow pad, and the tattered book from the squeaky top drawer of my desk, but before I could begin coding my message, I heard footsteps in the hall. I shoved the book and the writing pad back into the drawer. Dickinson barged into my office waving a telegram and wearing his most supercilious smirk.

Alistair Algernon Smythe Dickinson. The second offspring from the venerable middle tier of the British aristocracy. Entitled, skilled in bluster, and superior in every way. He was only an inch shorter than me at six foot even, but he could grow a respectable moustache, and that was reason enough to hate him. My upper lip steadfastly refused to produce any decent foliage. And if his parents really were cousins, as rumour had it, he was probably proud of the fact; keep the riffraff out of the bloodline.

Amongst those kinds of families, the first son inherits the father's title and usually custody of the estate, becoming literally lord of the manor, with tenant farmers kowtowing to him and everybody in the local village referring to him as 'your Lordship'.

Second sons, therefore, had a massive chip on their shoulder, resentful of the spoils bestowed upon the elder sibling by virtue of nothing more than the accident of birth. Second sons had to make their own way, often in the military with bought officerships. Dickinson senior had bought his second son an upper-strata position here at the IMCS, Alistair being far too stupid to be put in charge of men and weaponry. At least, that's how I liked to imagine it.

Dickinson stood in my doorway and leant against the doorjamb. "The enquiries I made with the Australian authorities have borne fruit. This little gem arrived this morning." He waved the telegram some more like he was trying to dry the ink. "It's for Nelson himself." That was the nickname of the head of the IMCS, Dongying office—so named because he had only one eye and insisted on wearing his Navy tie every day. "It's from the Darwin Police, demanding that you be sent back there for questioning."

I sighed loudly and stood up, making a pantomime of extreme lethargy to conceal my concern. I sauntered to the doorway as casually as I could and went to grab the telegram.

He snatched it away, out of my reach. "You're for it now. I told Nelson he shouldn't hire a chink, especially one as uppity as you."

"If more of you Brits could learn the Chinese language, the IMCS wouldn't need to hire a half-caste *chink* from the colonies. But none of you can master it, can you? Too many generations of aristocratic inbreeding have left you bereft of wits." I let the insult sink in for a moment and then continued, "Why don't you show me the telegram? Huh? Could it be that it doesn't say what you claim?"

"Lowly clerks don't get to peruse management's communiques."

"Then, fuck off."

"Having a British papa won't help you now. Your demise is imminent, and I'm going to enjoy every minute of it." He turned and minced swiftly down the hall.

Dickinson was a mid-level administrative functionary, technically only one level above me within the IMCS hierarchy. But he was right; there was another, unspoken hierarchy, based on parental wealth and country of birth. I worked under an invisible ceiling made of class.

Now I was annoyed. How dare he question my bona fides for this job? My Australian references were beautifully crafted by the finest forger in the southern hemisphere. Thankfully the IMCS was always desperate for bi-lingual staff, and I speak Mandarin like a native, thanks to Mother, and English like a Brit toff, thanks to Father. And it pleased the Chinese government officials when they could see a few 'local' faces among the IMCS workforce, which didn't want to be perceived as a foreigner enclave, a club. So no one looked too closely at my references. Thank goodness, as they were one hundred percent fiction. I thought I'd made them impossible to check, but Dickinson was resourceful and determined, damn him. I'd had the signature of a recently deceased lieutenant-colonel forged at the bottom of the fabricated service record. I'd thought that was a clever touch by Giuseppe, the forger. But Dickinson's queries may have been able to poke holes in the veil of lies. We'd see.

I liked it here, and I wanted to stay. At home, I was a half-caste chink nobody, but in China, I was faring better. I could pass as Chinese well enough. I was tall for a Chinaman, but my brown eyes and black hair meant I was regarded as one of them. As an IMCS staffer, I enjoyed a little respect, though that was tempered by a hint of resentment from the locals when they saw me in uniform. Somehow the Chinese people can harbour both resentment and respect at the same time. Yin and yang, I suppose.

Largely staffed at senior levels by foreigners, the Imperial Maritime Customs Service was notionally controlled by the Chinese central government. Only it wasn't. It was effectively established by foreign consuls in Shanghai in '54 to collect maritime trade taxes that were going unpaid due to the inability of Chinese officials to collect them during the Taiping Rebellion. Its responsibilities soon grew to include customs administration, postal administration, harbour and waterway management, weather reporting, and anti-smuggling operations. We mapped, lit, and policed the China coast and the Yangtze. We conducted loan negotiations, currency reform, and financial and economic management. The IMCS published monthly Returns of Trade, a regular series of Aids to Navigation, and reports on weather and medical matters. It also represented China at world fairs and exhibitions, ran some educational establishments, and conducted some diplomatic activities. Brits dominated the staff of the IMCS, with the help of some Chinese, Germans, Yanks, and Frogs.

The IMCS collected about one-third of the revenue available to the government in Beijing. Additionally, foreign trade had expanded rapidly now that we had made international trade regulated and predictable. Foreign governments benefitted because there was a mechanism to collect revenues to repay the loans they had imposed upon (by force of guns) or granted to China.

This massive growth was the work of the venerable Robert Hart, who had joined the service back in '63 and had been running it ever since. He transformed Chinese Customs from an antiquated setup, anarchical and prone to corruption, into a well-regulated modern organisation, which contributed enormously to China's economy.

The Imperial Mandarins had wanted to supplant Hart with one of their own but were terrified of making any changes to the great cash cow. It helped that Hart was loved by the Empress Dowager Cixi. Her recent retirement, however, threatened to change Hart's favoured status. He'd been awarded the Qing dynasty's Order of the Double Dragon, among other accolades.

The diminutive Bible thumper enjoyed high status in the Middle Kingdom, a status that would never have been granted to an Irishman if he'd worked with the British government.

Speaking of status, I needed to get that cable away to Spratt. Infuriatingly, though, my masters had a new torment in mind for me.

Chapter Four

Dickinson came back a second time, blast his eyes, and I only just got my notepad and book shoved back into the drawer before he reappeared in my doorway barely ten minutes since his last intrusion into my office. Much to my frustration, my coded telegram to Jack would have to wait. Something would have to be done about Dickinson. He wouldn't rest until I was out on my ear.

He must have seen me closing the drawer. "Don't bother trying to write to your mate, Spratt. Word of his incompetence has spread, and the problem now needs intervention."

Shit. How much does he know?

"You have been summoned to a meeting. Follow me." Dickinson led me upstairs to an enormous office at the eastern end of the hall, the posh end where the mould smell was replaced with sweet incense and the walls scrubbed and painted a duck-egg blue. He knocked on the richly varnished mahogany door, then opened it and went inside. I followed. A meeting was in progress, and Dickinson introduced me to two seated men, one Baron Hans von Heineken and his assistant William Ferdinand Tyler. They sat at a long table, and Dickinson took the only remaining seat. I stood at the head of the table like a schoolboy at an oral exam, ready to recite my times tables.

The one introduced as Heineken was sweating in his brown, three-piece woollen suit. He was a sizeable man, and his waistcoat buttons were stretched to their limit. His straight back made me suspect he was a retired military man. Some of his bulk looked to be muscle, the rest fat. He wiped his brow with a yellow silk handkerchief that had a monogrammed 'HvH' embroidered in blue thread at the corner. He spoke through a cloud of pungent cigar smoke. "Ah, Mr. Phillip Swageman, glad you could join us."

I was the only one in the room with only two names and expected to be given a laundry list of pointless tasks that these

25

multi-named management types doled out to minions like me after their meetings and luncheons.

I looked to the ceiling to try to place the name, though the answer wasn't written in the plaster above. "Heineken, Heineken..." I was damned if I would call him "baron." "I think I've heard of you. Were you at one time a military advisor to the Japanese?"

Dickinson shot me a look that said, unequivocally, *know your place.*

But Heineken gave me a benign smile. He didn't seem to mind that I'd addressed him by his surname. "You have good recall. I was hired to help them implement a system of military conscription. The old shogun warrior class was dead against the notion of conscripts. But there are just too few of them to fight in modern warfare. I convinced them otherwise, and they now have thousands of conscripts in training. That concluded my work there, and now I'm on assignment here with the IMCS."

Dickinson tried to insert himself into the conversation to show he kept abreast of current affairs, "That's the kind of thing the Chinese need. Their military is a mess."

Heineken replied to Dickinson's unsolicited opinion with just a touch of condescension, which was gratifying, "Thank God that the emperor is back in his rightful place. In charge. Now maybe we can see some real reform in this country."

I was reminded of my mother's words, "Cixi is a depraved despot". Thankfully, the Empress Dowager Cixi had retired, and the real emperor, though still young, could finally take the reins after decades under her thumb.

"What's your assignment here?" I said.

The assistant, Tyler, chimed in. "We are to go to Seoul. All communications with the IMCS office there appear to have been severed. There has been no news and, more poignantly, no funds coming out of Korea for two weeks now. Robert Hart is very concerned, and we have been asked to go there and find out the lay of the land."

Well, that would explain Jack's lack of contact.

Heineken picked up where Tyler left off. "The political situation there is tense. The Chinese and Japanese military are there, the Korean Royal Family are always having little tantrums, and there are still remnants of the Donghak rebellion yet to be extinguished. The IMCS office could be working perfectly and merely have had their telegraph wires cut; or they could be all slaughtered and the office set ablaze. We just don't know."

Dickinson spoke and his eyes bore into mine. "Besides, there are administrative anomalies to investigate. Opium tariff revenue has been lower than expected, and it has been suggested that there might even be some corruption—"

"No one's suggested corruption," Heineken said, cutting him off. "Really, Alistair! We're just going there to see what we'll see. We'll deal with what we find. We make no assumptions ahead of time."

I enjoyed hearing Dickinson being smacked down and hoped I'd hear more of it. I was taking a shine to this German. I asked, "Respectfully, Herr Heineken, why am I here in this meeting?"

"Your language skills, my boy. We've had Alistair here compile a dossier of all matters relating to Korea, and we need you to translate the parts that are not in English. Especially transactional data. Here's the file." He tapped a manila binder on the table.

So, it was to be tedious minutiae, as predicted. Understandable, though. There were some subtleties and nuances to the Korean patois and characters that few native English speakers, no matter how well trained in Mandarin, could decipher. But I could.

I picked up the dossier, though it was little more than a bundle of loose papers inside a binder. It would be a simple enough task, and I had to admit that I was just a little flattered that I was the only staffer that could do the job. As to the transactional data, I'd be keeping my eyes out for anything about opium smuggling. The illicit endeavour that Jack and I had embarked upon was unlikely to have any kind of paper trail—Jack wasn't that careless—but I'd check and redact from the dossier anything from which the wrong inference could be drawn. Or the right one.

I was dismissed, and I took the file back to my office and dumped it in a drawer.

I had only been back in my office for ten minutes when I realised it was almost lunchtime, so I decided to head out for a celebratory lunchtime smoke on the old pipe. Celebratory because at least I had learned the reason why I hadn't heard from Jack. Maybe the shipment was already on its way, but Jack couldn't tell me because the telegraph was down?

Hope triumphed over pessimism, and I headed for my usual den. Unlike most of the opium dens frequented by the locals, the one I was on my way to had private cubicles that contained a reclining chair and a table, atop which was all the accoutrements for a euphoric foray into the abyss. It was still a dark basement, like all the dens, but this one serviced a better-heeled clientele and had an entrance on a secluded back lane, away from prying eyes. The perfect place for a respectable IMCS man to imbibe discretely.

Out on the street, the day was stiflingly hot and dusty. I slung my IMCS blazer, inside out, over my shoulder. I was trying to be incognito. My route took me from the clean and orderly business and administrative district, which was nearest the water to take advantage of the infrequent cooling sea breeze, to the grimy and chaotic residential area where the Chinese lived.

A straw hat shielded me from the worst of the sun's rays, while sewage flowing in the gutters made my nose hairs curl. I wiped the sweat from my neck with my handkerchief. As always, it came away brown. I should buy brown handkerchiefs.

As I rounded the corner of the lane, I saw and heard that a loud argument was in progress in front of the circular gate in the wall of the opium den's courtyard. Four people were shouting and gesticulating. Their shouts were loud enough for me to discern the languages, which told me that the argument was between two Korean women and two Chinese men. As I got closer, I could make out more of the shouted words and could see that the men were wearing the dusty beige uniform of the Chinese infantry. The topic under heated discussion was the power struggle between China and Korea. I stopped walking and hovered about ten yards away to wait for the antagonists to move (or be moved) away from the den's entrance. I found a shady spot under an apricot tree overhanging the lane and was joined by a merchant. We watched the drama unfolding across the lane.

The merchant turned to me. "We'll see more of this in the coming weeks."

"Why do you say that?" I was interested in the merchant's take on the topic. I was privy to all kinds of reports that the IMCS circulated to its staff, but it was always worthwhile to hear the word on the street.

He pointed his chin toward the two harridans remonstrating with the two Chinese soldiers. "You heard about the uprising by the unpaid Korean soldiers? Those women. They're widows. Here looking for work. They're saying their husbands were killed by Qing troops. The men they are arguing with are Manchu, same as the Qing."

I remembered the reports. Heineken had not been exaggerating. There sure was big trouble brewing in Korea. The drought of '92 meant the soldiers didn't get their usual wages, which were normally paid in rice. What little rice was harvested was snatched by corrupt officials. The soldiers mutinied, killing Japanese and Korean officials alike. The rather sexy Queen Min escaped, dressed as a peasant. The

Chinese Empress Dowager Cixi, who was still in charge then, sent Qing troops to quell the uprising because she worried the Japanese might use the incident as a prelude to war. "Fair enough. I'm glad Queen Min escaped the trouble, though."

The merchant gave me a gap-toothed grin. "She is sexy, isn't she?" I smiled, and he continued, "Her husband, the King Gojong, signed a trade treaty with the USA and a couple of European countries. The Japanese are going to get savage in Korea, just you wait and see."

He was right about the treaty, but it wasn't the only thing infuriating the Japanese. They'd apparently demanded reparations for the soldiers that were killed during the uprising. By way of reply, Chinese troops arrested King Gojong's son, Daewongun, and imprisoned him near Beijing. He was still there today, two years later.

Korea was thus reduced to a semi-colonial tributary state of China, with King Gojong unable to appoint diplomats without Chinese approval and with troops stationed in the country to protect Chinese interests. "You might be right. If the Qing wanted to humiliate the Japanese, then it's job done. You heard about the attempted coup? King Gojong just can't take a trick."

The merchant let out a brief chuckle. "Just when we'd all hoped it had settled down, a coup was staged by pro-Japanese reformers. The idiots thought China was too distracted fighting the French in the south to get involved."

"Yeah. That was pretty stupid." I took out two cigarettes, lit them both, and handed one to the merchant. "The Qing troops were reinforced and thrashed the Japanese." This defeat had marked the nadir of Japanese influence in Korea and an increase in Chinese influence. The Japanese seethed.

The merchant scoffed. "That's not the real problem. What really stinks is that treaty. Why should we have to make deals with those Jap savages? We beat them fair and square!"

He was referring to the Convention of Tianjin, which pledged China and Japan to withdraw their troops from the peninsula, and each had to give prior notification to the other if troops were to be sent to Korea in the future.

My boss, many rungs above me, Robert Hart, wrote at the time, "So we win all-round," about the Convention of Tianjin. More recently, referring to a possible Sino-Japanese conflict, Hart wrote, "Big China is blithely confident that it can defeat Little Japan." There was more than a little sarcasm in that missive. I said to my companion, "I wonder how long it'll be before the Japanese have the strength and the audacity to attack China."

The merchant snorted again and spat some green-brown phlegm onto the ground. "It'll never happen."

"I hope you're right." If the rumours were true and the Japanese military machine had grown as strong as some believed, then they might just have a shot at clobbering China, whose underfunded, corrupt and antiquated military would struggle to repel them, despite superior numbers.

The argument in front of the den wasn't the first one I'd seen over Korea. The fight had gotten physical, and much as I didn't want to get involved, I didn't like the idea of two soldiers beating up two women. It looked like that was imminent.

I put the blazer back on, walked over, and stepped between the antagonists, pointing to the IMCS crest on my breast pocket, while I gave them my best withering stare. I held my arms out like I was Moses parting the waves and told them to cool off and walk away. I wasn't police, but an IMCS uniform still commanded a little respect among ordinary people, especially when the wearer spoke their language. It helped that I was at least a foot taller than any of them.

After a few parting insults and hand gestures, the men turned and walked away down the lane. I turned and told the women to walk away in the other direction. They spat on the ground and walked away. Finally, the entrance to the den was unobstructed.

Alas, the chat with the merchant and watching the argument had consumed my lunch break. A smoke would have to wait until tonight. I'd better spend the afternoon at the office like I'm supposed to, especially with a new Prussian VIP on the premises. In hindsight, I should have taken the afternoon off and smoked myself silly.

Chapter Five

With my blazer slung nonchalantly over my shoulder, I walked across the road to Customs House. The building was a three-storied affair of stuccoed brick with a handful of polished marble highlights here and there. I'd been told that it was modelled on the imposing edifice of Customs House in London, only about one tenth the size. Apparently, the British had built similar buildings all over the world using the same template. Even though ours was stucco pasted over locally produced bricks, it looked like solid stone and gave the desired impression of British permanence. The marble over the entrance and surrounding the windows was a mere cladding, not more than an inch thick. It was an impressive façade concealing a utilitarian structure.

I skipped up the granite steps and entered the cool vestibule. The streets had been quiet on my short walk back from the opium den by virtue of the post-lunch nap that the locals favoured. It was a most civilised custom and one I wished we would adopt. The reception desk pointed at me like the prow of a galleon, and I was about to skip around it and head upstairs when I was stopped by Mary, the friendly and officious receptionist and gatekeeper. But she wasn't her usual cheerful self; she was in a state of high agitation, and the blood had drained from her already pale face. She scurried out from behind her counter and grabbed the lapels of my blazer. She'd never before come within two feet of me, or any man as far as I knew, so this much intimacy meant something very serious indeed if she needed to use my jacket to prevent her from collapsing.

"The Seoul office has been bombed! One dead, two injured!"

I felt like the floor had fallen away, like it does on a gallows. Stunned, I plied her with questions. "When? How? Who's dead?" She had no answers, she just buried her face in my chest and sobbed and sniffled, while I was jumping out of my skin to find out more.

We remained in that embrace at the foot of the stairs for minutes. I gave her my handkerchief and she dried her eyes, then filled it loudly with the contents of her nose. "Keep it", I said, when she offered it back to me. She stopped crying and took a step back, turned, and walked to her desk where she sat down, eyes downcast.

I raced downstairs to the basement where the telegraph machine and its operator were ensconced and asked the inscrutable Harry for more detail. He looked up from his chaotic desk and turned his pale and jowly face to me. There were no windows down here, and the dearth of sunlight was making Harry look more like a mole every day.

I spoke first. "I thought the telegraph wires were out. Cut, probably. How did this information come through?"

I liked Harry. Unpretentious and detached, he wasn't about to dampen my jacket with tears. He'd give it to me straight. In addition to operating the telegraph, he was also in charge of the archives, and to talk to him, one would think he'd read every document in the building. "The bombing happened three days ago, and yes, the wires were cut. Took that long to find the break because it was in the underground section of the cable some miles from the office building. They were only reconnected this morning, and this was the first message through. The head man in Seoul, a German named Möllendorff, sent the message as soon as the break was found and fixed."

There was only one staff member whose welfare concerned me. "Do we know who's dead? Who's injured?"

"Unnamed as yet. It's probably political."

I had a feeling in my bones that the dead man was Jack. It could be anyone. I knew that. And maybe I was paranoid because I had so much riding on him. But the hairs on the back of my neck were standing on end, and a shiver ran through me as if someone had walked over my grave.

A bombing, no less. Korea must be far more turbulent than I thought. With so many antagonistic factions running about with their own ideas of what's best for them, I guess violence shouldn't be so surprising.

But terrorism? I doubted it. In my experience, the more someone claimed to be doing something for the good of the people, the more certain it was that they were lining their own pockets somehow. Whether it be a peasant uprising or a military action ordered by royalty, the motives were usually equally venal, the only difference being the degree of sophistication. Somebody's snout was deep into the trough.

The more I thought about it, the more dread I felt, and the more convinced I became that Jack Spratt was almost certainly targeted. As a Customs man in charge of enforcing tariffs, he would have made enemies as a matter of course, as had I. But as a fledgeling opium smuggler, he'd attract antagonism of a higher magnitude. It'd be easy to make enemies that were far less squeamish about violence.

Or maybe Jack simply screwed the wrong person's wife. He had serious Yellow Fever, falling in love or lust with every Asian woman he met, bless him.

Whether or not Jack was the target, this plunged me into serious trouble with my dealer, who would find out about the bombing sooner or later. Probably sooner, his being the most extensive, almost mystical, grapevine I'd ever encountered. The dealer knew that Jack was my partner-in-graft.

Harry broke my reverie. "Have you met the German?"

"What? Oh, you mean Heineken?"

"Yeah, the broke baron."

Broke, was he? "We didn't discuss his financial position."

"He's Prussian aristocracy, that one. Family fell on hard times. That'd be why he's slumming it in the colonies. Has to work for a living."

I could see it. Heineken had an air of the ruling classes about him. A bit like my father, whose demeanour resembled that of an unjustly impoverished aristocrat. "Maybe he's here to rebuild the family fortune."

Harry pondered that a moment. "Maybe. Rumour has it that the family pitched their last hopes on buying up silver. Thought the Yanks would keep on buying it forever, pushing the price up. Spent their last pennies on it, I heard. Even borrowed. Like a lot of people. But it crashed, as I'm sure you know, when the Yanks changed their mind. Bought some myself. The wife still gives me grief over it."

"Maybe he should have bought gold. The silver thing pushed up the gold price."

"That's what the wife tells me I should have done. Everyone's an expert after the fact."

I thanked him for the information about the bombing and declined his offer to go out for drinks after work. He'd have to find another way of avoiding going home to his wife. I left the basement, heading for my office. I needed more information, and I needed to think, and I figured that having a stimulant and a suppressant at the same time was the way to do it.

On the way, I bumped into one of the coolie staff on the stairs. Jim, we called him, though his name was Cim. I asked him to fetch me a cup of coffee from Miss Sophie's coffee house across the street. Most everyone in the building drank tea, which I detested. After some instruction from me as to the finer points of preparing good coffee, Miss Sophie's had rapidly become a popular establishment. Thus it was that my coffee was always free and first in the queue.

Coffee order placed, I proceeded to my office. I sat at my desk and rolled a cigarette. Tobacco, obviously. Any IMCS staffer found merely in possession of opium, let alone imbibing it, was dismissed on the spot. I stared out of the window and watched the street below and saw Jim coming out of Miss Sophie's carrying a silver tray with a teapot—inside which I knew the ground beans were steeping—two small cups, and a little milk jug.

Before he could cross the road, a burly Chinese man stopped him. It was not the same man who had been watching me earlier. I had to lean out of my window to watch the two men. They spoke only a few words to each other before Jim crossed the road and entered our building. When he arrived in my office, I basked in the coffee aroma for a moment as he set the tray on my desk. I handed him two coins and asked who he had been speaking with in the street.

"I don't know him."

"What did you two talk about?"

"He asked who the coffee was for, and I told him."

"Nothing else?"

"Nothing, sir."

I doubted that. Jim left my office, and I poured some coffee. I could see out of my window the man who had spoken to Jim loitering near the entrance of Miss Sophie's. He'd have to be another of my dealer's henchmen, of that I had no doubt.

The caffeine and nicotine now coursing through my bloodstream didn't do its usual magic for my thought processes. I needed to formulate a strategy that would secure my opium shipment in the likely event that my partner was dead. Knowing I had a shadow watching me from across the street made it hard to think. I finished my coffee, butted out my cigarette and walked out of my office and went downstairs. As I passed other offices, I heard snippets of worried conversations: "I knew it could be dangerous here, but bombs?" "Might that happen here?" "Surely, the IMCS is too valuable to be put at risk?" "The Qing need us, need the money we make...", and such like. The building held an aura of stunned anxiety.

But until we knew more details about the bombing, there was nothing to be gained by worried speculation. I walked behind the reception counter, through the kitchen and slipped out the back door. It was mid-afternoon, and no one would miss me. My role often required me to be out of the office, visiting merchants, and so forth. I needed to think things through, away from here.

Behind the IMCS building were the stables, with their own gate out onto a laneway. Mistral stopped chewing straw when she saw me approach.

"Yes, things are tense. Let's ride."

She spat out the straw, and it hit me in the face. She neighed loudly, which was horse-speak for, "About bloody time!"

I grabbed her saddle and bridle off the hook on the wall.

I'd been speculating for weeks that the opium enterprise Jack and I were starting might need a personal appearance in Seoul. It had been too nerve-wracking to be so dependent on Jack's diligence in the matter. Two heads would have been better than one.

I was coming round to the view that I simply needed to get to Seoul. The bombing made it a necessity. Jack might be dead, and he might not. But too much of my life was not under my control. With a dealer on the warpath, and Dickinson trying to get me fired or worse, it was time to regain control. I would try to get myself on the team that Heineken had put together to sort out the Korea operation. I needed to be there.

I led Mistral out of the back gate and down the lane, confident we couldn't be seen from the street in front of the building. Her coat could best be described as golden caramel, and her mane and tail were blonde. She was handsome, and she knew it. At seventeen hands, she was tall and thus stood out from a crowd, by far the tallest horse any Chinese had ever seen, which made it difficult to go about unnoticed. I doubted that my watcher was the only one of my dealer's henchmen tasked with keeping an eye on me, but no one this side of the Yellow River had transport as fast as Mistral.

After a few turns down narrow cobblestone lanes, Mistral having to duck her head under overhanging ginkgo trees, we joined the main road west. I jumped into her saddle, and she cantered. The foot and cart traffic thinned as we traversed the outskirts, and I was just about to give her a nudge with my heels when she broke into a gallop. One day I'd figure out how she knew these things before I did. She set a good pace, fast but not so fast as to exhaust herself. In her former abortive racing career, she was being trained as a distance steeplechaser, so she knew how to conserve her energy.

After passing smaller settlements outside of the city, we soon had the landscape to ourselves and began to ascend. There's something very special, something cleansing about motion. Most people talk about travel in terms of destinations: *"Darling, I'd like to see Constantinople,"* or *"Wouldn't it be just divine to see Paris in the spring?"*

Phooey. I didn't care where I was, just so long as I could move through it. It's simply the movement, and I was sure Mistral shared my feeling. Travel is a verb, after all.

As we climbed, the track narrowed, and Mistral chose to slow to a canter, the terrain being a little rockier. We moved on up to the kind of mystical landscape that one sees depicted in so many Chinese paintings. Limestone pinnacles shrouded in humid mist, dotted with ghostly trees clinging tenaciously to steep hillsides, and precariously balanced boulders of red or grey granite. The kind of landscape that inspired the holy men and philosophers to pen their cryptic tomes. Every Chinese person had a memorised store of enigmatic philosophical life-lessons to draw upon for any given situation. It was maddening sometimes, but in a landscape like this, I could understand it. Even empathise a little.

I dismounted when we got to the top of a little mountain. I unsaddled Mistral and removed her bridle, and she went off in search of tasty alpine lichens and mosses, which she loved.

I reclined against the crumbling walls of an old, neglected temple, got out my pipe, and packed it with the dried opium-tobacco mix. I lit the pipe with some American wax-tipped matches and drew deeply. I closed my eyes and rested my head on the stone. I could almost feel my bloodstream extracting the elixir from my lungs and journeying to all corners of my body and brain. My imagination began to expand gradually, and it dawned on me that our office in Dongying was not the closest one to Seoul. The IMCS had quite a large office in Dalian, on the Liaodong Peninsula, which was just a hundred or so miles across the Yellow Sea from Seoul. Before the news of the bombing, the problem that Heineken was being sent to solve was one of mere severed communication with the Korean office. He and Tyler were going there to find out the communication problem and solve it. What had Heineken said? Something about having been asked, by the big cheese himself, Robert Hart, to go to Seoul and find out the "lay of the land." There had to be more to it than just severed communication. One could send a technician for that. What'd happened to the IMCS Seoul's technician?

Now that I thought about it, why send a consultant and military expert like Heineken, at all? There must be some other agenda, something from higher up the chain of command. Something well beyond merely finding out the "lay of the land".

A bombing is a lot more serious than a severed telegraph cable. The IMCS would have to send a proper investigation team to Seoul, maybe even a platoon of soldiers. And we, in Dongying, were not the closest.

Heineken must know more than he let on. It was equally apparent that he was calling the shots about Seoul. He had some secret remit, and I didn't need to know it to know that I must go to Seoul with him. I hoped that news of the bombing necessitated a complete change of plans. Whatever the real agenda, I had to insert myself into Heineken's team.

The peaceful surroundings and the opium had given me my next step, as I'd hoped. I didn't have a longer-term strategy, but I had made one decision, and that was enough for today.

Besides all the practical reasons, Jack was my friend. One is supposed to do something when one's friends are murdered. Assuming he is the dead IMCS officer. He saved my life on the ship from Australia the day I learned that no matter how loudly the voices in my head tell me I can fly, it's not true. Opium strikes again.

I'd need every ounce of the Swagger charm to make sure I was at Heineken's side if and when he departed for Korea.

We rode back to town while the sun set. It was too late by the time we got back to town to put Mistral back in her pen at the stables, so I left her to spend the night in the yard behind the apartment house where I lived. She'd be okay in the open. Rain was very unlikely tonight. I kissed her goodnight and entered the building via the back door and went upstairs to my room. My landlady brought me up some dumplings for dinner. I ate them and turned in early, formulating a devious plan for the morning.

Chapter Six

I woke before the sun, and my dim room still held the scent of the previous night's dumpling feast. Through my grimy window I could see the pre-dawn glow. I burped and farted simultaneously and rolled out of bed. The window squealed when I opened it, and crisp air came in to replace the funk. The street below was already alive with carts clattering their way to the markets hauled by both men and beasts. I gave myself a 'sailor's bath'—wiping my face, armpits, and nether regions, in that order, with a damp cloth—dressed and left the room, taking the back stairs to the yard. I needed Mistral; there was something I needed to do before I got to the office.

My apartment building was one of the few in town with electricity, and all unmarried IMCS personnel lived there. My apartment was small, or 'cosy' as the landlady described it that first day. Most of my colleagues aspired to get married and live in one of the larger houses with outer walls, gates, courtyards, and servants scurrying about taking care of one's every need. I was happy here. It was compact, but it contained everything I needed, and the staff took care of laundry and some simple meals. More space would just mean more complications and more expenses. The apartment building wasn't much to look at, especially from my vantage point in the back yard. It was four storeys tall, constructed of red brick with a terracotta roof. It had little tile dragons on each corner of the roof to protect us, and almost every window had some kind of improvised clothesline holding drying garments. There were shirts, underwear and even dresses strewn around the yard, having fallen from their owner's clotheslines. I didn't know why they bothered. The landlady did laundry for a very modest fee.

Mistral was up and ready in the yard when I got there and gave me a nibble on the back of the neck as I secured the buckle of the saddle under her belly. I noticed a mattress nearby with most of its stuffing missing. The contents of the mattress were strewn about the yard. It must have had cotton stuffing. Mistral loves the taste of cotton, for some reason. The stable hand at the IMCS stables, old Mr. Ting, nowadays sported a tunic with leather patches on the shoulders. The poor fellow had had the shoulders of his cotton tunic bitten into, not just nibbled, when he turned his back on Mistral one day. He'd needed stitches. I'd paid to have him stitched up by the local sawbones and barber and had a silk tunic made for him. I'd had the shoulders covered with leather, just for good measure.

The landlady here sometimes left a smelly mattress outside to air, but this one must have been too delicious for Mistral to resist. So we fled the scene before anyone saw the incriminating evidence.

We rode through the misty morning light to Dickinson's compound, which was one of the larger walled houses in the posh foreign dignitary district. It was typical of the kind of houses the IMCS appropriated for its executives. This was a seven- or eight-room villa surrounded by a high stone wall. I could see that atop the wall broken glass was embedded in the mortar. The entrance gate was a circular archway, inside of which were two semicircular wooden doors with an ornate iron framework. Quintessentially Chinese and all aligned with auspicious feng shui. Dickinson and his family managed to get by with only five servants. One's status within the IMCS could be measured directly in terms of the square footage of one's abode and the number of fawning coolies.

I dismounted from Mistral, and we stood together on the footpath opposite the gates to Dickinson's compound. As I'd hoped, his driver was just pulling his shaded rickshaw up to the gate. I left Mistral and rushed across the road. I got to the uniformed driver before he had put down the poles. "Mister Dickinson won't be needing you today. He's not well and will spend the day at home."

I handed him two silver coins. He bowed and pulled his rickshaw back the way he'd come. That should delay Dickinson's journey by about half an hour, which was all I needed. The irritation he'd experience was merely a bonus. It was impossible to get a rickshaw for the morning rush without having booked it in advance. He'd have to walk to work, like the lower ranks.

I remounted Mistral, and we cantered the four blocks to the office. The sun was well above the horizon and the day was warming up fast. Mistral took odd detours to either side of the road to try to walk in the shade. Our strange zig-zag course drew indignant curses from pedestrians and cart-haulers as we cut them off. I smiled and waved. Road rules weren't Mistral's strong suit. When we got to Customs House I dismounted and led her around to the stables at the rear. Then I handed her reins to old Mr. Ting, who said he'd heard us coming. I walked across the dusty courtyard and entered the building through the iron door at the rear, the tradesman's entrance. My mouth watered as I walked along the corridor past the kitchens billowing spicy steam. This area, the back end of Customs House, was where the 'help' worked and thus had low ceilings and was poorly lit, giving it a gloomy countenance. The next doorway I walked past was the scullery, and the clang of pots being scrubbed was deafening. I caught a glimpse of the women up to their elbows in scalding soapy water. I went through the heavy door at the end of the corridor and entered the more presentable section of the ground floor and headed for the staff pigeonholes under the counter behind the reception desk. Mary wasn't in yet, and there was nothing in my pigeonhole. But there was a folded piece of paper poking out of Dickinson's. I looked around to make sure I wasn't being observed and then pocketed the paper.

I left the building via the front door, dodged a rickshaw and an oxcart as I walked across the road and entered Miss Sophie's. The collection of brass bells and wooden chimes above her door announced my arrival in the crowded café like a fanfare. I took a stool in the window and sat watching the entrance of Customs

House. A coffee arrived at my elbow without me asking. When I'd first arrived in Dongying, there was no competent coffee maker within a hundred miles. For my own selfish reasons, I schooled Miss Sophie and her niece in the finer points of brewing coffee, and I like to think that the subsequent prosperity her café enjoyed had something to do with me. I sipped contentedly, wondering what to have for breakfast.

I was just finishing the coffee when I saw a hansom cab pull up in front of Customs House. The driver got down from his seat and opened the door of the cab. Heineken stepped down to the pavement. I jumped off my stool and rushed across the road, nearly getting cleaned up by another hansom cab, whose driver had a few choice words of rebuke for me, but I didn't have time to stop and tell him that my mother was not, in fact, a rodent. Heineken must have heard the commotion because he turned to face me as I arrived at the pavement.

"May we talk, Herr Heineken? Can I buy you a coffee before you go inside? Miss Sophie makes the best, in fact, the only drinkable coffee in town."

"Why, yes, thank you. Though I can only stay a few moments, we have a lot to organise. Can you be ready to leave by tomorrow?"

I stared at him for a few moments before my wits returned. "Leave? Where? To Seoul?"

He chuckled. "Where else? Forget the dossier, we need your language skills in person. The bombing," he added, as if I might have forgotten.

Ah, that was a relief. That was what I wanted to achieve and the whole reason for orchestrating this time alone with him. He'd answered the question I had not yet asked in exactly the way I'd hoped. Perhaps he was telepathic.

We crossed the road together and entered Miss Sophie's. I held up two fingers and nodded to Sophie behind the counter. Heineken and I took a stool each at the bench up against the front window next to the entrance and looked out onto the street.

Heineken gave me an appraising look. "The unfortunate event doesn't change our remit; in fact, it merely broadens it. In addition to examining the operation, we'll need to recruit replacements for Mr. Spratt and the two injured assistants. As well as coordinating the investigation with the local police to bring justice to the perpetrators."

I felt like someone had punched me in the solar plexus. "You've received confirmation that the deceased was Jack Spratt?"

Miss Sophie delivered our coffees and withdrew.

He tilted his head and imbued his words with a sympathetic tone. "He was a friend of yours, I gather. Yes, we received a second telegram this morning. It was his office that was bombed, and given the location of his office, the back corner on the second floor, it is obvious that he was the target."

He sipped his coffee in silence, perhaps knowing that I needed a moment to digest the information. Minutes passed. I stared into my untouched coffee cup. Heineken took me by the elbow and led me out of Miss Sophie's and across the road.

By the time we began to ascend the steps outside the IMCS building, I had recovered my voice. "I see. Thanks for letting me know."

"My friend, you might even get a chance to avenge him. Officially, your role will be to help me recruit his replacement, but I also want you to do what you can to assist the local police in finding the bombers. What with all the turmoil in that blighted region, I imagine the police will be an inept bunch, corrupt and slovenly, so you must push them to arrive at a satisfactory result."

"That would be my pleasure, sir." It would be the least I could do for Jack.

"I've left a sheaf of papers on your desk. They're carbons of all the most recent telegrams received at the office from Spratt. They're all routine, but you might see something in them I missed."

"You think they might contain some clue as to why Jack was targeted?"

"Perhaps. You might have a better idea than I who he might have, er, irritated."

A rickshaw pulled up at the kerb behind us, and that seemed to signal the end of our chat, the end of my allotted grieving period. The big German turned to go through the doors at the top of the steps, then stopped and turned back to face me. "Keep a weather eye on the chief of the Seoul office, Möllendorff, too. He's a little too chummy with the Korean King."

"Really? What should I—" I didn't get to finish.

Dickinson appeared on the footpath. It must have been he who had alighted from the rickshaw I'd heard behind me. So, he'd found one after all.

Heineken saw him too. "Morning Alastair, you simply must try the coffee across the road. Only back home in Königsberg have I tasted better. Swageman, be sure and study those telegrams, then go home and pack." He turned and entered the building.

I plastered onto my face my smuggest grin and faced Dickinson. "Yes, Dicky, you simply must try the coffee."

He stood close to me and tried to look menacing, though with his full lips, he just looked petulant. "Don't think getting pally with that Prussian prat will save your bacon. Let's see if you still have a job here when you get back. I have eyes everywhere. Any day now I'll receive a reply to my enquiries with the Darwin police. Then your goose is cooked, buster!"

"Do let me know when I'm in any serious trouble, Dicky. I'll be shaking in my boots until then." I turned and went up the steps and entered the building. As I went through the double doors, I pulled the paper from my pocket, the one I'd taken from Dickinson's pigeonhole. It was from the Darwin police insisting that I be returned to Australia on the next available steamer.

I felt Dickinson's eyes on my back as I walked past Mary, now at her desk, and ascended the stairs to the second floor. I went straight to my office.

Having gotten onto the Seoul team solved one problem, but I'd be closely supervised and scrutinised. Dickinson almost certainly had 'eyes' in Seoul, as he'd claimed, possibly Tyler or Möllendorff, or maybe both. The telegrams Heineken had spoken of were on my desk. There were only about a dozen, and I shoved them into my pocket.

The rest of that day and the morning of the next saw me preparing for departure with high hopes. I said farewell to Mistral and told Mr. Ting that I'd be away for a week or so. He knew what to do, knew that she needed to be taken out once in a while, or she'd get claustrophobic and kick the stable to splinters. He was a little afraid of her, but I knew he'd take good care of her. I spent a lovely evening in the opium den and later slept like a log in my apartment. By three in the afternoon the next day I presented myself at the gangplank of the *ZhenYuen*, a German-built battleship of the Beiyang Fleet, the best of China's fledgeling Navy. She had been ordered to go to Korea to keep an eye out for any Japanese Navy arrivals, and we were hitching a ride aboard her.

I always enjoyed visiting the docks. My work brought me here often. The whole area was a hive of activity with an air of exotic industriousness. The *ZhenYuen* was tied to the southern end of the wharf and as I looked northwards, I could see the thousand-foot-long wharf stretching into the misty distance. The rust-streaked hulls of the ships nuzzling the wharf rose imposingly skyward. To my left were rows of warehouses where goods and people—both considered commodities here—were processed for import or export.

Docks were places of leaving for adventures and of triumphant homecomings. Places of trade and entrepreneurialism. People were busy; trading, negotiating, departing, and arriving, goods and people. Here it felt like I was in some kind of portal where modernity arrived to push its way into a sleepy land. Countries grow through trade, and here it was apparent to all that China could never again be the insular kingdom it once was. Goods, humans, and ideas were coming here in an unstoppable wave like an advancing army. The world was entering China through her ports, whether she was ready or not.

But a rising tide does not, in fact, lift all boats. Boats with holes sink. Foreign powers knew all too well the strategic value of controlling ports. They'd been commandeering ports all over the world for centuries. Here they'd fought wars to swipe the ports and then demanded to be compensated for their casualties during the war they'd started. The Chinese would never forget such humiliations, but they were powerless to stop them. They had long memories, though.

Nevertheless, I liked the docks, the gateways to the world. I was both early and hungry, so I bought some tofu soup from a cart by the wall of one of the warehouses and sat on a rough teak bench blowing on the steaming liquid.

The soup seller apparently felt the need to make small talk with his customers. "You going somewhere interesting?"

"Korea."

"Aboard that big ship just there?"

"Yup." I held the bowl up to my lips and took a gulp.

"You working for the Brits?"

I showed him the IMCS logo embroidered on my blazer pocket.

"Customs man, eh? Stamping out corruption in the lawless lands. So you can pocket the spoils yourselves."

Marvellous. A soup seller with a chip on his shoulder. I was glad he hadn't figured out who I worked for before he served me. He'd have spat in my soup. I drank faster.

"The Brits took this port by force from the Qing. About six years ago now. Did you know that?"

By way of reply, I slurped soup as loudly as I could.

"Course you did. You know what that was like? Imagine someone broke into your house and beat you up and stole your stuff. Then imagine they stood in the doorway and demanded payment every time you wanted to use the door. That's what it's like when—"

Mercifully, his diatribe was interrupted by a coolie wanting some soup.

I'd finished mine, and I stood up, grabbed my bag, and strode quickly away.

At the top of the gangplank, I was welcomed aboard by a deferential Chinaman in lieutenant's uniform and shown by a steward to my cabin. I was delighted to find that I had it all to myself. It wasn't a stateroom, but the simple fact that I didn't have to share a cabin made me feel that I'd been elevated in status. It felt good. I'd already forgotten the soup seller's rant.

I dumped my bag, left the cabin, and took a turn around the shaded lower deck. After a lap of the ship, I took the stairs to the upper deck and completed a lap of that too. Ships can be so labyrinthine; it takes a little time to get one's bearings. On the sunlit upper deck, I stopped and rolled a cigarette. Leaning against some kind of funnel, I watched British officers drilling Chinese sailors on how to use the equipment, both the machinery for operating the ship and the artillery mounted to the turrets. One group was being schooled by a very proper looking brigadier, who had a smartly pressed khaki suit complete with waistcoat and tie. Sweat ran in rivers from his brushed peaked cap and soaked his collar. His ginger muttonchop sideburns glistened in the sunlight. The Chinese listened respectfully as he showed them the breech slide of a turret-mounted cannon, but they hadn't received the memo about ironing one's uniform, and at least three of them were barefoot, hopping from one foot to the other on the scorching steel deck.

I was pleased to see the enormous guns, barrels twelve inches in diameter at least, one of which was pointed at me. The rifling inside swirled into blackness. There were two guns in each of the two rotating turrets, one to port, one to starboard, and just one of the shells to feed these monsters took two men to lift. I felt safer seeing such large and brutal ordnance. If there were Japanese warships out there prowling the Bohai Sea, they'd think twice about tackling the *ZhenYuen*.

I turned and left the officers and the rumpled but eager trainees and walked along the port side deck to the stern rail. From that height I could cast an affectionate eye over the city. Though I was keen to get to Korea and sort out my future, I was missing Dongying already, just a little. Over the low slate roofs of the waterfront warehouses, I could see the usual bustle in the streets and the dust it kicked up, swirling skyward. I had a sense of place here. I hoped I'd return soon, and I hoped I would return triumphant.

Heineken joined me at the stern rail, catching me ruminating upon how precisely to get things sorted in Korea swiftly. They targeted Jack, I felt sure, but why? And who? Was it because of our modest graft? Or was it something political?

"You look pensive, my friend." He smiled at me like an uncle.

I wanted to gently sound him out, wanted to know his attitude vis-à-vis business dealings that might be not quite by the book. "To tell the truth, I'm a little worried that our investigation into the bombing might find something less than savoury about Spratt's dealings in his role as Tariff Officer. Business is not always straightforward in our line of work..."

His smile broadened. "Rest assured, Phillip. Whatever we uncover, I see no advantage in broadcasting anything that might tarnish the late Mr. Spratt's reputation. None of us is blameless. Glass houses and all that."

If only you knew, mate. Or maybe he did? Some of the biggest opportunities for graft can be found near the top of the tree. Maybe Heineken's 'bent'?

Tyler arrived at the stern rail and whispered something into Heineken's ear. Heineken excused himself, and the two of them left the stern. I walked to the starboard side and looked out over the ocean to the horizon. I could hear the shouts of the dock men and the rumble of the engines. I felt the ship leaving the dock.

I stayed on deck, and within an hour, Dongying was merely a brown smudge on the southern horizon. There's something special about the sea. The knot in my stomach subsided with every mile we put between the ship and Dongying. I hoped my gut was wiser than my head, which was apprehensive about the coming days.

Chapter Seven

Dinner was served at the captain's table once we were well underway and out of sight of land. I'd watched Shandong recede to the south-west and had stayed at the stern rail, daydreaming, when a steward tapped me on the shoulder to ask if sir was ready to come down for dinner.

At dinner I met Captain McGiffin and his senior officers, and an air of jovial bonhomie accompanied the four-course meal. We had schnapps as an aperitif, Beaujolais with dinner, and cognac and cigars as our digestif.

The officers' mess was cramped. It was entered through an oval doorway and the steel door had one of those wheels in the centre. I asked about it, and the steward explained that it was a watertight door and would protect the ship from sinking if a torpedo tore this section of the hull apart. He spoke with pride about the ship's protections, and I'm sure he was trying to reassure a landlubber that he was in safe hands. But by painting a picture of explosions, torn steel and drowning, his words had the opposite effect.

After dinner, I went to my cabin. I sidled sideways through the narrow door, grabbed the sheaf of papers from my bag and sat on the edge of the bunk. It was time to have a thorough read of Spratt's IMCS telegrams by the weak light of the bare bulb in the ceiling. Maybe, as Heineken had suggested, there'd be something I could glean from them. As I skimmed each page, I found that they had a lot to say about legitimate opium movements and tariffs but gave no indication of anything about our clandestine shipment of Bengali Gold and how it would be shipped to Dongying. That was good and bad. I was itching to find the trail of our opium, but I was glad that Jack had kept his cards close to his chest.

The telegrams were mostly political reports on the deterioration in Chinese/Korean relations. Collectively, many of the telegrams outlined the problems caused by Japanese influence in Korea. There were some telegrams reporting on meetings with diplomats, some giving a precis of missives from King Gojong and his Queen, the enigmatic Min. Some telegrams summarised local newspaper reports. Standard tariff officer weekly reports.

One telegram gave details of a meeting of diplomats where the king's representative restated the palace's rejection of Japanese reform proposals. Mention was made of the Japanese representative there, a certain personage named Masamoto, but no surname was given.

Everyone knew how badly the Japanese wanted Korea, and every action they took, every diplomatic meeting they attended, was directed towards that end. The game in Korea had become one of simply holding the Japanese at bay.

The IMCS was supposed to be a disinterested observer in such matters, but of course, we were anything but. The Japanese would surely take over the customs service if they invaded. Our revenue would be just too tempting to resist. But did they have the balls for that? Could they even pull it off?

What was furrowing my brow, though, was one question. Could eliminating an IMCS staffer, Jack, serve that Japanese agenda somehow?

And who was this Masamoto character? It was vexing. How could Spratt take notes at an important meeting and neglect to give the surname of the Japanese representative? He might be guilty of many things, but sloppy admin wasn't one of them. If he neglected to properly identify someone in an official report, he would have had a damn good reason. I needed to know what it was.

Near the bottom of the pile of telegrams was one from Spratt to the IMCS regional director, Eastern China, Nelson. Spratt had asked for formal permission to marry a local girl, whose family name, Yi, rang a bell somewhere in the belfry of my brain. I remembered there had been a noble family, part of China's landed gentry, with the family name 'Yi'. It was a common name in China, less so in Korea. In fact, if memory served, King Gojong's son, Daewongun, the one imprisoned in Beijing, carried that family name.

If Jack had fallen in love, then good luck to him. Unless it was a distraction from our important business, I couldn't begrudge him that. But could Spratt's death be an elaborate crime of passion? A family spat? A lover's tiff? Maybe there was a cuckolded husband? A jealous ex? Moreover, why hadn't he told me, his best friend, that he was in love? Private and confidential it may be, but I, his friend and co-conspirator, needed to know everything. Keeping me in the dark put me at serious risk. I confess I felt a little snubbed.

The telegram at the very bottom of the pile gave details of the trial of an opium smuggler. Reading between the lines, I thought I could detect Spratt's influence in the man's acquittal. Perhaps this acquitted opium smuggler was Spratt's other partner? Now *my* new partner? I resolved to find this man as my first priority once we disembarked in Seoul. Good. I had something tangible to do.

Looking at them practically, though, there was nothing solid in the telegrams that pointed to a motive or a culprit for the bombing of Spratt's office. Only fodder for fruitless speculation.

I stuffed the sheaf of papers back into my bag, kicked my shoes off and slipped under the blanket. But sleep proved elusive. When I closed my eyes, my head swam with ideas and theories that precluded sleep, even though I knew there would be no conclusions until I got my feet on the ground in Seoul. I gave up and let insomnia have its little victory at about five in the morning. I rolled out of bed and put my shoes back on. I left the cabin and went on deck. I passed Tyler on deck, who was heaving his dinner over the rail. I patted my stomach and silently congratulated it on its fortitude.

After staring at the horizon for an hour, I went downstairs to the mess where I found Captain McGiffin, who invited me to join him for breakfast. I found him to be more loquacious than he'd been at dinner the evening before, and I became very interested in his history. His American background and his work with the Chinese military machine gave him a rare insight into the Korea situation, which he believed was much closer to war than I realised. I knew right away that here was a man I should listen to.

He was tall, muscular, and lean, his face almost gaunt, his grey eyes were piercing and missed nothing. His bushy brown beard was flecked with grey, and his Chinese Navy uniform was clean but rumpled, as if he'd slept in it. Over my steaming noodles with bony chicken chunks, I asked him just how afraid he was about the likelihood of naval conflict with the Japanese over Korea.

"Concerned, not afraid. *Concern* is worry without fear, and yes, I'm concerned. We are a little too complacent for my liking. Your boss, Hart, got it right when he wrote 'Chinese are sure big China can thrash little Japan' and 'Japan will dash gallantly and perhaps successfully...' He's one wise Irishman, that one, which is why the Qing keep him around, I suppose."

By "we", did he mean the Chinese? I said, "How long have you worked for the Qing yourself?"

"Since '85. Had no luck getting into the US Navy, and I heard they were recruiting foreigners here. I came and signed up. Best decision I ever made."

He went on to explain how much he loved being in China and enjoyed a status and level of respected responsibility he'd never have achieved in America. A navy man didn't need to buy his commission here. This simple Pennsylvanian had gone one hundred percent native. I watched while he used his chopsticks northern China style, with a scissor action between the index and middle fingers. He said he loved China, and whatever conflict it found itself in, he would be on China's side. It surprised me. I'd never met a Westerner who had 'become' Chinese. Most, even Hart, were just visiting, working to some end here in China while looking forward to spending their spoils 'back home'. McGiffin loved the place even more than some Chinese I knew.

He wiped some broth from his beard. "Too many Chinamen seek their fortunes overseas. When I was a kid, my Pappy pointed them out, heading to the goldfields. He'd say, 'Look at them, stupid chinks. Don't they know the gold rush was over a half a century ago? Things must be pretty bad back home if they're desperate enough to come here.' My Father hated being a farmer and couldn't understand why anyone would aspire to try to eke out a living from the land."

"Plenty of Chinese in Australia, and our gold rush has been over for a few decades too."

"You said 'our'. Are you an Aussie or a Chinaman?"

"I can't be both?"

He shrugged his shoulders and pushed his empty bowl to the side of the table. "Maybe. But in trying to be both, careful you don't become neither."

Breakfast over, he stood up and walked to the door, but he turned back at the doorway. "Wanna see the Bridge?"

We continued our conversation as we went up the steep stairway that led to the bridge. McGiffin opened another watertight door and entered the room, where three officers saluted the captain then turned back to their duties. He looked out of the large, slanted windows and pointed. He may have been a fearless, grizzled old salt, but I saw the concern lines on his face deepen when he pointed out a Japanese Navy boat about five miles to starboard.

While he got busy with charts and orders for the officers, I stood in an out-of-the-way corner and gazed out of the broad windows. Jack's murder needed to be solved when I got to Seoul, and the clues would lead where they lead. No need to speculate on them now. Just be sure that the murders are solved and the new opium supply line re-established. Simple.

McGiffin roused me from my reverie and pointed out a flotilla of five ships on the horizon. He said, "Japs. There sure are a lot of them." Not afraid, concerned.

Chapter Eight

Before dawn the next day, we arrived at the port of Dalian for supplies. I went ashore. I had about six hours before the *ZhenYuen* was due to cast off, and I needed to see if I could find any sign that my shipment had passed through and was on its way to Dongying. If Jack had been able to send it on its way before the telegraph cable was severed, there was a chance that it would have come through Dalian. I had a nefarious contact in town that I'd met the very first day I arrived in China. He had tried to pick my pocket and received two broken fingers for his efforts. I'd been able to follow his career as a half-legitimate trader through IMCS despatches and memos over the years and had kept his name filed in my mental address book in case he became useful to me at some future date.

As I headed into the township from the docks precinct, I soon found myself in a busy street lined with retail stores. Even in the pre-dawn glow, there were industrious shopkeepers sweeping their storefronts and shooing away cats, dogs, and rats, while they arranged their wares for best advantage. If I were them, I'd have done the same thing; get started early before the real heat kicked in.

My memory of the town was rusty. I walked along a road that I thought led to the address I'd remembered, but it ended up curving back on itself, following a contour of one of the steep hills that broods over the waterfront. Realising I'd taken a wrong turn, I stopped, turned around, and walked back the way I had come. That's when I spotted him, my tail, who was amateurish enough to have gotten himself flustered by my about-face and clumsily ducked into a ladies' fashion store.

I didn't recognise the man. It was extremely unlikely that any of the dealer's henchmen could have gotten themselves aboard the ship. My instincts told me it could be Tyler's doing. Heineken's tight-lipped assistant. There was no one else on the ship that it could be.

While my follower was presumably trying to bat away enthusiastic sales clerks, hoping he'd buy something nice for his wife, I ducked through a medicine store and came out amongst rubbish bins in a back alley. I strode quickly down the cobblestones, made a couple of turns, and found what I was looking for, mostly by smell; a dark and dingy street store selling fishing supplies. I slipped under the stall's awning and grabbed off the pile a grubby, second-hand fisherman's hat, a jacket and waders, and a sack to stuff my other clothes into. I stripped and changed right there behind the counter, untroubled by the stares of the proprietors. In Chinese culture staring is not prohibited. It's not considered rude, and one must simply get used to it. One member of my gawping audience had a money pouch around his belt. I shoved some coins into the pouch and made my exit.

Back out in the alley, I slung the bag over my shoulder and walked casually like a fisherman who'd just returned from his nightly toil and was on his way to his bed. I was confident I'd lost my tail.

The search thus resumed, I finally espied the café where I remembered my pick-pocketing friend grudgingly buying me lunch that first day, as amends for the attempted theft, broken fingers notwithstanding. The café was further south than I had remembered; it was five years ago, after all, and I went inside to order breakfast. My friend wouldn't be here so early, so I settled in to wait.

The proprietress raised her eyebrows at me when I ordered some steamed buns and tofu soup. It was my accent. Too posh to come out of the mouth of a fisherman. I smiled and asked if they had any coffee. She replied that yes, of course, they had coffee! What was I, stupid?

What came to my table with the food, however, was simply strong tea with lots of sugar and chicory flavouring. I sighed and thanked her. I could never fully accept China as worthy of the term 'civilised' until they got the hang of coffee. I concede that that's an irrational yardstick by which to judge a country. But screw gross domestic product. If they can't make coffee, they're still living in the stone age.

I finished breakfast, but it was still only six o'clock. I picked up a rumpled, day-old copy of the *Dalian Examiner* from the counter and ordered another 'coffee', went back to my table, and rolled a cigarette.

I was taken aback to find that the *Dalian Examiner* was not so much a newspaper but a propaganda organ of the Japanese. The front page led with an opinion piece about the 'heinous injustice' of China keeping Korea all to herself and about how the Korean people deserved to be 'liberated' from the yoke of the Qing dynasty, presumably to then find themselves under a new, Japanese yoke. The penny dropped when I realised the paper was a subsidiary of the *Shanghai Chronicle*, whence the opinion article had come. That syndicated newspaper network was Japanese owned, and the article was by Okamoto Kido, a well-known Japanese propagandist and famously hyperbolic. He'd had a great deal to say about the decaying and corrupt Mongol Qing empire in other articles I'd read. But unlike many Chinese newspaper opinion pieces, he was always careful not to mention any need to rid China of foreigners. Despite Europeans believing all Asians look the same, the Japanese were foreigners here.

After reading every word of the newspaper and drinking four cups of the chicory and tea brew, my former-pick-pocket friend entered the establishment. The years since I last saw him had been unkind. He no longer had any hair on his head, and his shiny dome was dark brown and pock-marked. He was shorter than I remembered and stooped as he made his way between tables. He was wearing the same capacious coat he'd always worn, which served as a hiding place for small stolen goods liberated from the pockets of the good people of Dalian. He waved at the proprietress who presumably knew what all the regulars usually wanted to eat and took a booth in the back corner. I grabbed my drink, left the newspaper on the counter, walked to the booth, and slid in beside him.

"Fuck off, stinky." He said without looking at me.

"Charming. I missed you too. Your fingers look nice and straight, all healed up."

He looked up, and I watched recognition spread across his scarred face. "Hell's teeth, where did you spring from? And when did you take up fishing? I heard you got a job with the Brits." He smiled, and his teeth looked like broken tombstones in a vandalised graveyard.

I sat down and caught him up on my life during the years since I'd seen him last and why I was wearing smelly clothes.

After fending off his efforts to sell me a watch and some jewellery, I told him what I wanted. "I'm trying to locate a shipment of opium that might have been organised for me. It should be at least eight bales and will have come from Seoul, destined for Dongying."

"I don't know such stuff."

"But you know who does, right?"

"Maybe. Tons of the stuff comes every day. Who could tell yours from anyone else's?"

"Mine will be marked as tea, and as belonging to Fyodor Ltd." Fyodor, as in Fyodor Dostoyevsky, the author of our number code reference book. "I'll give you four taels to ask around, then get word back to me on the *ZhenYuen*, which is leaving at noon."

He said he would, and maybe he was telling the truth. He was my best and only hope of finding out anything while I was here in Dalian. It was worth a shot and four taels.

I asked after his health and his family, for form's sake, and we left the café together. We parted on the street, and I headed downhill, in the direction of the waterfront. I changed back into my regular clothes in a laundry I found on the way.

Did my opium ever even leave Korea? I hoped so. Nevertheless, I despaired. If there's any opium at all, it's probably still in Korea. I'd probably just wasted four taels.

There were more Westerners in Dalian than I had expected—it was certainly a cosmopolitan city. On my way back to the *ZhenYuen*, I had been surprised to see some Russians, or maybe they were Prussians, in civilian clothes but with notably military haircuts and bearing despite the civvies. Shore leave? Sightseeing? I saw no European ships at the wharf, only Chinese Navy ships and Chinese and Japanese merchant vessels.

I arrived at the ship and ascended the gangplank, then waited at the rail for the remaining three hours until we were to cast off. No one came with any messages for me by the time the dock lines were taken aboard, and we lumbered away from the dock. Four taels not so well spent. Damn.

It only took another two days' sailing to get to Korea, and the *ZhenYuen* dropped anchor in the little bay to the north of the city of Seoul. I'd had little to do during the journey; mostly just bumbled around the ship getting in people's way. Now I stood at the bow watching the huge anchor splash into the water and had to cover my ears as the massive chain clattered through the hawse pipe. I could feel through the soles of my shoes the engines ramp up and watched as the bow backed away from the place where the anchor had splashed. The ship kept going in reverse, the chain stretching out in front, until we shuddered to a halt and the engines were shut down. The anchor was dug into the seabed and the manoeuvre complete. I turned to see Chinese sailors untying the lashings on the wooden shore boats, under the supervision of a smartly dressed British officer.

McGiffin had shown me the chart of Seoul's coastline over tea in the bridge. Apparently, there was no room at the docks due to the number of merchant vessels and Chinese and Japanese Navy ships. McGiffin said he preferred anchoring out. He liked to have a little distance between himself and the Japanese Navy, and at anchor he could get underway faster.

Heineken, Tyler, and I were rowed towards the shore by four strong Chinese sailors and one British officer. I sat in the little shore boat facing astern and looked at the solid and safe steel structure of the *ZhenYuen*. I felt naked out there on the water while we left the sanctuary of the ironclad warship and became unaccountably nervous about entering an unknown country. We and our luggage were deposited on a small stone jetty and met by a uniformed man who beckoned us to follow him. At the end of the jetty were four rickshaws, and we took one each, one for the luggage, and began the journey into Seoul.

From the jetty we took a road that ascended over a shallow ridge, after which the road began to descend into Seoul proper. From the ridge, the city looked like a cramped mess. The dark brown, slightly domed roofs of densely packed dwellings looked like a random scattering of beetle shells. Taller colonial buildings poked up through the scrum here and there, and I guessed that one of them must be Customs House.

I thought back to Dongying, which was a sleepy backwater compared to this crowded and bustling metropolis.

We descended to what appeared to be the main street of the city, which was a wide boulevard with low, grey brick buildings on either side divided by dark, narrow alleyways. From my rickshaw, looking over the top of my driver's sweaty back, I counted three pickpockets operating in the crowded slate footpaths and saw military uniforms of many ranks from many countries. I watched as one of the pickpockets slipped a handful of silver coins into the palm of a policeman on a corner who quickly slipped them into his pocket, then went nonchalantly back to his supervision of the street. A hundred yards further on, as we passed a shaded and narrow alley, I caught a glimpse of a group of policemen beating someone up with thick clubs.

The street snaked to the right and then followed the wide, brown river. A long wharf was on our left and weathered, low warehouses on our right, and I saw three ships being loaded by cranes with huge bales of soybeans—I recognised the Japanese writing stencilled on the bales as we passed. I recalled that during the drought of '89, the Japanese got very spooked when the Koreans cut off soybean supplies. It was a painful reminder to them of their dependence on Korean-grown food. Hence their interest in wresting control of the country from the Qing. The Qing regarded Korea as a 'tributary' state, nominally self-governed but subservient to the Chinese government.

Looking at the streets of Seoul, I figured that the Qing better send more troops here if they want to retain any semblance of control. But they probably didn't have many to spare. Bubonic plague had broken out down south in Guangdong and decimated the army there. An IMCS memorandum I'd seen last month estimated the deaths at seventy thousand. With a scarcity of Chinese troops, the Japanese would stand a better chance of taking over here.

Some of the more excitable coolies in the bowels of the *ZhenYuen* had told me Seoul was a hotbed of spies, thieves, pimps, racketeers, corrupt officials, Japanese, Germans, Brits, Chinese, rebels, royalists, and the most skilled and prettiest prostitutes this side of Honkers, and now I believed them. I wondered where the latter congregated.

From the smooth-riding rickshaw chair—which had leaf-spring suspension, no less—I noticed no gaiety, heard no laughter. People looked worried. There were almost as many beggars on the street as there were targets for them. We passed a small park that had a little fountain in the middle. The fountain was empty and there were no children running around, or old men playing Mah-jong and laughing. The grass was brown and dying.

The city brooded. I could almost smell the tension, or maybe that was urine.

We stopped at a regal-looking hotel and were told to stay put. Some coolies ferried our luggage inside while some uniformed hotel staff with batons strapped to their belts stood guard nearby. Our luggage deposited into what I presumed was to be our accommodation, the rickshaws got moving once again and after three blocks pulled up at a building whose sign, in red and gold, proudly boasted the building as being 'Chinese Imperial Maritime Customs Service, Seoul Branch Office.' The addition of the word 'Chinese' to our usual IMCS livery probably seemed like a good idea years ago but now looked like a provocation to the Japanese, which tickled me a little.

Customs House here was extruded from the same mould that had been used by the British everywhere, only this one looked to be made of sandstone. I guess that was what was locally available. As we alighted from our rickshaws and ascended the stairs of the four-storey building, Tyler hung back. Once I got into the shade of the doorway, I turned around and saw Tyler speaking furtively to one of the rickshaw drivers and pointing at me. He saw me looking and immediately put his hand down and broke off the conversation. He turned away from the driver, and as he came up the stairs and drew level with me, I said, "He's to be my watcher, is he?"

Tyler tried to scoff, but it came out like a cough and triggered a short coughing fit. There was dust in my throat too. When the coughing subsided, he said hoarsely, "driver," and scurried into the building and down the hallway ahead of me.

I was going to have to be on my guard night and day here. I had to figure out quickly how to navigate this world of spies and intrigue. Nothing would be as it seemed. I'd need eyes in the back of my head.

But I was up for it. There was a time when I rubbed shoulders all night and day with thieves, pimps, and assorted ne'er-do-wells. I could blend in and deceive as well as the best of 'em, and I would start today and try to swiftly figure out who was friend and who was foe. If only it'd been that easy.

Chapter Nine

Tyler hailed me from the top of an ornate central staircase, as if I were a coolie, "C'mon, Swageman, get a move on."

After we had arrived at Customs House, I'd given myself a tour of the ground floor to do some snooping. It was fruitless, as it turned out. The ground floor was just your run-of-the-mill British colonial administrative enclave; waist-high oak wainscotting lined the halls and rooms, and modest electric chandeliers hung from the plaster ceiling. I encountered about a dozen staff as I wandered about, all European and all smartly dressed in clean and pressed uniforms. I received some quizzical looks, but only one staffer asked me if I was lost. By my count I was the only non-European in the building, though presumably there was a basement where some genuine work got done, like cooking and cleaning.

When Tyler hailed me, I'd returned to the foot of the stairs. I muttered, "Go fuck yourself," and ascended the stairs using my most lethargic gait, hoping to irritate him.

"What was that?"

"What?"

"I say, what was that you said?"

"What? When?"

This went on, like a game of badminton, back and forth, until I drew level with him and overtook the little twerp.

I heard voices off to the left down the corridor and followed the sound. I arrived at a charred doorway, with Tyler bringing up the rear. I stood in the doorway, barring his entry. Every surface of the small room was covered in soot, and one side of the upturned desk had a semicircular burn as if someone sitting there had combusted. Jack's bombed-out office. Tyler squeezed past me and in his best grown-up voice introduced me to a big man in an IMCS blazer with gold epaulettes.

Paul Georg von Möllendorff was as tall as me and held his head tilted back, aiming his blonde goatee at me like an arrow. His receding hairline had marched all the way to the top of his skull, but he'd resisted the temptation to adopt a comb-over. He wore his shiny dome proudly, and it set off his muscular jaw, which looked strong enough to gnaw through tree branches. His piercing blue eyes probed mine, searching for my sins, which were legion.

I was introduced to a policeman of indeterminate rank, whose eclectic insignia looked to have been put together by toddlers who liked shiny things.

I needed to search this room thoroughly. I needed to find out the who and the why. There was a sheet of wood covering one broken windowpane, and there were three chairs, two blackened but largely unbroken. All that remained of the third was its castored base. A few threads of what must have been a tapestry wall hanging clung to the wall behind the place where Jack would have sat.

The burn marks on the wall were darkest under the remnants of the tapestry. The other three walls were browned, not blackened. The embroidered rug on the floor, while sooty, was unburned.

"Where's Heineken?" I asked.

Möllendorff's eyebrows shot almost all the way up to his hairline.

Tyler spoke before anyone else could, "The baron is meeting with a representative of His Majesty King Gojong."

The shiny policeman spoke up in Korean. I was pleased to find that it was similar enough to Mandarin for me to pick up almost all of it. As he spoke, I realised the role of the other man in the room, the one I had not been introduced to. He was a translator and spoke softly into Möllendorff's ear. The gist of it was that the plod was satisfied that local rebels dynamited the office by throwing a couple of lighted sticks through the window. It was believed that some unhappy opium merchants, the ones that traded with the IMCS's blessing, were furious about recently raised tariffs and hired some unemployed Donghak rebels to do the deed, thus concealing the merchants' involvement. Cut and dried. The policeman looked at Möllendorff as if to say, 'the prosecution rests, m'lud' and pulled a red sash from his pocket. He waved it in the air. "Donghak."

Tyler and Möllendorff nodded sagely.

I groaned audibly and rolled my eyes.

Möllendorff aimed his beard at me. "You have something to add, Mr. Swageman?"

I held his superior gaze and said, "Not dynamite, and not thrown through the damn window." More staring, I let the silence linger. He blinked first. I won our first staring competition.

I continued, "One stick of dynamite would have blown out not only all the windows but much of the wall. This room would have been a fireball and would have burned down the entire building before any firefighting service could have made it here."

I walked over to stand in the space where Jack would have sat. "Jack Spratt sat at his desk here. He was left-handed and thus needed the light from the window to come in over his right shoulder. This spot is the centre of the blast, a blast that killed Spratt, destroyed his chair, desk, and the tapestry behind him, but did little damage to the rest of the room. This bombing, gentlemen, was done with less than a quarter of a pound of black powder. The bomb would have had a lit fuse and been thrown into Jack's lap from the doorway."

Almost a minute passed in silence. Tyler spoke first, wanting to flex his intellectual muscle in front of Möllendorff, "But the broken window—"

I cut in, "If something was thrown through that pane from the street, there would be broken glass on the floor. Do you see any? That pane, and only that pane, blew *out* from the small blast. Black powder makes a lot of smoke compared to dynamite, hence the modest amount of actual damage to the room. Most things are blackened with soot, yet unburned." I stopped there. Enough showing off.

The policeman again waved the red sash like he was bidding farewell to a lover. He spoke, and the translator said, "Then the bomber must have dropped this as he fled."

No, it was too clean—there was no soot on the sash. But it made me wonder, if Jack caught a bomb with a lit fuse in his lap, he'd surely throw the bloody thing away, in whatever direction was available, out into the corridor or out through the window. Fuses were notoriously unpredictable. Six inches of fuse could burn down in anything from five seconds to a minute. And a bomber wouldn't wait nearby to make sure the target didn't throw the bomb away before it went off.

The best way to ensure that an unpredictable bomb went off in someone's lap was if that someone was unconscious. Jack's position at his desk next to the window meant no one could sneak up on him. To knock him out and blow him up, one would have to get close enough to clock him on the scone with something heavy and hard. Jack wouldn't have let a stranger get close enough for that.

The more I thought about it, the more certain I became. Jack was acquainted with his killer. I made a mental note to check his body, if I got a chance to view it, for skull fractures.

I looked up at the others in the room, and they were all looking at me.

I focussed on Möllendorff as I spoke. "That sash is a beautiful piece of shiny red silk. Wonderfully unburnt and thus was never anywhere near any explosions. I doubt it's ever even been worn."

Möllendorff pursed his lips and frowned while he thought of a reply. "Then I suggest that the sash must have fallen under the rug and thus was shielded from the blast." He was looking at the policeman while he said it, as if he were encouraging the man to concur.

I sighed. "Under the rug? Where you'd like this investigation to be swept?"

Möllendorff turned back to me, his face scarlet.

Tyler jumped in, "Now look here, Swageman—"

"Where's Spratt's body, anyway? I need to see it." I interrupted.

"In the cemetery. Where else would it be?" Tyler looked genuinely surprised by my question.

Möllendorff had remained red-faced but silent and now turned and left the room.

Even Spratt's remains were now buried under a rug.

So, that was the way it was. Everyone in the room except me was intent on getting back to business as soon as possible and bring any 'investigation' to a speedy and palatable conclusion.

After a few polite goodbyes, Tyler and the policemen left me alone in Jack's sooty office. I snooped around among the debris. I pulled out all the drawers in the upturned desk. They had all suffered major damage being so close to the blast. I found the one I was looking for, the one with the false bottom. Before opening it, I got up and checked the corridor. There was no one there. I hoped to find some papers, some clues as to the status of our opium. I didn't want any prying eyes to see what I was doing. I went back to the desk and pulled out the drawer. I slid the false bottom out of its cavity. I was disappointed to find that the only item the secret drawer held was a silver locket. I pulled it out and opened it. Inside the locket was a picture of a woman, the fiancé presumably, and the outside showed some kind of family crest. I pocketed it.

I searched the rest of the room until I was thoroughly sooty and sweaty. I found nothing that would help me pick up the trail of my opium.

I left Jack's charred office and went downstairs to the ground floor, then took the narrower staircase down to the basement. I was looking for the records room. When I found it the gatekeeper, who had the job of making sure all records searches were authorised, just like Harry back in Dongying, stood at a chest-high wooden counter that barred the entrance. He was not European, like Harry, but Asian. But his suit, waistcoat and watch chain told me he had embraced the attire of his British masters, at least when he was at work.

The counter was hinged at one end, like a bar in an inn. I tried to sound authoritative. "Open up. Möllendorff sent me."

He looked up from his ledger and eyed me through thick, tinted glasses. There was a strong musty smell that I suspected wasn't just coming from moulding files, but from the man in front of me. He paused before he replied, and his eyes narrowed ever so slightly. "I need that in writing."

"No time. Urgent."

He folded his arms across his chest. He would not be moved. Harry would have opened up when he saw me coming. But this fellow was far less amenable. I thought I'd detected a throaty twang to his Chinese. Nothing major, just a slightly deeper register and some flattened tones. Back when my mother was teaching me Chinese, I'd had endless trouble with the tones. If you got them wrong, while, say, trying to ask for directions to the train station, you could find yourself, by way of a reply, being handed a freshly caught octopus, still wriggling. The tones conveyed meaning. Mother told me, "You learn tone, or you no be understand."

I looked at the gatekeeper and ventured a guess as to where he learned Chinese. "Your Chinese is good. When did you arrive from Japan?"

He was taken aback for only a moment and covered it well. "Why? Are we about to become friends? Exchange Christmas Cards? Friends or not, you can't come back here without the right credentials."

Sarcasm. My jovial repartee needed work. In my defence, I was distracted by my urgent need to be doing something investigative, and this peon was in my way. "For heaven's sake, there's been a murder. Möllendorff will throw you out on your ear for hindering the investigation."

He sighed heavily and removed his glasses. He took a yellow silk handkerchief from his pocket and began polishing them. I seized the opportunity of his temporary blindness to grab his ledger. The leatherbound book in hand, I took two steps back, out of his reach, and began thumbing through the pages.

"Hey! Give that back!"

I turned my back on him. "Well, this book is certainly riveting. How does it end? No, don't tell me."

I heard the click of the latch. I threw the ledger down the hall, and he rushed past me to fetch it. I spun on my heel and walked through the doorway past the open counter. I went straight to the bank of bookshelves at the gloomy rear of the room and ran my finger along the spines of the leatherbound volumes. The gatekeeper came scurrying up behind me, making unintelligible protestations. I found the three volumes I wanted and pulled them off the shelves.

"You can't take those!"

I summoned my most menacing timbre and loomed over him. "I only want to look in them. Shut up unless you want a permanent injury." I held the volumes above my head, and he soon gave up trying to reach them. "Go back your counter, and I'll be out of your hair in a moment."

"Management will hear about this", he said as he shuffled back to his post.

I put the volumes down on a table. I pulled the locket from my pocket and examined the image pressed, in relief, into the face. Thumbing through the pages of the book, I found a family crest similar to the one on the locket. The book gave the Chinese characters for a Hongxia family and a potted history of the family line. It was the usual once-noble-but-fallen-on-hard-times story that is so common in the East, especially for a tributary protectorate like Korea.

I recalled the telegram Jack had sent asking for permission to marry a local girl. The name he used was 'Yi'. I checked through the book again but could find no such name as having a noteworthy family crest.

For all his bonhomie, Jack was never really a pants man, a player, never much of a swordsman with the ladies. He could more often be found obsessing over one woman or another. The poor fellow fell in love rather easily and hard. I couldn't credit any notion that he might have had more than one woman as the target of his affections. So, the locket almost certainly came from his fiancé, Miss Yi. Perhaps her mother's maiden name was Hongxia? The fiancé would carry the father's family name, obviously, but if the mother's name was once noble, then she might well think of herself as one of that family's line, despite the family name she carried. The only Hongxia listed in the citizens' directory lived on a street that the street directory told me was a mile and a half south of the office. Say what you like about the IMCS, but the Brits sure know how to keep impeccable records.

Just how far should I go with this investigation? All I really needed to do here was secure a new opium smuggling route while giving the appearance of doing my assigned IMCS job, getting Spratt replaced, and his department up and running again. Maybe I should take a deep breath, button my lip, and let the local police and IMCS bosses bring the whole thing to a perfunctory conclusion.

I shook that thought off. I couldn't do it. I felt that the tasks of finding Jack's killer, finding my opium (if it existed), and getting it back to Shandong were linked. Jack knew his killer. That's the only plausible explanation for him allowing himself to be knocked unconscious and roasted with black powder. A lovesick fool he certainly was, but a dupe? Never. Getting the drop on Jack was something few would attempt, and fewer still could achieve. I had to keep investigating and see if it had anything to do with our graft. And to see if I could re-start said graft.

Nothing in the office had pointed to the identity of his smuggling contact, so I'd have to chase down the culprit with what little I already had from the telegrams, which wasn't much.

The next logical step was to see if the fiancé lived at the Hongxia address.

It was time to leave, but my intuition told me there was something else I should look into before I go. I pulled the financial directory down from a shelf and looked up Barings Bank. The listing was right where it should have been, and it gave the address of the head office, a concise history of the institution, and the names of the board of directors, correct as at the time of publication, which was last year. There was an Ernst Heineken on the board, along with several members of the British aristocracy. I wondered how common the name 'Heineken' was in Germany and whether it should surprise me to find that name on the Barings Bank board. Did it mean anything? Probably not. My intuition was often way off the mark. But I'd file this little nugget of information away in my head just the same.

I closed the volumes and left them on the table for the gatekeeper to put away. I smiled inwardly, knowing that he'd need to use the ladder to get them back up to the top shelf. As I approached him, he slid off his stool, opened the counter, and took three steps back and to the side. As I drew level with him, I reached up to run my fingers through my hair. He flinched and took another step back.

Swagger the bully. Father would be proud.

Chapter Ten

I left the IMCS building to go and find the Hongxia house. Only two blocks south-west of the office, the neighbourhood became what I would call 'impoverished residential'. The smell of Jack's bombed-out office, barbequed flesh and black powder, clung doggedly to my nostrils but soon became mixed with the smell of steamed mandoo—Korean dumplings. I followed the smell into the open doorway of a house, the front room of which appeared to be a miniature café.

A kindly lady gave me a one-toothed smile, scooped half a dozen mandoo onto a wooden plate, and placed the plate on a narrow shelf in front of the room's only window. She nodded at the plate and at me as she handed me some chopsticks.

They smelled great but were too hot to eat, so I blew on them and gazed out of the window at the narrow street. That's when I spotted him, my rickshaw driver from earlier in the day, the one Tyler had had a word with. He was walking briskly along the street, looking fore and aft in the manner you'd expect of a hunter who'd lost his quarry.

My follower would enter this makeshift café sooner or later—probably sooner. I was annoyed that I'd have to ditch the man by hurrying out through the house, leaving my delicious-smelling meal.

I pulled two coins from my pocket and went over to the proprietress and tapped her on the shoulder. She turned, and I put the coins in her hand and told her I wanted to lose a tail by ducking out of the back of her home.

"No problem. Take your food and eat it in the back room. Relax. No one will get past me."

Bless her. I picked up my plate and utensils and walked to the back of the room and through the beaded curtain which depicted a bucolic rural scene in a mosaic of dried and painted lychee husks. I heard a door slam behind me, which cut off the sounds from the street.

I walked along the corridor through her home, glancing briefly into the dark and airless rooms I passed. One contained an old man reclining on a chair with a tea set on a table within reach. In another, there was a woman my age reading to a child, and in the kitchen, at the back, there was another woman slaving over large woks that smelled of noodles and chilli. She gave me the briefest of glances, then returned to her work. There was a rough teak table with four low stools. I sat on one of them, put down my bowl, and popped a mandoo in my mouth. It was delicious, just the right amount of spice and a tasty combination of green vegetables and what I was fairly certain was goat meat, though it could have been pork. I savoured the flavours and looked around the room. Dark and dank though it was, there were plenty of simple decorations that told me the place was the happy home of a family. For some inexplicable reason, it felt good to be there in someone's poor but cared-for home.

The Chinese can be very proud, and if they feel that their home would fail to impress, they won't invite any guests to it. I could count on the fingers of one hand the number of times I had been invited into the home of less well-off Chinese. Of course, I had been feted at the homes of the upper-middle class. But peasant homes were usually closed to me.

Maybe people were less house proud in Korea.

The house had no courtyard, and the glassless kitchen window faced the back lane. There was a hessian curtain that was pulled back to allow the steam to escape. I looked up from my plate just in time to see my follower pass the window. I stood up and rushed to the wall next to the window and pressed my back into the brickwork. I pulled the curtain off its retaining nail and let it drop across the window. I pulled a small scrap of the corner of the curtain aside to try to see my follower. He was about thirty feet along the back lane, looking left and right, fretting that he'd lost me.

Good. I let the curtain drop and looked at the woman cooking, who stared back at me. I sat back down and put another mandoo into my mouth. She returned to her woks.

I finished my food and put the bowl on the counter next to the sink. I sat back down and rolled myself a cigarette. I offered it to the woman and was delighted when she took it. Chinese women who considered themselves more civilised than the peasantry would never do such a thing. With their bound feet and their elaborate brocaded robes, they aspired to being admired and cared for. Smoking was for men.

But this peasant woman was happy to take a thing offered, and I rolled myself another one. She turned down the heat on the woks and sat down opposite me. We smoked together in silence, our ash falling to the floor.

My pleasant interlude over, I took a peek through the curtain and was happy that my watcher was nowhere to be seen. I gave a thank-you wave to the woman and left.

The IMCS directory was wrong, as is to be expected in a bustling and lawless town like Seoul. People move house, and even street names get changed. The search was pleasant, though. I toured several blocks of shaded streets with birds twittering in the trees, even plucked a ripe apricot from one overhanging tree and munched contentedly.

I found the house eventually by examining the Korean characters on little varnished wooden plaques over the circular arched gates of the most ornate looking homes. I knocked on the one marked 'Hongxia', and a servant let me into the courtyard. He asked me my business, and I told him I was here to see the fiancé of Jack Spratt of the IMCS, a Miss Yi. Either he'd tell me there was no such person here, or he'd ask me to wait while he checked with his master or mistress.

It was the latter, and when he emerged from the red lacquered door of the house, I was shown into a well-lit and tastefully furnished front room that presumably had only one purpose, that of entertaining guests. Standing and waiting for me in the room was a petite and excessively beautiful woman. Nice one, Jack. She was just Spratt's type, mine too. Though well out of our league.

She was about five feet two and slim, draped in a yellow, brocaded, floor-length gown that left her well-defined shoulders bare. The makeup on her face was minimal, and it was nice to behold such a blemish-free complexion. Her manner was demure and deferential, as dictated in this society, but I could tell that was a façade. There was an unmistakeably feisty undercurrent behind her eyes. My heart skipped a beat, and I hoped she didn't notice my sharp intake of breath.

There's something about short women. Short men compensate for their lack of stature with belligerence and pugnaciousness. The same syndrome has a magnificent effect on women, however. They seem to develop a stronger will as a result of their reduced height and rail and argue against those who attempt to dominate them. I always found that terribly sexy. Demure decorum bored me.

But I wasn't about to flirt with Jack's fiancé, his dead status notwithstanding. I have *some* scruples.

I had earlier entertained a notion that Jack's murder could have something to do with his intended nuptials. One look into her deep, black irises almost swept that notion away.

"I'm Cuifang, but please call me Anee."

"Enchanted. I'm Phillip Swageman, but my friends call me Swagger. I've been friends with Jack for years, though I haven't seen him since he transferred here. Allow me to express my deepest condolences for your loss."

"Thank you. Tea?"

I lied and told her that tea would be lovely, and she rang a little bell on the mantlepiece, above which was a portrait of a formidable fellow in full battle dress. She beckoned me to a settee, and we sat a respectable distance apart. Her robe rode up slightly as she lowered herself onto the settee, enabling me to catch a furtive look at her shoes. Her feet were not bound. She wore Western shoes, 'pumps', I think they are called, with a two-inch heel.

"Are you of the Yi family?"

"Distantly, on my mother's side."

"Jack's telegram asking for permission to marry you used the Yi name, not Hongxia."

She tilted her head and allowed herself half a smile. "He thought that might make his request more likely to be approved."

Ah, I had it arse about. Yi is the name that must carry some prestige, not Hongxia. "So, your actual family name is Hongxia, your father's family name?"

"Yes."

A different servant came in and placed a tray on the low table in front of us. He knelt and poured the insipid liquid into two small cups, replacing the silver teapot on the tray with the spout pointed at me.

Anee shouted with a vehemence that nearly made me jump out of my skin. "What are you doing! Fool! Get out! I'll deal with you later." The servant, terrified, backed out of the room on his knees, head bowed and muttering apologies. I couldn't figure out how he could see where he was going, but he made it through the doorway backwards without banging into anything. He must have had practice.

She turned to me and smiled sweetly. "Sorry about that. Do you know about the tradition? It's very bad luck to point the spout of the teapot at a guest. It indicates contempt. I'm very sorry for the insult."

I *did* know about that. But it wasn't a tradition, it was a superstition, and one of the stupider ones, in my view. "Think nothing of it. A simple mistake. Don't be too hard on him."

The event over, she handed me a cup. I sipped some tea. It had honey in it.

Time to dive in. "What have you been told about Jack's passing?"

"His murder. Please, let's not dance around the subject." That suited me fine. "Jack was worried that his wage would not be enough to marry me and build a family. I told him I cared not about such material things, that we'd manage. But he was determined to augment his income. He wouldn't give me details, but I worried that he was doing something dangerous."

"Were you aware of any people that might wish him harm?"

"No one I could name, but Jack was definitely worried these past weeks." She lowered her head, her grief getting the better of her. It was brief, and she shook it off and raised her damp and glistening eyes to meet mine. "You will find his murderers."

A statement, not a question. "I will."

A silence passed between us. I was delaying. There was something I needed to ask. It would hurt, but I saw no way out of it. I girded my loins and reluctantly asked, "Your family has fallen a long way from its former glory, is that why you needed Jack?"

I could see in her face that my gold-digging implication stung. I felt like a cad. Her mouth fell open in wounded shock, but only for a second. Then defiance burned in her eyes as she raised them to meet mine. "I loved him!", a pause, then, "I didn't latch onto him if that's what you mean. We were going to make a life for each other. I'd had plenty of opportunities to find myself a man who could keep me in style and comfort, for whom I could be a dutiful trophy wife. But that kind of life is no life at all! Jack didn't want a live-in sex slave and attractive social accessory. When I was with Jack, he made me feel like I could achieve anything, like I could be my true self. He gave me wings."

I believed her. Her inner strength was written all over her face. My heart skipped another beat.

A sliver of scepticism remained in my mind, however. Marriage to an IMCS man would go some way to regaining lost legitimacy. Why else would her father countenance such a match? Maybe every word she said was true, but she'd still need her family's approval, and Jack looked good on paper.

"Is there anything you can tell me that could point me in the right direction? Anything at all that might lead me towards finding his murderer?"

"Could be anyone in a town like this. Japanese, Chinese, Rebels." I noticed she didn't mention Royalists. I supposed that even long-expired noble bloodlines held a torch for the good old days of kings and landed gentry. A family like hers would remain loyal to a royal family line.

I pulled the locket out of my pocket and handed it to her. "This was in Jack's office. I presume it came from you?"

She gave a demure gasp and clasped it with both hands, then held it to her breast with her eyes closed for a few moments before she spoke. "Yes, thank you for returning it to me. It's precious to me."

"You mentioned other suitors, before Jack. Anyone I might know? Anyone significant?"

She lowered her head again as if she was embarrassed that she wasn't a virgin. Like I cared. "When I first met Jack, I was at a garden party held at the Japanese Consulate. I was there with a diplomat. I was his mistress. His wife was back in Japan."

I tried to sound reassuring, hoped a matter-of-fact tone would let her know that I didn't think less of her for being someone's mistress. Happens all the time. "The diplomat's name?"

"Masamoto."

Bingo. That name loomed large on my list of things to find out about. One of Jack's telegrams mentioned it. It was a first name, not a family name, and the odd thing about Jack's telegram was that no family name was mentioned. Unusual in official communications like IMCS telegrams. "That's a Japanese name. And his family name is...?"

She paused. "He's not important. He had nothing to do with Jack's murder."

"Please, I need to find out everything I can. Jealousy is a powerful motive for murder—"

"No! That is impossible. Masamoto is a sweet man, and I'll not allow you to embroil him in this."

Maybe she's still in love with him? Maybe she remains his mistress to this day? Or hooked back up with him before Jack's corpse went cold? Such suspicions tainted my affection and sympathy for her. I let her words hang there and let the silence between us lengthen. Nature abhors a vacuum, and I hoped she'd fall into it and tell me more.

She fell eventually, but she didn't give me the surname I wanted. "You will avenge him, won't you?"

I answered with a few platitudes, told her I would try, but there were too many possible motives and too little evidence to go on.

She seemed to accept that, and without a word, got up off the settee and left the room. A minute later, she returned and handed me a leatherbound book. "Jack kept a diary. You should have it. It may help."

"Thank you. I'll return it when I'm done." The leather cover was unadorned, and the yellowed pages were well thumbed and curled. When I untied the string, it fell open to the day when entries stopped, the day of his death. A sheaf of loose folded papers fell onto the floor. I picked them up and put them and the diary in my pocket. I'd examine it more closely later, in private.

"No need to return it. I have plenty of things to remind me of him." She glanced around the room as if her eyes would fall upon reminders of her fiancé, but the faraway look told me her keepsakes were not so tangible. They were memories.

I finished my tepid tea and sighed as I stood up to leave. She stood too, and I think she sensed my feeling that I'd achieved little, that she'd not been a great deal of help. "Despair not. You'll find the murderer. Look to the stars. There are planets we cannot see, but we know they are there by the gravity they exert on their neighbours. Find the gravitational pull, and you'll find the planet."

I guess she thought she was being helpful. She'd re-worded an old proverb. A customary way of ending a conversation and not a good one. After I observed a few appropriate and tedious politeness protocols, I left. I was eager to examine Jack's diary. When the sheaf of papers had fallen to the floor, I caught a glimpse of some newspaper clippings in the bunch, and the name 'Mason' jumped out at me from one of the headlines. Studying that was going to be interesting.

Chapter Eleven

No, Anee, I'm not in the avenging business.

Walking away from the Hongxia house, I became more frustrated by the conversation I'd just had. I chastised myself for not pushing Jack's fiancé harder. Excessive beauty can have that effect on me. The diary she'd given me might have some use, but essentially, she'd given me no insights into the case. I was miffed and suspicious that she wouldn't come clean on the surname of this Masamoto character.

The image of her beautiful face and graceful physique remained, however. She was just my type, though I'd make a terrible husband if I ever wanted to be one.

As I approached my hotel, I saw my watcher leaning against a lamppost on the opposite side of the street. After losing me, he must have come here to wait and pick up my trail. He did not try to conceal his role as my shadow. Presumably, because he'd realised that I could always spot him and usually lose him. I didn't need to shake him off just now, so I strode into the hotel, collected my key from the smartly dressed and elegantly quaffed concierge at reception, and went upstairs to my room.

This was a foreign-built hotel, and some plasterwork looked French to my untrained eye. Plaster swirls in the cornices and flowing friezes high on the walls. My room had a solid mahogany door and a Persian rug on the floor. The furniture, however, was bamboo and unvarnished teak. I wondered what had happened to the original Frog furniture when the Koreans requisitioned the hotel. Out of the floor-to-ceiling windows that opened onto the narrow balcony, I could see my follower down in the street. He was looking straight at me, making no attempt to conceal his intent. He knew where my room was. Must have a contact at the hotel.

As I was looking at him, a platoon of neat Japanese infantry marched down the middle of the street. Civilians stopped walking and talking and stood aside, watching the soldiers silently as they went past.

I sat down at the little table and opened Jack's diary. The sheaf of loose papers fell out. This looked promising. I went through the papers one at a time. There were a few mundane telegrams; the first three in the pile were duplicates of the ones I'd seen already from the Dongying office. Another two gave further details of the hearing and acquittal of that opium smuggler, who I hoped to find as soon as possible. There was a handwritten note in German that said: "*Nutzen Sie die Gesellschaft der älteren Brüder, von denen es viele im Gericht gibt.*" Using my rusty high-school German, I translated it and wrote what I thought could be the meaning below it. "*Use old brother, he is many in house.*" Made no sense. I made a mental note to browbeat my archives gatekeeper friend into lending me a German-English dictionary.

There was a receipt from a jeweller that looked like it might be for an engagement ring that Jack was having made for Anee. The collection date for the finished ring was two days ago. Maybe I should collect it and give it to her. It'd give me an excuse to see her again.

There were some envelopes addressed to Jack, but they were empty, with no return address on the back. The postmark showed that they were posted in Seoul, and they had large stamps depicting the Korean Royal Family, children, and all. I wished their original contents were folded inside. They might have been illuminating.

There were some newspaper clippings. One about the Mason affair, which read like a propaganda piece; very pro-Japanese and sympathetic to the KoLaoHui. I remembered the kerfuffle and handwringing over that thorny event. An IMCS staffer, Charles Mason, joined the KoLaoHui, a mystical and secret society bent on overthrowing the Qing and expelling, or simply killing, all foreigners. Arms were bought by the sympathetic Mason for this purpose but were seized in Shanghai. Mason was arrested but acquitted during a British show trial, making the Qing incandescent with rage. The Chinese members of the KoLaoHui were rounded up and beheaded without trial, though some remained at large, their escape from custody attributed to magic by their credulous followers. The IMCS as a whole, and Robert Hart in particular, were extremely embarrassed about both the fact that an IMCS staffer had joined a conspiracy to murder the Empress Dowager Cixi, and the fact that the culprit was given little more than a slap on the wrist and sent back to England to enjoy a comfortable retirement. It was speculated in at least one newspaper that the secret society was founded by Freemason Jesuits during the sixteenth century. But that was obviously balderdash.

The incident left a stain on the IMCS that it had never quite shaken off.

One telegram in Jack's pile caught my eye; it was the same as the one I had seen before about the acquitted smuggler, but handwritten on this copy was the man's name and address. Ying, and the number of a warehouse on the waterfront. Progress at last.

The diary itself was not a journal, sadly, just a record of meetings and appointments. There weren't even any notes about the meetings themselves. I put the loose papers in my pocket and left the diary under the mattress, there being no other hiding places in the sparse room.

I hung my IMCS blazer on a hook on the back of the door and threw on a linen jacket. I left the room and the hotel and headed straight for the docks to try to find this Ying fellow. My watcher peeled himself off his lamppost and followed about a hundred feet behind. I knew I could lose him in the labyrinth of lanes and alleys near the seedier quarter of the dockyards.

While walking east past the Russian consulate building and past another hotel, I gave myself a quick summary of what I knew so far.

Suspect one: Opium suppliers angry at tariff increases. I decided to use the records in the basement to compile a list of likely traders when I got back to the office, but I wasn't enthusiastic. It just didn't seem likely. Tariffs go up all the time, there's even an appeals process within IMCS policies and procedures for traders to avail themselves of if they felt the increases were too steep. They never won, of course, but there *was* a process. I'd never known of a merchant committing murder over increases. They sought redress in a court, and perhaps surprisingly, they usually got a fair hearing. Then lost.

But it was, at least, conceivable, and thus remained the favoured motive of the Seoul police and of my colleagues. Their apparently iron-clad belief that a Donghak rebel had been hired as some kind of hitman to do the bombing was, however, plainly ridiculous.

What might make more sense is Donghak rebels doing damage to the IMCS on their own account. They were fanatically anti-Chinese. The IMCS was an arm of the Chinese Qing government even though it was run by an Irishman and staffed mostly with foreigners. Whoever wound up running Korea, they'd want the substantial customs revenue to stay in Korea. That could mean that the Donghak might be doing the bidding of King Gojong. De-stabilise the IMCS and separate it from the Qing and divert the revenue into the royal coffers, using loyalist rebels. The idea was plausible if I also considered the revenge motive. The king's son was still rotting in a Beijing prison. But, as horrific as that was, could the king be stupid enough to attempt to take a revenue stream away from the Qing? He'd be safer fighting a dragon with a spoon. But royalty isn't immune from idiocy. I mentally filed that theory under 'improbably plausible'.

Alternatively, perhaps the Japanese could have convinced the Donghak leadership that they'd be better off if the Japanese were in charge. After all, they share a common enemy—the Qing.

Suspect two: Japanese diplomat Masamoto. Motive? Jealousy. I needed to find out his surname as a matter of urgency.

Citizens of Japan seemed to feature repeatedly in my ruminations. Gawd, I definitely did *not* want to go up against the Japanese. They take no prisoners, *literally*. Whether it was at the behest of King Gojong or the Japanese, if the Donghak murdered an IMCS man for whatever reason, I'd seriously consider letting sleeping dogs lie on that score.

I decided that after I'd got the ball rolling on my opium, I'd look into Masamoto.

One problem at a time, and mine was more pressing than Jack's. Avenging him wouldn't bring him back.

The acquitted smuggler I was setting out to find, Ying, wasn't a suspect as such, but you never knew. Maybe he and Jack had had a falling out, serious enough for one to murder the other. If so, I hoped Ying's enmity toward Jack did not extend to me.

Murderer or not, I had to talk to the man. I had no idea he'd be so well protected.

Chapter Twelve

From my hotel the docks were precisely due east, and I covered the mile and a half in about twenty minutes. I needed to see this Ying fellow, then I'd go and eat. I was ravenous. I arrived at the T-intersection where the street I'd been on ended and the waterfront road stretched away in both directions. I turned left and as I walked along the waterfront, ships unloading cargo to my right and warehouses to my left, I saw four Japanese troop ships with soldiers streaming down their gangplanks. Once on the wharf, they lined up neatly in rows so they could be shouted at by their superior.

Anywhere in the world, the docks could be a violent place, and here in tense Seoul, I reckoned everyone would be that much more on edge. A smuggler has minders, and I had no way of predicting how vigilant and skilled Ying's would be. But I knew these kinds of people. At one time, I had a similar role.

As I walked along the wharf, the ships and the warehouses gradually became smaller and less well kept. My watcher remained a discreet distance behind, and that didn't bother me. He'd report my presence at the docks, and that would accord with my role as the investigator of Jack's death. The prime suspects, in the minds of many, were opium merchants. Whoever he was reporting to, it was better to be watched while seemingly doing my job than having him report that I'd given him the slip. If my activities were too mysterious, I might get asked some troublesome questions.

I found the structure I was looking for. On the outside, it looked like a small, ramshackle warehouse. Single storey, constructed of water-stained and unpainted wood, with four menacing-looking bouncers leaning on the wall next to a rusty steel door, their arms folded. I walked up to the biggest, thickest, and ugliest one. He was a good two inches shorter than me, and I said a silent prayer to the god of genetics that had blessed me with a height of over six feet.

"I have business with Mr. Ying."

"No, you don't, customs man." All four of them sniggered.

Okay, so a linen jacket wasn't much of a disguise. Or perhaps my reputation had preceded me. But they knew who I was talking about, which meant he was probably inside.

"Matter of fact, I do. Not customs business, personal. Send someone in there to tell him Jack Spratt's partner is here."

He unfolded his arms slowly, then gave three heavy knocks on the door, followed by two, then one, and jerked his thumb toward the door. I took a step forward, but a big, meaty hand on my chest barred my way. I'd misunderstood. He wasn't beckoning me inside. His thumb gesture was for one of his comrades, the one with an angry golden tiger embroidered on his scarlet shirt, the image failing to make up for his paucity of rippling muscles. Tiger shirt pushed himself away from the wall. The door opened, releasing sounds of boisterous chatter inside. He went inside, and the thick door closed, cutting off the sounds from within. Meat hand went back to his folded-arm stance.

I took a step back and turned around, rolled a cigarette, and lighted it. I took one drag and then gave a casual salute to my watcher, who was leaning against a warehouse wall a hundred yards away. He didn't return the salute.

"Friend of yours?" meat hand asked.

Without turning to face him, I said, "We're not formally acquainted, but I feel we're becoming firm friends."

The door opened, and tiger shirt beckoned me inside. I gave meat hand my cigarette and entered the gloom of the building.

My eyes took a moment to adjust, and when they did, I saw that the structure was one capacious room with a bar running the length of the wall to my right. The room was full of people smoking and drinking and talking, sitting on low stools at low tables. Many eyes turned my way and followed me all the way to the back of the room, where tiger shirt directed me to one of the booths that lined the back wall.

"Ah, the other half of the great Spratt corporation emerges from the ashes. Have a seat."

"Mr. Ying, I presume?"

"And what appellation attaches to the one asking?"

Sarcastic and verbose. Marvellous. Here was a grinning Chinese petty tyrant I could develop a serious dislike for. "My friends call me Swagger, but you can call me Mr. Swageman."

His grin faltered for just a moment and then returned. "Yes, I am Mr. Ying. What can I do for you?"

"With my partner dead, I am here to finalise the arrangements for the shipment of opium he was in the process of sending me. He told me that if anything happened, I needed to visit the honourable Mr. Ying, in whom Jack placed the utmost trust." None of which was true, I only learned Ying's name a couple of hours ago. I was laying respectfulness on thick. But the Chinese love that, even when they know it's insincere.

He was indeed susceptible to flattery, or at least pretended to be. "Some wine for my friend here", he said to one of his hangers-on, who exited the booth and went in the direction of the bar. "I'm afraid I have some grim news for you, Mr. Swaggerman."

The mangling of my name didn't bother me, not when it came out of the mouth of someone I didn't care about. "Now, let's not get off on the wrong foot here. My partner Spratt has paid for eight bales of the finest Bengali Gold. I'm here to see them on their way."

"Two. Spratt paid for only two bales."

That was a kick in the guts. I eyed him suspiciously. I had sent my half of the investment to Jack two months ago, fifteen hundred taels in silver ingots. Jack was to put in the same amount. That should have bought eight bales at least. I couldn't believe that Jack had stitched me up. He couldn't have, could he? He was, after all, courting a woman who he felt deserved the finer things in life. I shoved that suspicion to the back of my mind and preferred to regard this Ying as less than truthful.

Before I could think of a deft way to call him a liar, respectfully, of course, he said, "And I will not be able to arrange shipment of the two bales. I got a better offer, so now all my available cargo space is to be used sending weapons to Dalian."

For whom? Not the Chinese, they have their own ships. Who in Dalian needs weapons? And who do they plan to use them against?

"Mr. Swaggerman?"

"Are you saying I will have to arrange shipping myself?"

Just then, I heard a scraping noise and saw two men dragging two large bundles along the floor. They stopped at the table, and I saw that the bundles were tied hessian cubes, each about three feet square, marked 'tea'.

"There, that's your opium. I wish you luck finding a ship to take it to the mainland. You may just have to carry it yourself, as luggage." Ying grinned smugly. His cronies tittered.

I was on my own here, outnumbered and out of my depth. And they knew it. I had no option but to accept the two bales.

"Thank you, Mr. Ying. Alas, I can't take the cargo myself. Perhaps you know of another 'agent' who might accommodate me?"

"You might have some luck with the tobacconist."

We exchanged a little more polite, though wary, chatter, and Ying agreed to hang onto the bales until I sent word about whether the tobacconist could arrange shipment. I was told the address of this tobacconist, who apparently had no other name, and I opened up one corner of one bale to make sure there was opium inside. There was, and I scooped a handful into my pouch and re-tied the twine binding. Ying nodded to his men, and they began dragging the bales back in the direction they'd come.

I was disappointed, but at least Ying was honouring the chain of ownership of what little opium there was. He could have denied all knowledge of the transaction, and I'd have had no grounds on which to challenge him. And he had muscular bouncers. Our transaction complete, or as complete as it would be, I asked, "Is there a back way out of here? I am being followed. Nothing to worry about, but now is the time to ditch him."

We bid our farewells, and one crony led me out of a side door. I was in an alley perpendicular to the wharf, and I walked through some winding alleys in westerly direction.

So, I was the proud owner of only two bales of opium, not eight. Where was the rest of Spratt's and my money for the buy? Did Ying pocket it? Or did Spratt keep it for some other purpose? Would my dealer back in Dongying be mollified with only one-quarter of what was promised? No, he wouldn't. He might not kill me, but I was likely to lose some fingers. I only had ten, and I was fond of all of them.

Even so, better some than none. Opium, I mean. I needed to find another ship fast.

Chapter Thirteen

I went back to the IMCS building after my meeting with the smuggler, Ying. It was evening, and the receptionist was preparing to finish for the day, stuffing her belongings into a capacious handbag. She testily gave me directions to the office that had been seconded for Heineken's use for the duration of his visit. She told me I was supposed to have seen him hours earlier. I should have snuck in the back way.

When I got to the top of the stairs, Heineken was already beckoning me from the doorway. I entered the office, and he went around the desk and sat in the chair. The office décor was opulent, with tapestries adorning two of the walls, an enormous bookcase covering the third, and large French windows beyond which was an inviting balcony. It must have been the best-furnished room in the building. Someone important had been dislodged to house Heineken in style.

He told me to sit. I did so in the ornate but uncomfortable straight-backed chair facing his intricately carved mahogany desk. Sculpted dragons at the desk's corners scowled at me. It was evening, and the sun was setting. The red sunlight streamed in through the window behind him, and I had to squint to see his silhouette.

"We've missed you around here, my boy. Where have you been, and what have you learned?"

I gave him a heavily abridged progress report, leaving out my nefarious activities at the docks.

He leant back in his chair, his hands together and his fingers forming a steeple, fingertips touching one of his three chins. "You think it unlikely that Spratt was killed by a disgruntled merchant?"

"I do. That doesn't wash at all. There are plenty of perfectly legal ways for merchants to seek redress for punitive tariffs. And even if one was in a murdering mood, he'd have to know that Jack was merely a mid-level functionary. That killing him wouldn't change tariff pricing policy."

"Yes, I see what you mean."

"I'd like to explore the Japanese angle a little more, you see—"

"You're barking up the wrong tree there, my boy." He cut me off with a wave of his hand. "If the mighty Japanese want to make a statement, they'll simply march in and take the place. No, there's no reason for any Japanese involvement here. Don't look so sceptical."

Oops, I regained control of my face quickly. "Do you know anyone named Masamoto?"

"The civilian diplomat? Affable fellow, a little effeminate if you ask me. Name of Okori."

Good to know. I'd look him up later. "I think I'll call it a day, continue my investigations tomorrow."

"Tomorrow, I need you to accompany the local Polizei. They plan to make an arrest. You really can't go running off on your own the whole time. I expect you to be here to report to me, and only me, frequently."

"Must I? Accompany the local plod, I mean? I'm confident they're just fitting up some patsy for appearance's sake."

Heineken looked down indulgently at me through the red sun haze. "Yes, indeed, you must. See you in the morning when you return from that expedition. Think of it as a diplomatic one." His implication was unmistakable; it was an essential part of correct protocol to show a little respect for the local police, whether or not they deserved any.

Oh well, I must follow some orders, I suppose. I might even find out something I needed to know. Unlikely, but possible. I suppose it was 'good form' to invite an IMCS man to the arrest, and I had to toe the company line.

Given that the police almost certainly had the wrong man, I anticipated that I'd have to clash with them too somewhere down the line.

I left his office, but before leaving the building, I went to the basement. The bespectacled gatekeeper opened the counter and stood aside as I approached. I looked up the address of one Okori Masamoto. Fifty-One Sajik Street in the diplomatic quarter. Definitely worth a visit.

I left the building and went in search of an inn where they served food and drink.

• • • •

I WAS LATE FOR MY APPOINTMENT with the police. I'd had a pleasant evening of food and drink after my meeting with Heineken and fallen into bed to enjoy the dreamless sleep of the exhausted drunkard. By the time I had arrived at the address Heineken had given me, before I'd even alighted from the rickshaw, I watched the police already leading a bleeding and cowering man out of the door of his rotting wooden shack. His face was a bloody pulp, and a brand-new red bandana had been placed askew on his head.

I had hailed a rickshaw from the steps of my hotel, and my driver was visibly relieved when we finally arrived. The address was in the hills to the east of the city, and the ascent had left him very short of breath. I climbed out of the shaded cabin, and he immediately dropped the rails and slumped down on the ground. He rolled himself a cigarette to soothe his lungs. I told him to wait for me. The air was cleaner and cooler up here, though the terrain was arid. The winding dirt road whence we'd come was dotted with one-room shacks along both sides at intervals of about fifty feet. They appeared to be constructed from discarded planks and sheets of corrugated iron. The area here was treeless, the only flora being scrubby bushes, doggedly clinging to the dry soil.

From the purple bruises on the prisoner's face and from his limp, it looked like a 'confession' had already been extracted from the handcuffed wretch that was being bundled into the oxen-drawn police wagon by two stone-faced police constables. I hoped to never find myself on the wrong side of the local constabulary and receive similar treatment. My opium activities might just see me at the wrong end of their clubs.

I sidled up to the policeman with the most gold trinkets on his uniform, who was standing just outside the doorway to the shack. He also had the shiniest boots and was thus obviously in charge. He looked me up and down spoke to me with a straight face. "The prisoner is a known lieutenant of the defeated Donghak Rebellion. I hope you'll report our efficient resolution of the case to your superiors?"

"My 'superiors'? I'm yet to be convinced I have an equal." I grinned at my little witticism.

Alas, flippant irony wasn't part of his vocabulary. He blinked at me for a moment, still not sure what to make of me. "I hope Mr. Möllendorff, and Mr. Heineken will be pleased."

From this I inferred that he believed my remit to be nothing more than being present to observe the fine job he and his men were doing. But his hope of pleasing the IMCS hierarchy was no concern of mine. "I need to see inside."

My demand to inspect the suspect's dwelling was met with bemused expressions from the other two policemen, but they grudgingly allowed me inside. It was a one-room hovel and smelled of stale opium, cheap rice wine, and excrement. A sparse peasant's bachelor pad, with a bamboo mattress on the floor, a table with one chair, a dirt floor and no bookshelf or personal touches at all. It smelled lived-in but didn't look it. It was merely a place to sleep. The digs didn't look like the home of a lieutenant in an army, albeit a defeated rebel one.

It took me only a minute to search the place, and there was nothing there that could give me any insight into the bombing, certainly no revolutionary material, or any other evidence of the man's political leanings.

That was no more or less than I expected, though it was interesting to note how important it was to the local police to be showing efficiency in front of the IMCS. I guess they 'saved face' today. It left me wondering who they thought their employer was—their king or the IMCS? Maybe they just wanted to ingratiate themselves with every possible government instrumentality, hedging their bets so they'd emerge unscathed after the coming power struggle.

I wondered to what other lengths they might stoop to ingratiate themselves with the IMCS and with Möllendorff in particular.

I left the sordid dwelling, thanked the police, and had the rickshaw driver take me to Jack's apartment. He spent most of the journey using his sandalled feet as brakes to keep us from hurtling down the slopes, kicking up quite a little dust storm. Downhill was, apparently, no easier than uphill for a rickshaw driver. I missed Mistral.

Jack's apartment building was on the fringes of the foreigner quarter. It was a red brick, three-storey structure with a red tile roof and utilitarian architecture. Practical rather than pretty, apart from the little terracotta dragons at each corner of the roof. The entranceway and portico faced north—no Asian architect could ignore feng shui.

All the non-executive IMCS personnel lived here, and the building had a Chinese manager and caretaker who occupied a small booth just inside the front door. He put down his newspaper, slipped on his sandals and led me upstairs. As we walked down the corridor, I heard raised voices coming from behind the door of the apartment opposite Jack's. The caretaker pulled a keyring from his pocket, unlocked Jack's apartment door and then turned and went back downstairs. I opened the door to my late friend's digs, and I saw at once that the entire place had been thoroughly searched. Like mine, it was a one-room affair with one door and one window with floral curtains. Strewn on the wooden floor were the contents of the wardrobe, whose doors stood open to reveal empty coat hangers. The mattress had been overturned and slashed, and all the drawers in the bureau had been removed and upturned.

Standing in the doorway, I could tell that no effort had been made to conceal the ransacking of the apartment, and it was evident that it had been more of a looting than a search for clues as to the identity of Jack's killer. It had to be the work of the police. I mentally chalked up another black mark against Seoul's finest. While I had no objection to a little victimless graft, police looting was a horse of another colour.

I'd tried one time to explain to a Manchu official—the minister for justice, no less—the importance of the rule of law if China was to ever join the ranks of modern civilised countries. He blustered at first about how ancient China had been civilised for millennia at a time when Europeans were still living in caves, and I had to concede that salient point. But he ultimately lost the argument when he pointed out that without some corruption, how would a policeman get paid?

That was the day, at a lavish diplomatic garden party to which I was mistakenly invited, that I learned how the dynastic government service worked and how it had worked for millennia: government officials didn't get paid by the central government, they were expected to make their own 'salary' through graft and corruption, hopefully not too excessive. Any official accused of corruption was thus being accused only of *too much* corruption because there was understood to be an acceptable level. It saved the central government from having to pay and transport wages. That was why government posts required one to pay a large sum to the outgoing incumbent to effectively buy the position.

I searched Jack's room, tidying up as I went. I put the mattress back on the iron bed frame and shoved all the clothes and loose mattress stuffing under the bed. The more I searched, the angrier I became. Was this all the justice Jack was going to get? Just me snooping about aimlessly, alone? I had my own life-threatening problems to deal with, but this was getting under my skin. I knew that if there was to be any justice for Jack, I'd have to get it myself. When I got the chance. When I had everything else under control.

While shoving things under the bed, I encountered, of all things, a high school blazer. Why Jack kept it, I had no idea. I hung it back up in the wardrobe where it looked lonely and sad. I went through what remained of Jack's wardrobe, his empty desk, his toiletries that were strewn about, and I'd even looked under the threadbare rug to see if there were any loose floorboards. I sat down on the bed and lit a smoke.

There was one of the new Kodak folding cameras on the shelf above the radiator. It would have cost him a week's wages. I took it down from the shelf and opened it up. Alas, it contained no film. I made a mental note to ask Anee if there were any photographs of Jack's I could have.

I sat back on the bed and sighed. I couldn't stop investigating now. I had nothing that could be called a trail, but what little I had I'd chase down. Maybe take on the avenging business for just a little while. Anee would appreciate that.

Anee. Given their love, I doubted that Jack even spent all that much time in this apartment. I wouldn't have. Just a place to keep clothes. But he must have kept some things here, things he wouldn't want to keep either at Anee's house or at his office.

Clothes. Why had he kept his old high-school blazer? He'd hated every minute of his schooling. Who didn't? I went and pulled the blazer from its bamboo hanger and sat back down on the bed. There was nothing in the pockets, but the hemline felt stiff. Something was sewn inside. I got my little pocket knife out and attacked the stitching. Out came some large pieces of paper. They were share certificates in the Rocky Mountains Railroad Corporation. Six of them, granting the holder one hundred stocks each. *What the hell?*

Could *that* be where the rest of our opium money went? A goddamn share investment?

Or could the stocks be payment for some other favour? Were they valuable?

I pulled out the clothes I'd shoved under the bed and rummaged through all of them, even underwear. None of them had anything sewn into them.

Did Spratt blow our opium money on some bloody stocks? What was he up to? Was he stitching me up? Were the stocks even transferable? No, I knew the answer to that one. Not transferable, not unless I was his heir. Was Anee his heir?

I lay back on the bed and blew a smoke ring up to the water-stained ceiling. The mysterious Mister Jonathan Spratt. *What were you up to?* A gorgeous fiancé who was once mistress to a Japanese diplomat. A fiancée from a formerly noble family line. Missing opium. Corporate stocks. Possibly bought with some of my money.

I began to wonder if I knew the man at all.

Attached to the last share certificate was a list of stockholders. I read the names. The biggest stockholder appeared to be Barings Bank. Möllendorff's name was on the list, along with several other members of the executive class of the IMCS.

Could Spratt have bought the stock just so he could get a look at the names of the stockholders? Was he investigating Möllendorff? If so, this was an expensive way to go about it. Could such costly digging have come to the attention of the wrong people? Murderous people? I was going to have to look into my German superior a little more closely and see if there was any way, legitimate or otherwise, to turn these stocks into cash.

Chapter Fourteen

The stock certificates needed serious further investigation. But one problem at a time.

Mr. Lu was a jolly fat man in a dapper waistcoat and cravat, with gold front teeth. He was expecting me.

I'd walked to the merchant quarter, one street back from the docks. With a bulging inside pocket full of the papers from Jack's diary and folded stock certificates, I'd left his apartment and gone in search of some lunch, after which I found the tobacconist's shop at the address Ying had given me. Stepping from the bustling street and through a beaded curtain, my eyes met a narrow but deep store. Both walls were covered with small glass-fronted wooden drawers. If they were all tobacco, then this was a bewildering range. I wanted to sample all of them immediately, such was the intoxicating aroma of the place. On my left, the proprietor was standing behind a glass-topped counter. I told him who I was and why I was there.

Mr Lu, who'd told me his name, smiled, his eyes sparkling over the tops of his reading glasses, perched on the very tip of his nose. "Dongying, I'm told by our mutual friend, is to be the ultimate destination of your packages. I can accommodate you, sir, rest assured of that." He bowed his head slightly.

"How much?"

He hesitated at my abrupt question and looked me up and down. "Fifteen silver taels. Ingots, not coins."

Yes, obviously ingots. No one trusted the locally minted coins. Each province had its own mint, producing silver and copper coins of widely varying purity. Even the IMCS didn't trust them to be wholly made of the metal that they claimed to be. Ingots, however, could be easily tested and exchanged anywhere.

"I'll pay no more than ten, and I'll take a pound of tobacco as part of the deal." My bargaining position was weak. I would normally have offered him one-third of the price he asked, then walked away if he refused. I was a dab hand at the haggling tango. But his foreknowledge of my predicament gave him the advantage.

He countered with, "I'm afraid space on ships is at a premium at the moment. Much profit can be made from war and even from merely preparing for war. War may not come, but supplies bought for such a contingency cannot be returned either way."

I waited. It was his turn to counter with an actual number. If I spoke now, I'd have to give a number higher than ten. I let the silence vacuum grow, and eventually he fell in. "I can go no lower than twelve, and you must bribe the petty officer of the ship yourself."

Everyone had their hand out. I sighed. "Done."

It would have to do. With a possible naval battle in the offing, maybe sea freight would be dicey, but the land route from here to Dongying was out of the question; it'd be about seven hundred miles around the Bohai gulf and would traverse three provinces. Best to send the goods with an experienced expert and standing behind the counter in front of me was the most expert person in Seoul that I knew, which meant almost nothing.

Mr. Lu nodded his assent. "Day after tomorrow, present yourself at the loading bay of warehouse forty-five, at the north-west end of the wharf, wearing that customs blazer. You will be met by my man, and the transaction concluded."

I handed over twelve ingots.

The deal done, he reached under the counter and pulled out a large, lacquered red box with gold trim and proudly laid out some of his under-the-counter tobacco stash for discerning customers. "Hand-rolled on the thighs of virgins." I took some and stuffed it into my pouch.

"Boys or girls?" I asked.

He smiled and snorted and took two ready-made cigarettes from the lacquered box. On the counter, there was an oil lamp under a bronze tray. In the tray was some scented oil, the vapour of which wafted gently upwards. He used the burner to light the two cigarettes, passed one to me, and put the other between his lips. We smoked together in silence as a kind of ritual conclusion to our arrangement.

Between fellow smokers, small talk is usually called for. When our cigarettes were half-way smoked, I asked, "Know anything about railroad stocks?"

"You looking to buy? I know a man—"

"No, no, just curious. I live in Shandong, and I've seen no railroad construction. I heard the Qing forbade it. Bad feng shui."

"Bah! Ancient superstitions standing in the way of progress."

I looked around the store. "I notice *your* doorway faces north, and your stairway is off to the side, invisible from the door. You're a feng shui believer."

"No, but my customers are. You're right, though, railroad stocks are worthless just now. But if the damn Japanese take over, and I think they will, construction will start all over Korea. If the Qing haven't figured out that being behind the times means being swept aside, then they deserve everything they get."

I took a long drag on the cigarette. It got better with time. "They say that now that the Empress has retired and the rightful ruler is in charge, reforms are imminent."

"Maybe, but they'll come too late. The Japanese got a head start years ago. If they're serious, they'll take this peninsula easily, and more besides."

"So, you think railroad stocks are a good investment? My late friend had these." I took the certificates out of my pocket and showed him.

"Sure. They're cheap enough. I have some myself. See? There's my name on the back page." And so it was. "The smart money is on someone, the Japanese, Brits, Russians, whoever, getting the rights to build the railroads. Which means the Qing must be softening towards foreigners. Or else they're being bullied by foreigners. Japanese, on the other hand, will give anyone a contract if they grease the right palms. Or if they conquer China."

That'll never happen, though the Japanese might succeed in seizing a little Chinese territory if they're determined. But the whole enormous country? They didn't have the balls.

Mr. Lu smiled and stubbed out his cigarette on the floor. "You should diversify too, don't put all your opium in one bastard." He laughed himself into a coughing fit.

We shot the breeze a little more, and then I asked him if he knew where a gentleman might imbibe some opium. And wouldn't you know it? Mr. Lu had a small den and brothel right above the shop. I went upstairs and availed myself of both facilities.

I stumbled back to my lodgings in the early hours, my purse significantly lighter, and went to sleep in my clothes.

I got into the office early the next day. Early for me being ten o'clock. I was fuzzy and grumpy and determined to make some progress with the investigation. Ask a few uncomfortable questions.

I trudged up the stairs. I passed Möllendorff's office just as Heineken was coming out, closing the door behind him. I cursed myself again for not entering via the rear of the building. Slow learner.

Heineken frowned at me. "Where've you been? You look like something the cat dragged in. Now that they have apprehended the culprit, it's time to turn our attention to hiring Spratt's replacement."

"I don't think even the police truly believe they've got their man."

"Whether or not they believe it, his execution tomorrow will put an end to the matter."

"So, that's it? Investigation over? We're all satisfied with such a perfunctory search for Jack's murderers?"

He stopped frowning and donned his paternal face. "We're not the police, Phillip. Usurping the local authorities would win us no friends here. And we'll need friends, believe me."

I was getting angry about the general disinterest in getting justice for Jack, so turned to go before I said something I'd regret. Besides, I felt nauseous. It wouldn't do to vomit on the Baron's shiny boots.

Heineken stopped me. "Wait. This telegram came for you from Dickinson." He handed it to me. "But I wouldn't lose too much sleep over it."

It was folded, but I had no doubt he'd read it before handing it to me. I put it in my pocket without reading it. Heineken smiled. "You must now turn your attention to getting that department up and running again. There are tariffs to be collected, import documentation to complete and sign off, et cetera. Director Möllendorff's secretary has written up a list of prospective candidates for Spratt's job and included a precis of their suitability. You are to conduct the preliminary interviews. I'll be very interested to hear your recommendations. Give their language skills a good going over. Put them to the test. Make them work for the opportunity. You're an expert judge of character." When had he drawn that conclusion? "Your list of preferred candidates will then be interviewed by the director."

"Understood. I'll get right on it." *After some strong coffee.*

We were still in the corridor outside Möllendorff's office. We parted, and I turned and walked the few paces to Möllendorff's secretary's office and went in.

I took the proffered list from the stone-faced though efficient-looking secretary and went to the temporary office they had allocated for me. Once seated at the desk, I pulled out Dickinson's telegram from my pocket. It read: *"I know what you've been up to. Your demise is imminent."*

I screwed it up and set fire to it in the ashtray. There'd be a carbon in the telegram room, but I still enjoyed seeing his missive turned to ash.

I would have to do some of my job, though Heineken was being a mercifully indulgent boss. I would have to sort out the department before I could continue my search for Spratt's killer. Eyes would be on me.

I'd have to start immediately. But I still had' one more errand to run.

Chapter Fifteen

I left the office and went looking for this Okori Masamoto chap, to either confirm or eliminate him as a suspect, if Jack's murder was a crime of passion by a cuckolded suitor. Out in the street, I felt a hot blast of wind on my face. It was only late morning, but I could tell the day was going to be sweltering. I could almost smell the previous night's opium oozing out of my pores with my sweat.

I needed to find out what Okori knew. I wanted to find out whether he was a military man and knew his way around weapons. Black powder in particular. Heineken had said he was a civilian diplomat, most of whom were usually retired military men. I only wished I had some leverage. I couldn't imagine a Japanese diplomat talking to me willingly without it.

I thought I'd try my luck first with the Japanese consulate, which was only two streets away. I slung my blazer over my shoulder and hit the pavement. I crossed to the shaded side of the street and after two blocks I was standing in front of my destination. The building looked nothing like a consulate. It looked like a military barracks and operations coordination centre. The building was set back from the street and had a high wrought-iron fence with spikes along the top. Behind this was a small parade ground, with the main building looming over it like a scolding parent. Brutalist, I think you call that kind of architecture. Every other building on the street had a high stone wall. I guess the Japanese weren't shy about passers-by watching their soldiers on parade. What's the point in flexing one's muscles if nobody is there to see it? Almost everyone coming or going through the gates of the entrance wore a uniform. I didn't like the look of it and decided I'd be better off catching Masamoto on his own. The building was imbued with serious officiousness, and I had an instinct that nobody within its walls would be free to talk openly.

I waited across the road in a café, nursing a German beer and watching the entrance. The beer was good for my hangover. My constitution wasn't yet ready for food.

At noon I watched a man leave the consulate building. He was not in uniform. He wore a mustard-coloured suit with a matching waistcoat and a pink cravat. His hair was puffed up upon his head, and his moustache had waxed curls.

Heineken had said that Okori was 'effeminate'—this had to be him.

I finished my beer, the one I'd been nursing for an hour, and left the café to follow him as he walked east. I stayed a discreet distance behind and scanned the street, looking for a suitable place to buttonhole him, but before he got a hundred yards, he turned into a lane. I hurried after him, but when I reached the corner, he was nowhere to be seen. I walked along the lane, looking at the doorways and any names over them to see if I could figure out which one he'd entered. I found it halfway along. A bathhouse. I could see steam wafting out of a funnel two stories above me. I could smell it, too, and I imagined that I was inhaling the salty and acerbic effluvia of the pores of dozens of Japanese men.

I could have done with a good sweat myself, but the iron door with its narrow peephole slit told me it was an exclusive establishment, unlikely to admit riff-raff like yours truly.

I was just going to have to watch the door and wait for Okori to emerge. Sadly, there was no inn or café from which I could hold my vigil in comfort. I loitered in a shaded doorway.

Over the course of an hour, I watched a dozen well-dressed men emerge from the door and lock it with a key of their own. The last of these men was Okori. He locked the door behind him and walked in my direction down the alley. When he drew almost level, I stepped out of the shadows and into his path.

"Why did you murder my friend Jack?" While waiting for him, I'd decided on a dramatic opening gambit. He was low on the list of likely culprits, but it never hurt to shake the tree.

The question flustered him for a few moments, after which he composed himself. "What on earth are you talking about? You're accusing me of being a murderer?"

I noted that he didn't ask who Jack was. "Yes. You blew him to bits in a jealous rage."

He frowned at me for a half a minute. Then his face softened. "Ah, I see what's happening here. You don't believe anything of the sort. You're trying to find something out by catching me off guard. Fair enough, I've used the strategy myself. Who are you?"

"Swageman, of the IMCS." Recognition flickered behind his pretty eyes. Now that his face was close to mine, I saw how heavily made up it was. There were no eyebrows, just a brown line drawn over each eye, perhaps tattooed, and long eyelashes. He had some powder on his face and a little rouge in the cheeks. And he reeked of some European cologne. If he'd been wearing an evening gown, he'd have looked like one of those lady-boys Jack and I had danced with one night in a bar in Bangkok. One of them had Jack completely taken in, partially thanks to a particularly lethal local liqueur. He was exceedingly embarrassed the next morning when he woke up beside one of them and swore me to secrecy on pain of death, and I thought I detected a slight limp to his gait. Good times...

Okori snapped me out of my reverie when he spoke to me in English, "Ah, yes. I see the logo on your jacket pocket. I gather you were hoping to catch me... how do the English say it? On the hind leg?"

"Back foot. From cricket."

"A baffling game."

"And less entertaining than watching bamboo grow."

He let out a brief chuckle. "Really, Mr. Swageman, you don't need me on the back foot. May I call you Swagger?"

"You know who I am?"

"Our late friend Mr. Spratt spoke of you often. Let's not talk in this smelly alley. Can I interest you in some sake?"

I told him to lead the way, and we walked together out of the lane and back in the direction of the diplomatic quarter. We didn't talk, and I was trying to put the pieces together in my mind. This man said he was a friend of Jack's. But Jack stole Anee away from him. Or did he? Why would Jack have need of a friend in Japanese diplomatic circles?

Okori held open for me the door to a small storefront. A suited man led us down a corridor lined with sliding doors to a private room where we sat cross-legged on cushions on the floor with a low table between us. The suited man exchanged some words in Japanese with Okori that were too fast for me to understand, then he closed the paper-clad sliding door, and we were alone in this little slice of Japan installed in Korea.

I got comfortable on the hard cushion. "How did you come to be friends with Jack?"

"Wait a moment." He looked to the door, and an elaborately dressed woman with her face painted white entered and placed a tray on the table and then retreated, sliding the door closed behind her. Okori poured two small cups from the steaming sake jug and handed one to me. He raised his cup, and I mimicked him. We drank.

Rituals. The Japanese, and indeed the Chinese, love their elaborate rituals. They tried my patience.

The first cup consumed, now he was ready for conversation. "I met Jack at a function at our embassy about six months ago, and I'm very glad I did."

"The one you attended with Yi Cuifang, English name Anee?"

He wasn't taken aback. "Yes. You've met with her." Not a question, a statement of fact; they still talk to each other. "I used to ask her to accompany me to functions. My colleagues are almost all married, and their wives are here in Korea with them. It's good protocol to have a lady on one's arm."

"She described herself as your mistress."

He smiled. "How sweet of her. I allowed my colleagues to believe that she was, and she was happy with the façade. But I lost her as a party companion the evening her eyes met Jack's. What passed between them was akin to electricity, and when he began courting her in earnest, I gave them my blessing."

I couldn't be sure, but I began to suspect that Okori wasn't likely to be interested in *any* women. I suspected that he played for the other team, as it were. I had no problem with that. My father had said more than once, "Only a fool would resent the existence of the queers. By taking themselves out of the game, they improve the ratio for the likes of us, boy. More skirt for you to chase, what?"

Okori poured more sake and offered me one of his cigarettes, a Woodbine, which I knew to be hand-rolled in Bristol, England, and very expensive in China if they could be bought at all. I took one, and while he was lighting it for me, he said, "You're investigating the death of your friend?"

I drew deep and discovered why they were so expensive. With my larynx coated in what felt like honey, I replied, "Yes. Though the investigation is more or less complete, the police were scheduled to execute the culprit this morning. He's probably in an unmarked grave already."

"You say, 'more or less'. You believe they have the wrong man?"

"I do. You described Jack as a friend. You met with him often after that function?"

Okori Masamoto sat still and stared at me for a long time, apparently making an assessment, weighing up some question in his mind. The ash of his cigarette lengthened and fell onto the table. After almost a minute, his face changed. He appeared to have made some decision. He dropped his cigarette on the floor, leaned forward conspiratorially, and said, "Many times, but in secret. He and I shared a common aim."

The room had paper wal"s. If leaning close and speaking softly was his idea of clandestine tradecraft, then he had a lot to learn. He could get himself killed. Or someone else.

He stared at me again, hoping I'd give him some indication that he could continue without fear of... *what?*

"It's okay Masamoto, Jack and I have no secrets from one another. Had," I corrected myself. "I reckon I know what you're about to tell me, I merely need to hear it from your own lips." I took a sip of tepid sake.

He relaxed and took a deep breath. "Then you know we were spying for each other."

Chapter Sixteen

You what? I couldn't help it, I involuntarily sprayed him in the face with coughed-up sake. I turned my face away and continued to cough uncontrollably, sending an acidic spray of bile, tobacco, and sake onto the floor. It took me a full two minutes to compose myself.

The effeminate Japanese diplomat sitting cross-legged across the table from me, in a private room of a Japanese restaurant, stared open-mouthed at me with my spit dripping from his chin. He wiped his wet and stunned face with a scented lilac handkerchief. His reaction to my reaction made it obvious to him that I did not, in fact, have any idea that there was any spying going on. That Jack had indeed kept secrets from me. Okori's expression was one of regret, presumably for revealing a secret. He looked frightened.

Regardless, I needed to hear more. Much more. "Relax, Masamoto, you have nothing to fear from me. Please explain things to me as if I was Jack's confidante. I have no loyalty to any government, and I'm only loyal to the IMCS to the extent that they pay me. Nothing you tell me will leave this room. I only want to find out why, and by whom, Jack was killed."

He called for the waitress, and when she came, he ordered more sake, perhaps needing some Dutch courage. She returned with a rag to clean the table and another steaming jug. Okori poured us both a generous amount, and we drank deeply of the scalding liquid.

"Okay, I'll fill in some details for you. But this information is most dangerous. You're new here. You won't know who to trust. So, trust no one. Please say it."

"I will trust no one."

Cautiously satisfied, he took a deep breath and plunged in. "Jack and I shared a belief that the peoples of the east should not fight with each other. We, Japan, China, Korea, et al., share a common enemy: Europeans. If we fight amongst ourselves, we weaken each other, paving the way for rapacious powers to plunder us. It is well known that the European aristocracy considers us to be little evolved above monkeys. Many call us yellow monkeys. Jack saw the inherent injustice in the European worldview, and we became fast friends over our shared desire to prevent the East deteriorating into squabbling among ourselves."

It was true that Jack had 'gone native' with some alacrity. Despite being a white New Zealander of good, if poor, Anglo-Celtic stock, he became smitten with every Chinese woman he saw and found the food, the philosophy, the medicine, and the culture as a whole, far superior to the venal and oppressive colonial culture we had both fled.

Okori went on, "We exchanged information and compared notes regarding our respective masters. Jack didn't trust the IMCS or the Qing, and I don't trust the Meiji, who do everything the old shogunate families tell them."

My Japanese history was sketchy and had many gaps, but I recalled that they had ended a warlord period about thirty years ago and reinstated an emperor-style system. The shoguns were the ruling class, nowadays united under an emperor named Meiji. But as I understood it, Meiji rubber-stamped any and all military matters that the aristocratic shogun families decreed.

"Despite our growing friendship, Jack remained anxious. He was willing to collaborate, but only up to a point. I understood his reticence. I decided, as a show of faith, to share with him a list I had discovered at the embassy. I had chanced upon a telegram I was not supposed to have seen while sorting through the correspondence of an admiral who'd been taken ill."

"Some kind of strategic plans for war?"

"More incendiary even than that. It was a list of the names of members of the Qing government and of the IMCS who were providing material support to the Japanese military."

"You mean, like, double agents?"

"I am unfamiliar with the term, but I suppose it fits; people who appear to work for one master when their true loyalties lie with the enemy."

Incendiary indeed. "You gave this list to Jack?"

"To prove I trusted him. I had copied down the names, then re-sealed the telegram into its envelope and sent it on its way to the admiral."

I had found no such list, but then Jack's office and home had been thoroughly searched long before I got to them. "What did Jack do with the list?"

"He put it in his pocket and said he needed to talk the matter over with someone. He wouldn't say the man's name. He simply referred to him as 'the German'. I cautioned him against such a course of action. He promised he would keep my name out of any discussions and that I had to be satisfied with that."

"Did it work? Did your giving him the list make him trust you? To compile a similar list of double agents among the Japanese that were supplying information to the IMCS and the Qing?"

"That was his promise. He said that he'd prepared the list already and would hand it to me at what he called 'a suitable time'. Sadly, he never got the chance to fulfil his promise."

Phew. This was hard to swallow. My friend Jack, the spy. How would Jack even know what double agents we had embedded with the Japanese? I asked, "Where did you meet him to give him your list? It would have had to be somewhere very private indeed."

"Cuifang's home. Anee's", he corrected himself. "It was safe there, far from prying eyes."

Except for hers. I wondered what made Okori and Jack feel so safe there. Jack was always too trusting of women. It's why he had to flee New Zealand. Whenever things went awry for any man, my mother used to say *'cherchez la femme'*—look for the woman. And getting a black powder bomb dropped in one's lap is about as awry as things could get.

My head spun with questions, but Okori told me he had to leave. He'd been away from his office for too long, and he didn't want his superiors to get suspicious. We agreed to meet again, though we didn't set a time. He told me I could get a message to him through Anee.

He left the sake house first, and I waited a full fifteen minutes before leaving, and even then, it was via a rear exit I found. Can't be too careful.

I ambled along the lane behind the sake house, and the thought of going to the office filled me with inertia. Today was July 21st, a month after the summer solstice. I watched some women in the street exchanging decorated fans and eating lychees, this being a traditionally auspicious time on the calendar. I couldn't remember why.

Okori had given me a lot to think about, yet I couldn't quite regard him as an ally, though I had so few. Who were these double agents? If they killed Jack for Okori's list, were they now complacent enough to call the matter closed, their secrets safely unrevealed? Or would they come after anyone looking too closely into Jack's murder?

It was entirely possible that everything Okori told me was bullshit. A story made up to... what? Deflect me from investigating him, the jilted lover, as suspected of murdering Jack? Did I believe that he was not jealous, that he gave his blessing to the besotted couple? Would he risk torture and execution for giving state secrets to Jack? Merely to earn Jack's trust? Did I believe that Okori and Jack were fellow travellers, conjoined by their mutual pacifism and love for the peoples of the orient? Too many questions. I needed to focus on what I knew. The unnamed 'German fellow' was probably Möllendorff, the head of the IMCS in Seoul. If he had had Jack killed for the double agent list, I'd be next if I didn't cease and desist from my enquiries. That made evading my watcher doubly important.

Come to think of it, was I still alive because the list had *not* been found among Jack's possessions? What if Möllendorff himself was one of the double agents? He'd want to avoid exposure and find and destroy the list. Maybe he had? And thus, knew that there was no danger of me finding it?

I had seen no indication that any spies had been rounded up, no surprise arrests of IMCS personnel or mysterious staff disappearances. That told me that Okori's list hadn't been found by the right people, the people who could use it to reduce hostilities, as Okori, the supposed pacifist, would want. If Möllendorff, or whoever, had found it, the threat would evaporate, and no action would be needed. The identities of any double agents embedded in the Japanese camp would be safe, the problem contained.

I bought a bag of lychees and munched away, spitting the pits into the street as the locals do. As I turned the corner to the block my apartment building was on, a cool sea breeze hit me in the face. I buttoned up my blazer against the cold and felt the stiff cardboard of Jack's share certificates in my inside pocket. I stopped walking.

Jack was no patriot, not the Jack I remembered. If he had valuable information, his first thought would surely be to sell it. I would have. Maybe he was playing Okori, his fiancé's ex-lover, pretending a mutual love of the Asiatic peoples to get his hands on a very saleable commodity, then bought stocks with the proceeds. Or perhaps the stocks *were* the proceeds.

Whatever, I walked on. My head was a maelstrom of facts, half-truths, suspicions, and questions. *Just put one foot in front of the other, Swagger, and watch your back.*

Find the killer and the motive. Find justice. Whatever other worms wriggled out of the can after I opened it. Deal with them later if needed.

Möllendorff was my new suspect number one. Though there was no way I would be able to interrogate him, he'd have no motivation for answering my questions, and the asking would tell him what I knew. I'd continue to treat him like the German mushroom he was. Keep him in the dark under a pile of manure.

I hadn't yet talked to any of the Koreans about the bombing, except that nameless policeman. Heineken had told me to make an appearance at the palace for form's sake and simply update "any official they offer up" on the investigation. Though if the purpose of such a visit was merely diplomatic, why not send the big cheese, Möllendorff?

Okori's information gave my intended visit to the palace a new slant. I would, delicately, sound them out about intrigues between the intimidating powers facing off on Korean soil. Koreans had been resisting Japanese 'help' for years—maybe I'd find an ally? After all, only three weeks ago pro-Japanese Korean revolutionary, Kim Ok-gyun, was assassinated in Shanghai. The Qing sent troops here to Korea at the request of King Gojong to quell the Donghak rebellion. Japanese claimed this to be a violation of the Treaty of Tientsin, which forbade the Qing or the Japanese from putting any extra boots on the ground here without informing the other. With the treaty 'violation' as their excuse, the Japanese were sending eight thousand troops to Korea. I'd seen them unloading at the docks and heading for the barracks. The Qing government had smugly turned down the Japanese 'suggestion' for the two of them to cooperate to reform the Korean government. When Korea demanded that the Japanese withdraw their troops from Korea, the Japanese refused.

Yes, it was time to have a chat with someone in the Korean government: the higher up, the better.

While my brain cogitated, my feet brought me to the hotel. I went upstairs and opened the door to my apartment. My ennui hit a new low. My room had been ransacked, and the diary was gone from its hiding place under the bed. Thankfully, the most valuable documents I had were in my bulging jacket pockets.

As depressing as it was, it told me one thing: my faceless enemy didn't have Okori's list because they were still looking for it.

Faceless, yes, but also impatient. I had a premonition that things were about to come to a head.

Chapter Seventeen

I vacated my still-dishevelled room after a fitful night of fighting insomnia and losing. Washed and dressed, I went and sought out a young street urchin. I found one in the lane next to the hotel and gave him a handful of coppers and a note. I told him to deliver the note personally to a Herr Heineken at Customs House. The little fellow treated me to a broad, gap-toothed smile, hoisted his loose hessian trousers tied with string, and scurried off in the wrong direction. I hoped he'd ask someone where the building was and find it eventually.

The note merely said: "Making progress, will be in later to debrief."

The seat of the Korean king's 'government' was the Gyeongbokgung Palace, eight miles away across the river. I hailed a shaded rickshaw and relaxed into the ride along one of the main arteries of the city. There was a traffic jam on the bridge, and I gazed at the river life. In the distance I could see the docks where the big ships were berthed, but closer I was treated to a kaleidoscopic display of small boat river life. Long, narrow boats, laden with fruit, grain sacks, fabrics, timber, or even passengers were being sculled by dark brown men whose muscles and taut sinews glistened in the sun. How they avoided collisions I'll never know, but avoid them they did, and they plied their craft with skill and efficiency.

The traffic thinned with the help of my shouting driver, and we soon found ourselves on the broad boulevard that circled the palace just outside its walls. I alighted, paid the driver, and walked through the tall stone gates under the watchful eyes of two Japanese soldiers who guarded the entrance.

An IMCS uniform, even if it was only the blazer, still denoted some status with the Korean king's government, and it was enough to get me past the officious gatekeeper at the administration building of the palace complex, which was just inside the gate. He directed me to another gatekeeper on the second floor. I ascended a wide and sturdy wooden staircase. This was a building for administration, not royalty, and the timber floor, plaster walls and ceiling were undecorated and painted in plain beige.

The fact that the king's 'government' had been usurped by the Japanese was neither here nor there to me. Some months earlier, a handful of Japanese troops had staged the weirdest of coups. The king now had to run all his edicts and memoranda through a Japanese general, but the country managed to muddle along even with that impediment. Why the Qing military hadn't taken this as an act of war, I could not understand. I knew the Chinese military had been weakened somewhat after fighting with the Frogs down south, but I wasn't sure that justified letting the Japanese get away with occupying the king's palace.

But occupy it they did, and somehow, in typically mystifying Eastern style, Korea went on much as it had before, while the Chinese and Japanese generals eyed each other warily, like a cobra and a mongoose.

Thus it was that I had to convince a palace functionary in a Japanese soldier's uniform to allow me to see someone senior in the Korean government administration.

I blustered and charmed my way in to see a man whose title, 'foreigner controller', made me smile. Throughout the entire region, for the last six decades, any attempts to control foreigners had been rebuffed with savage force. To assign a functionary such a title showed a very oriental inability to detect irony.

I knocked on the door marked Foreigner Controller and a voice within told me to "Come".

His office was a smaller, cheaper version of a Qing official's office. The furniture was plain and made from cheap pine, and hanging on the wall behind the desk was a tapestry depicting heroic battles, no doubt, but the images were too faded to make out. The room was airless and hot. The foreign controller was standing in front of his desk, and I walked in with my hand held out. He wore the uniform of a major in the Korean Army, which was essentially a khaki three-piece suit with brass buttons, epaulettes, and stripes on the arms.

There was no shaking of hands. The man before me was already scowling. I received one of the coldest receptions I'd had in a long time—and I'd had some utterly frozen ones. Before I'd even introduced myself, his ranting began in educated English. "The IMCS is decidedly on the nose, my good man. We Koreans no longer regard you as friends, ever since the Mason scandal. You'll recall, I'm sure, that the KoLaoHui, for whom your man Mason was working, were not just anti-Qing but had plans to assassinate our own King Gojong too!"

Ah, the Mason affair. My hopes of extracting useful intelligence took a dive. Mason was an inbred aristocratic British moron, duped by the flattery and faux mysticism of deranged Chinese fanatics. His idiotic collusion with Chinese revolutionaries had been a stain on the IMCS' reputation for years. Even so, I felt compelled to uphold the honour of my employer. "Mason was tried and found—"

"Then sent home to a comfortable retirement! We do not forget such slights, sir, we most certainly don't!" My uniform may have gotten me in the door, but it was a liability now. He had a point to make, and I was nearest. He was just getting started. "Yes, the Qing helped quell the recent rebellion, but at what cost? The resulting Sino-Japanese spat over a treaty violation threatens to plunge my country into war!"

The activities of the Qing 'ere now my fault. Perhaps I was to blame for the KoLaoHui and the Donghak too. China, and Korea for that matter, had innumerable secret societies, each with various and often contradictory agendas. But a common theme was the expulsion of foreigners. It's a miracle the IMCS had survived as long as it had, mostly thanks to Empress Cixi's goodwill. In this bureaucrat's eyes, I represented the IMCS. I was half-foreign, and *all* bastard. He'd give me both barrels for as long as I was in his office.

"—and King Gojong has a good mind to take the local customs service over himself! He certainly has a use for the revenue!"

Well, he could try... It was time I butted in. "Sir! If I may get a word in. The service is doing all it can to restore diplomacy here," fancy me, being the IMCS's defender, "and that all I hoped to ask you today was if you knew anything about the murder of a customs officer, and my friend, Jack Spratt."

He calmed down a little, perhaps realising that he could rant at me all day and still not change the customs service one iota. "You should direct such matters to the chief of police. I'll have someone take you to him." He rang a bell on his desk.

"Thank you, but I have spoken to them extensively already. What I'm hoping to learn from you is a little more, um... *sensitive*."

A junior uniformed man arrived and hovered in the open doorway. The foreigner controller waved him away. I got up and closed the door, then sat back down. "We have reason to believe that my colleague was murdered because he had uncovered information about the Japanese and their probable intention of wresting control of Korea from the Chinese." I was being deliberately vague.

He snorted. "We are not now, nor have we ever been, controlled by the Chinese! We are a sovereign state, sir. We pay only tribute to the Qing, in exchange for military support when, and only when, we request it."

He was deluded on that score, and he knew it, but had to retain 'face'. Korea being a Chinese 'tributary' state was the very opposite of sovereignty.

I held up a conciliatory hand. "I misspoke. Nevertheless, is there anything you can tell me about Japanese underhandedness in dealings with the palace?"

"They want to take over, as you say, by any means necessary. But there's nothing of any substance that I would care to tell the IMCS."

Hmm, that could have been taken two ways; he knew nothing, or he knew something, but wouldn't tell me.

I opened my mouth to speak, but he cut me off. "If you want to know who wants the Japanese in charge, talk to a German!"

That shut me up. For a moment, anyway. "What an enigmatic thing to say. And it helps me not a jot. Why would Germans help the Japanese?"

He smiled and tilted his head, like he expected to have to explain something obvious to a simpleton. "They're late to the colonial party. The kaiser wants to catch up with his grandmother, Queen Victoria. Thinks the Japanese might help. Now, I am a busy man, and this meeting is at an end."

I hadn't heard him ring the bell again, but a muscular man appeared in the doorway. I left.

I should have known the Koreans would be no help, but if one doesn't ask, one doesn't get.

His bizarre parting shot rang in my ears. What could possibly have elicited such a non sequitur? The IMCS was rife with Germans—they're our allies. What did he think I'd do with his strange expostulation? Go fight the kaiser?

The foreigner controller was a proud, mad, ranting fool. He deserved to have his country taken over by anyone who cared enough to do so. I certainly didn't.

Germans again. People kept telling me to look out for them, and it was time I paid heed. Even Jack had something written in German amongst his papers, which I still needed to get translated. Möllendorff was the boss around here and was probably in the building when Jack was killed. No more putting it off. I had to know what he knew.

Chapter Eighteen

I walked out of the decaying palace complex, leaving the Koreans to their own devices. If they thought sovereignty could be retained with whining and ranting, they were in for a nasty shock. Vigorous trade and superior weaponry kept nations intact. Just ask the Brits.

I was annoyed at myself for losing sight of the prize. Politics, intrigue, and a vague notion of justice were diverting me from my more important agenda—personal wealth.

I took a rickshaw back across the river to the docks. Mr. Lu, the Tobacconist, had not given me the name of the smuggler who'd be taking my opium back to the mainland, and that made me uneasy. All I had was a location. Warehouse forty-five was where he'd said it would be, at the north-west end of the long wharf dominating a half-mile of Seoul's river. I paid off my driver, dismissed him, and went and stood near the open door of the loading dock. A scruffy, uniformed man came over to me, smiling widely, showing an impressive array of silver teeth.

I gave him a slight nod. "You're Mr. Lu's man?"

"Yes, sir. Everything has been arranged." He took me inside the warehouse and showed me the two 'tea' bales with their neatly forged customs stencil and the manifest showing my name. The name of the ship they were going aboard was the *Matsushima*.

I was astonished. "What the hell is this? You're putting my goods on the flagship of the Japanese Navy?"

He gave me what I'm sure he thought was a reassuring smile. "Relax, customs man, we do this all the time. She's been ordered to go directly to WeiHaiWei, via Dalian and Dongying, so your shipment should be in Dongying within a fortnight. The quartermaster is my cousin. Your goods will be well taken care of."

Blimey. Smuggling some opium is one thing, doing it on a Japanese warship is a whole other kettle of danger. But it was my only, and thus my best, option. Take it or leave it. I took it.

At a nod from silver teeth, a coolie put my bales onto a cart, and I walked with him to the loading bay doors. The coolie headed down the wharf. Silver teeth retreated into the warehouse, and I stood watching the coolie's progress. He stopped when he was a good three hundred yards away, near the stern of a large, grey warship. I couldn't make out much from that distance, but I saw the bales loaded into a net with a bunch of other cargo and lifted aboard by a small crane.

Again, I waited and watched the coolie on his return journey with the empty cart, as if watching him somehow gave me a measure of control of the fate of my wealth. I shook myself and walked away from the warehouse loading bay. For good or ill, my opium was on its way.

I knew I'd better make an appearance at the office, I needed to get Möllendorff alone and interrogate him. And the longer I put off reporting to Heineken, the more explaining I'd have to do. Seeing my investment get swallowed into the hold of a Japanese warship gave me a sudden urge to conserve my meagre funds. I chose to use my feet rather than another rickshaw.

As I walked through the merchant quarter, I passed a jewellery shop whose name was familiar. I stopped outside the shop and rummaged through the papers in my pocket. I found the receipt for the ring Jack had ordered for his fiancé. The doorway was framed with two enormous elephant tusks, the ivory of which was elaborately engraved with Buddhist symbols. I entered the shop and handed the receipt to the man behind the counter who retreated through a beaded curtain behind him.

Jewellery didn't appear to be the primary inventory of the establishment. The shelves and cabinets held mostly exotic curios: carved ivory, certainly, but also tortoiseshell crockery and ashtrays,

Pangolin scale scrubbing brushes, and every possible incarnation of porcelain knick-knacks. There was an entire wall devoted to little drawers, the contents of each described with Chinese characters on the facing. They appeared to contain everything from the innocuous chrysanthemum flowers so favoured in Chinese medicine for every type of bronchial ailment, to ground Rhino horn for giving one's wedding tackle that extra oomph and longevity. I wondered if it worked.

"Your ring, sir." I hadn't heard the proprietor return from the back room.

I turned back to face him and took the proffered box. "It's all paid for, yes?"

"Yes, sir."

I was half tempted to hand it back and ask for a refund. Jack had squandered my money on stocks and fancy jewellery for his betrothed, after all.

But I had promised Anee.

I opened the box, only to find that I'd been holding it upside down because both the ring and its mounting plate fell to the floor and bounced under the counter. The proprietor gasped and dropped to his knees to search for the ring on his side of the counter, while a narrow slip of paper fluttered from the box toward the floor. I caught it before it landed and read it; "Darling, should anything happen to me, contact Swagger at the IMCS in Dongying. I have sent him two very important lists of names that he can use to avenge me should my enemies get the better of me. The lists are concealed in two bales of tea I plan to send him—"

Hell's bells!

"Found it, undamaged thankfully." The proprietor emerged from under the counter and handed me the ring. I remained still, not taking the ring, and stared at him open-mouthed while he took the box from my hand and returned the ring to its mount.

"Is everything okay, sir?"

I came to my senses. I put the note and the box in my pocket. I waved at the proprietor and left the shop in a daze, my legs working automatically. I broke into a run.

I had the spy list all along! Jack hid it in the damn opium. And I'd just put it on a Japanese Navy ship. And my name is on the blasted bales!

If the Japanese find it, I'm screwed. More screwed.

I stopped running and opted for a swift walk. I needed to catch my breath.

"Lists", Jack's note had said. Plural. Two lists. Jack must have prepared the list he'd promised to give Okori, a list of Japanese he knew or suspected of being double agents, passing information to the Qing. He was murdered before he could hand it over to the effeminate diplomat, if indeed he ever planned to.

Maybe he knew they were closing in on him. Whoever 'they' were. Why else hide the lists? In our opium, for goodness' sake?

And, via the note in the ring box, entrusting the information of the lists' whereabouts to Anee. What was he thinking?

He was thinking he might turn up dead. He must have been desperate.

My breath returned. I ran the rest of the way to the docks and headed straight for the *Matsushima*. There was a line of armed and uniformed Japanese sailors on the wharf, and I barrelled into them. They held firm, and one pushed me backwards onto my arse.

"I must speak to the quartermaster! He's been delivered the wrong, er..., spanners! Yes, and I need to retrieve them so I can deliver the right ones."

Spanners? I wasn't thinking straight.

The sailor who shoved me looked down at me, condescension written all over his face. "Too late, mister. The admiral." He pointed proudly to a man climbing the gangplank. I squinted at the figure lumbering up the steep stairs, trying to figure out who he was.

"Admiral Takagi", the sailor said, noticing my incomprehension.

I stood back up and watched the admiral arrive at deck level above, his chestful of medals glinting in the sun, where an honour guard awaited him with tasselled swords held aloft. The Japanese sure like their symbols of valour.

I pleaded with the sailor barring my way, pointing out my IMCS logo on my breast pocket. "Look, I just need a word with the quartermaster, or petty officer, or anyone about a package that went aboard only an hour ago. Just an administrative error, but we are very proud at Customs, and I need you to let me through so I can make it right. It would be dishonourable to the admiral if I do not."

I was babbling, and I must have looked agitated because the sailors saw right through me and started to get aggressive; four of them formed a semi-circle around me, ready for action. I retreated and went behind the warehouse buildings. I ran along the road servicing the rear entrances of the warehouses, looking for number forty-five. When I got there, I banged my fist on the closed loading bay door, and after an age, silver teeth emerged from another, smaller door to the left of the big one.

"We're closed. What do you want?"

"I must retrieve my bales from the *Matsushima*! It's a matter of national importance!"

"Not a chance. She sails soon, tomorrow or the next day. All shore leave cancelled, and the crew are preparing her for sea. It's impossible."

I argued with him, but I knew he was right. It was impossible. Jack's lists would have to stay where they were. I'd have to wait and hope that they would arrive in Dongying, two weeks from now. I sighed and scowled at the same time, then turned and walked away from the wharf. I had to get to the office. Given what I found there, I later wished I'd stayed at the wharf and become a stowaway on some ship, any ship.

Chapter Nineteen

My desultory amble from the docks back to the office in the late afternoon took far less time than I'd hoped. I chastised myself for allowing Jack's intelligence to fall into the hands of the Japanese. I wasn't looking where I was going and bumped into people on the footpath now and then, growling at them to look where they were going. I even swore at a tree I smacked into.

I tried to file the issue of the lists and their loss, under 'nothing can be done about it for now', but that didn't ease my funk.

I was angry with myself and everyone else. My investment was in the hands of the Japanese, as was the evidence that might point to Jack's killer. Both were on their way to the mainland with only a slim chance that they'd finish the trip undiscovered. I quickened my pace along the bustling street. I needed to wrap up my time in Korea, one way or another. My future was travelling to China, and I needed to shepherd it.

Whatever stupid job they needed me to do in this stupid country could wait. Or it could be left undone. I had more important things to do than play nice. With each step that brought me closer to the IMCS building, I grew increasingly irritable and impatient to do something, anything, about my plight.

Proof or not, for better or worse, I decided to confront Möllendorff with my 'evidence' and colluding-with-the-enemy suspicions. He was German. His name *had* to be on Jack's list. Push had come to shove. I hoped to rattle him by telling him I knew of the Japanese spy list. If nothing else, it would at least shake the tree. I'd see what, if anything, fell out of it.

I took the stairs at Customs House's entrance two at a time, strode past the open door of Möllendorff's secretary, arrived at the right door, turned the door handle, and charged inside. I stood, legs apart and hands on hips, while the door banged against the wall.

Facing me, surprised expressions on their pale stupid faces, crystal glasses and cigars in hands, were Möllendorff and... Dickinson. I was stunned and dumbstruck. I stood in the doorway, mouth agape. *How the hell did he get to Seoul so fast?* The threatening telegram he'd sent to Heineken, the one I'd intercepted, had only arrived three days ago. Maybe he sent it from Dalian while we were already in transit. Or maybe he sent it from right here in Seoul? Could he have come here on the very same ship that I had arrived on, the *ZhenYuen*, and kept himself hidden?

Such thoughts raced through my head in the blink of an eye. His presence was an infuriating surprise, but I wouldn't let it sway me or throw me off balance. While the two of them stared at me in their smartly pressed suits with eyebrows raised, I composed myself and forged ahead with my rehearsed allegation to Möllendorff. "You had Spratt killed to hide the fact that you're passing information to the Japanese and buying up railroad stocks. Banking on cashing in after you've helped the Japanese invade Korea."

Dickinson paused to absorb what I'd said, then closed his mouth and rearranged it into a sneer. "Ha! You are the stupidest—"

"Then the Japanese'll approve the railroad construction," I said, cutting the bastard off. "Your stocks' value will go stratospheric. Murder for profit, and I can prove it! Your name is on a certain list—"

Möllendorff held up a silencing hand, like a traffic policeman on a street corner. I shut up, having little more to say. Neither of their smug faces betrayed any kind of fear or even surprise. God, I hoped I was barking up the right tree.

Leaving his cigar in the corner of his mouth, Möllendorff put his other hand on Dickinson's shoulder, quietening him. "Alistair here is right. You're a fool, Swageman. Anyone with any brains is holding railroad stocks. The backward Qing can't halt progress forever, with their idiotic feng shui and simian superstitions. Hart encourages it and rubber-stamped my purchase without hesitation."

Shit. Not rattled, not even a little. Could I have it arse-about?

Dickinson smirked. "Thanks for giving me the last nail I needed for your coffin. Insubordination. Pack your bags, Chink, you're unemployed."

I punched him in his fleshy, smug face. Caught the bridge of his nose at the perfect angle. Seemed like the thing to do.

Möllendorff gasped and scrambled around his desk. His gritted teeth severed the cigar, and it fell to the floor while he ran at me, his arms out ahead of him, intending to grab me by the lapels. He seemed to be under the misapprehension that his seniority and bluster could cower any subordinate.

Instinct kicked in and I adopted the braced prayer stance; sideways on to your opponent, palms together in front of your chest as if praying, weight on slightly bent right leg, left foot out ahead of your body, toes pointed at your oncoming opponent. As his hands reached for my lapels, I pulled apart my arms, which connected thus with his forearms. That left him with arms akimbo, and his own momentum carried his face right into my head-butt. For the second time in the space of thirty seconds, I heard cartilage snap.

It was a simple trick I'd learned from a Chinese engineer on the ship from Australia. Trust the diminutive Chinese to figure out how to use a bigger opponent's momentum against them. While Möllendorff was stunned, I delivered a right jab to his solar plexus. He went down gasping, both hands over his nose.

Dickinson had recovered from his staggering, but on his way to where I stood, I delivered a swift kick to his balls that I hoped might prevent any continuance of his inbred family line.

I left them both groaning on their knees and made a speedy exit. I hurried downstairs, ran through the steamy kitchen and the scullery, and out of the rear exit of the building. I emerged breathless into the dusty rear courtyard. I didn't look back. I kept running. I zig-zagged my way through back alleys, heading for the docks. I had to try one more time to get hold of the spy lists Jack had hidden inside the opium bales before the *Matsushima* left the wharf. There *had* to be a way.

It was the pre-dinner rush hour, and it seemed to me that every resident of Seoul had come to this side of town as part of some grand conspiracy to thwart my progress. As people stood aside to let the big crazy customs man charge through, they laughed at the spectacle. The Koreans must share that joke with the Chinese; an 'important' person having to hurry can't be as important as all that. If he is in some kind of desperate rush, how important can he be?

I knew I'd flown off the handle back in the office, in the stupidest and most spectacular way possible. I was sure I was on the right track, but the cards I held did not trump Möllendorff's. So I had thrown a tantrum, and now I was unemployed and probably a fugitive. *Nice going, Swagger.*

I hadn't blown any conspiracy wide open. Not even a little.

As I rounded each corner, I listened for the sound of police whistles. Assault was not only a sackable offence but a criminal one. I'd already witnessed how eager the Seoul boys-in-blue were to please IMCS executive personnel. I was drawing far too much attention during my mad dash through town.

A possible silver lining occurred to me. Maybe my job was redeemable after all? Maybe I could get off with a disciplinary hearing and demotion? Surely Heineken would defend me? He'd said some things that indicated a dislike of Dickinson. Nothing blatant, but there was definitely an impatience and abruptness in the way Heineken spoke to the odious man. Might Heineken at least give me a fair hearing? He'd always acted like a kindly uncle to me. He'd at the very least let me explain how I came to suspect Möllendorff of conspiring with the enemy: *Herr Heineken, sir,*

Dickinson delivered a racial slur and sacked me. Surely my lashing out is, if not justified, at least understandable? Look. His nose is all healed up.

I turned down a less crowded alley. I stopped running and strode purposefully through the back lanes of the merchant quarter, trying to turn my mind to figuring out how to get aboard the *Matsushima*.

Möllendorff *had* to be the 'German' Okori had told me about. But even if he was secretly working for the Japanese, and the kaiser for that matter, his investing activities were apparently legitimate. His railroad stocks weren't indicative of wrong-doing and thus weren't a route by which I could catch him out. Perhaps Jack had simply made a wise investment when he bought stocks. Maybe acquiring the stockholder list was merely incidental? If that were true, then the only thing pointing to Möllendorff being a 'wrong'un' would be his name appearing on Jack's spy lists. And until I saw the lists, I couldn't be certain.

If Möllendorff was a double agent, I'd just alerted him to the fact that I was onto him by aiming the wrong accusation at him. Strategically unwise. But my forehead remembered the head-butt, and that gave me a smile. If I couldn't expose to justice the treacherous murderer, I could at least rearrange his face.

My pace slowed further. What if I *did* get my hands on the double-agent lists? What then? Keep pulling the string to uncover the mysteries? *What am I? Some kind of policeman?* Or should I call it quits and go home, with the hope that the shipment makes it to Dongying undetected? Spratt's murder was 'solved', and a man executed. I had a modest shipment of opium on its way to my dealer, which might keep him off my back for a few months. That's the only reason I came to Korea in the first place. Why was I allowing other agendas and purposes to creep into the caper? My opium was on its way home. That's what I came here to achieve. Sure, it's only a quarter of the quantity I planned, and sure, it's travelling under the watchful eyes of my enemies. But those two troublesome facts aside, I'd achieved what I came to achieve. I should just end the 'investigation' and ignore what I'd found out. Finding out more wouldn't bring Jack back to life.

Opium on its way—sort of—I thought I should now devote all my efforts to keeping my job. I would throw myself on Heineken's mercy.

Another, more delicious idea occurred to me. Perhaps I could use the lists for blackmail, squeeze a tidy sum out of the bastards before tumbling their game? That was a satisfying daydream, but no. Suicide. Geopolitics was a labyrinth too complicated for me alone. Though the spy lists might be useful for keeping my job, especially if Dickinson's name is on one of them, blackmail didn't strike me as a long-term money-making venture. It was much more likely to lead to death. It's probably why Jack was murdered. I was determined to remain *un*murdered.

That's what I'd do: Get Jack's lists and use them to try to keep my job and get back to the way things were in comfortable, anonymous Dongying. Justice for Spratt and his 'widow' was beyond me. Let those sleeping dogs lie, go back to life as it was, with fingers crossed.

I walked through the dock gate and froze. The enormous rump of the *Matsushima* was pulling away from the wharf. Leaving early. Not tomorrow. Today. I looked up and down the harbour, and there were no other Japanese ships around. They'd all left, and the *Matsushima* was the last to cast off.

As the ship's bow moved away from the dock, the ship's horn gave a blast which sounded just like an elephant's fart, and the stern loomed above me like an enormous monster flashing its arse in my face. Two figures appeared at the stern rail and looked down at me. Heineken! Wearing a German major's uniform, next to a Japanese admiral: Takagi. Both in full, glistening regalia.

I could actually feel the blood draining from my face. Astonishment, despair, and anger vied for space inside my thick skull. My God. I'd been so utterly duped. What a moron.

It fitted. Möllendorff wasn't 'the German fellow', Heineken was. He must have had Jack and his office bombed to cover his tracks. It was not about railroads and stocks; it was about Japanese military might. Heineken was still working for the Japanese, as a double agent, as their man in the IMCS.

Heineken spotted me below him and waved, grinning from ear to ear. I'd been so comprehensively buggered that all I could do was stare up at the chins and medals of the smiling bastards above me.

In addition to feeling furiously indignant for my defeat, a sudden kinship with the Chinese peasantry came, unbidden, into my head, despite the shortage of space in there. They, like me, were being clobbered from all sides. Not only did they have to contend with rapacious European powers snatching Chinese territory and with their Asian neighbour wanting to take the tributary state of Korea away, but now it looked like two antagonists, the Japanese, and Germans, had joined forces in a kind of imperial pincer movement. China was doomed.

This was not just about my murdered friend. This was about the Japanese, with German help, taking China. Had to be. The audacity, the balls they had on them. It was incredible, but on some level it seemed inevitable. Of *course* the shoguns and the kaiser are ganging up on China. How could they not? How else are empires built? By asking nicely?

At the *Matsushima*'s stern rail high above, Heineken pointed at me and said something I couldn't hear to Takagi. They both laughed. I raised my arm and gave him the middle finger salute. Childish and petulant, yes. But I was very glad I did because at exactly that moment, my raised upper arm was struck from behind by a truncheon. It hurt like hell, but if I hadn't raised my arm, the truncheon would have connected with my head.

I heard Dickinson's voice behind me, with its rounded vowels and its entitled tone, sounding like the lord of the manor chastising his servants.

"Arrest that man!"

Chapter Twenty

As the ship carrying my opium left the wharf with my new nemeses, Heineken, and Takagi, I felt a hand on my shoulder. I'd been violently belligerent all day, so why stop now? It was strangely soothing, purging. Catharsis with fists.

I grabbed the hand on my shoulder and bent back two of its fingers, hearing a satisfying crack. I spun around to see the hand's owner and watched as a policeman took two staggering steps back, grimacing and grunting, clutching his injured hand. Behind him was the smug face of Dickinson, in a sharply starched uniform. He must have changed his bloodied shirt. One of his cufflinks caught the sun and sparkled at me. He was standing a few feet behind two of Seoul's finest, whose brown uniforms were anything but sharp, one of whom had one hand out of action.

Keeping my eyes on the policemen and Dickinson, my peripheral vision detected movement over by the warehouse to my right. The policeman's squeals had apparently alerted some loafing dock workers nearby, and I was pleased to see them begin to saunter my way. I looked over and was even more pleased to see Ying among them, walking with his arms folded and a malevolent grin on his face. He'd made some money from our dealings, and I hoped that made him an ally of sorts.

I quickly turned my attention back to the trio in front of me and adopted the braced position again, silently thanking again that ship-board engineer, who I had dubbed the 'Kung Fu Spannerman.' The uninjured policeman took one halting step toward me, a scarred truncheon held up in front of him.

"Cyst and decease!" he said in English, which gave me a smile.

Dickinson shouted, "Arrest him, I said!"

I took the inexpertly swung baton on the upper arm. It hurt like hell. I ducked low and landed a blow with all my strength, just below his sternum. It knocked the air out of him, and he was neutralised until he could get his diaphragm working again. Usually, that takes about twenty seconds. He fell to his knees.

At that point, I had reason to bless Ying's criminal black heart. At an almost imperceptible nod from him, dock worker cronies closed around Dickinson and donged him on the head with a crowbar. He dropped like a sack of oranges. I wondered if they'd killed him.

One policeman was holding his injured hand and the other still struggling to breathe. But they both stood up and fled. They knew when they were outgunned.

A ship's horn blasted, and I spun around to see the stern of the *Matsushima* already three hundred yards from the wharf, steaming down the wide brown river, a trail of black coal smoke being blown eastwards. No one was standing at the stern rail.

Ying sauntered over to Dickinson's prone body on the ground. Blood trickled down his neck. I saw his chest rise and fall. He was alive. "You want him dead? No one will find him."

Ying's offer was tantalising, but I said, "Thank you, but no. I do need him out of the way for a while, though."

"How about a long vacation in a magical land? Cost you eight silver taels."

He was talking about heroin, the new poppy derivative I'd heard splendid things about. I'd been meaning to try it, but smoking opium was so much easier and safer than cooking up a substance in a dish and injecting it. I felt that the lungs were a simpler way of delivering something to the bloodstream, rather than poking holes in the skin.

"That would be perfect. He might return with a new, more enlightened, perspective." I handed over the silver.

I had a brainwave about how I might save my job. I told Ying to try to set Dickinson up with some naked women so I could take compromising photographs for blackmail. Ying smiled at my deviousness and nodded his assent. He gave me an address to return to later that afternoon with a camera. I figured a living, compromised Dickinson who had a vested interest in my well-being was better than a corpse. Marginally better.

Not my best plan ever. It lacked finesse, refinement, and thoroughness, but I was making it up as I went along. Possibly making my excrement quagmire deeper, but Father always said, "When in doubt, go full tilt. It may not improve the situation, but it will remove the suspense."

I looked toward the *Matsushima*, now five hundred yards away and disappearing into the mist. I bade my opium bon voyage and hoped for its safe arrival in Dongying.

When Dickinson resurfaced, things would get ugly for me. Uglier. Blackmail might not be enough. Möllendorff remained a problem, even though he was almost certainly not in cahoots with Heineken, he was still a supercilious Prussian bastard and a stickler for rules.

Bridges definitively burnt, it was time to leave. As I walked toward the gates, I saw Ying and his cronies carrying the unconscious Dickinson away to his appointment with oblivion. I strode purposefully through the gates on my way to Jack's apartment to retrieve his Kodak camera.

I was stumped about what to do with the revelation that Heineken was conspiring with the Japanese, in terms of how I could benefit from the knowledge. I couldn't yet see a way to use the fact to keep my job, but I hoped something would come to me. I had only just walked through the gates of the docks and across the road when an ear-splitting boom sounded from behind me, and a second later, a pressure wave threw me face down onto the pavement. Smoke billowed over my head and charred debris landed on and around me. I raised my head and looked around. There were two dozen people I could see through the smoke, all lying flat on the ground, too stunned to even shout out in fear. I rolled onto my back and heard the unmistakable scream of a cannonball travelling through the air above at eight hundred feet per second. The second floor of a building not two hundred yards from me exploded, and it took less than ten seconds for the entire structure to crumble to the ground, spewing high-speed dust in all directions. The building had been a Korean troop garrison.

Today was the twenty-third of July. People had been predicting conflict for months, while others, like me, had doubts about whether it would ever happen. But it had. The Japanese had finally started a war. And the departure of their last ship from the waterfront, the *Matsushima*, must have been the signal for the bombardment to commence.

The sound of cannons firing from the decks of ships both near and far now filled the air, along with the thwack of the balls hitting the ground, the buildings, the people. Seoul was under siege.

I clambered up off the ground and ran in a crouched position away from the docks, passing people of indeterminate race or gender—everyone was completely covered in brown dust. They'd recovered their powers of speech, and I now heard screaming and wailing. I sheltered for a moment under a sturdy-looking stone arch that was the entrance to a restaurant. Someone carrying a bundle that could have been a child saw what I was doing and joined me under the arch. I could tell her gender when she got close, and the bundle she was protecting was crying.

Could I still get the camera? Unlikely. Maybe Dickinson would be conveniently killed in the fighting? My arrangement with Ying was assuredly void in the event of a siege.

Cannon fire hit the store opposite where I was standing. I shielded my face, and shards of flying glass became embedded in my jacket. The stone arch we were sheltering under appeared sturdy enough, but it was no better than an umbrella when it came to cannon.

I wished the woman good luck—though I doubt she heard me—and ran. People were running in all directions with no discernible destination in mind. I was trying to put as much distance between myself and the docks as possible and to get away from the fort and its troop barracks. They'd undoubtedly be the earliest targets if the Japanese were aiming to take the city.

The diplomatic quarter was probably safe for now. There were no military installations there, and the area thus posed no threat to the Japanese. My route took me into the leafy residential district, where no bombs appeared to have landed. Nobody was running anywhere, but frightened families were standing in doorways or leaning out of windows, trying to see if they were safer where they were. Some of them shouted questions at me, but I had nothing I could tell them. I just kept running. I turned a corner and entered the wealthier end of town. Here I saw nobody on the streets. The residents of the large, widely spaced houses with surrounding walls were undoubtedly sheltering safely indoors.

I realised I was on Sajik Street. Okori Masamoto lived in this street. He might give me sanctuary. It certainly felt safer in this neighbourhood than anywhere I'd been since the siege began. A thought struck me: surely Masamoto would be able to re-create from memory the Japanese spy list he had given to Jack? Why he would do so and hand it to me was a question I couldn't answer. But it was worth a try. Besides, he was Japanese. Pacifist or not, it wouldn't hurt to make better friends with a Japanese diplomat. Someone on the side of the antagonists that would likely be the victors here. Maybe I'd live through this.

I found number 51 and banged my fist on the circular double doors in the perimeter wall of the compound. With all the ordnance noise, no one would hear knocking. I tried the handle, but it wouldn't move, latched on the inside, no doubt. I found a broken wooden cart, dragged it next to the wall and used it to climb over, carefully negotiating the broken glass embedded in the mortar along the top.

I tumbled down the other side, getting tangled in a peach tree on my way to the slate ground. I saw him as soon as I landed. Okori's body was on its side in the courtyard in a pool of congealing blood. I ran to him and took his pulse. He didn't have one, though his wrist was warm. I looked at his house and saw that it was so far unscathed by the siege. Cannon fire hadn't killed him. I looked back at his body and turned his head. A two-inch slash across his neck explained the method, though not the motive, of his murder.

In his closed, dead fist, he held something. I pried his hand open. It was some kind of medal. Torn red fabric was still pinned to the back. He must have grabbed it off his killer's chest as he was fighting for his life. And losing. The medal was an eight-pointed star with a red eagle in the centre. I knew this one, the Order of the Red Eagle, an order of chivalry of the Kingdom of Prussia.

Heineken. Had to be. Schemer, strategist, spymaster, and murderer.

I looked down at Masamoto's face. His hair was still perfectly coiffed, and his face powder and rouge were unsmudged. I closed his eyelids with their long lashes, and he looked like he was lost in a dreamless sleep.

I stood up and thought of Heineken. He'd presumably killed before today. He was a military man, after all. One doesn't get the Red Eagle for deftly organising military logistics. Only ruthless battlefield commanders get such accolades. Heineken was not what he seemed; he was much more. But he couldn't have killed Jack. Heineken was in Dongying when a bomb landed in Jack's lap and blew him to gristly bits. He must have had it done. Could some of his Japanese co-conspirators have done it for him? Or done it on their own account? If Jack's espionage revelations came to light, it would damage the Japanese the most. They'd have the strongest motive. But no Japanese would have a Red Eagle. A uniformed German killed Okori. Distant booms brought my mind back to the present. Right now, it was Japanese weaponry doing the most damage. Weaponry they'd learned how to use thanks to their German mentors.

I despaired, not for the first or last time, for the future of my opium.

Nothing I could do for Masamoto now. *Sayōnara, Okori san.* I hoped Anee was safe, because I doubted there would be anything I could do to help her either.

Blackmailing Dickinson was exceedingly unlikely now. And no doubt all IMCS staff had been ordered to abandon their desks and simply flee Seoul. The neutrality of the IMCS couldn't be counted upon if the Japanese prevailed. If and when things went pear-shaped, any Chinese and Koreans who remained alive would turn on foreigners like me.

An ear-splitting shriek followed by a ground-shaking thud gave me the unambiguous message that this neighbourhood was not as safe as it looked. Another shriek and thud told me it was about to start raining cannonballs, and my legs needed no further prompting. I ran.

Chapter Twenty-One

I ran out of the courtyard of the flamboyantly dressed, though very dead, Okori, and ran through the gate in a direction that I hoped would put some distance between me and the Japanese artillery bombardment of Seoul.

With such woefully limited options, I knew I simply had to flee. There was probably an evacuation plan in place for IMCS staff, maybe even a negotiated safe passage out of the country. But even if there was, I couldn't be part of it now.

Though I could still hear the thud of cannonballs hitting their targets, I heard none close by in this residential part of the diplomatic quarter. Most of the sounds of carnage that met my ears sounded like they were coming from the north-west. That made sense. The naval bombardment seemed to be centred around the harbour in the part of Seoul called Pungdo.

While I had seen loads of Japanese troops disembarking from ships during my many visits to the docks, I could see no Japanese troops on the streets. A newspaper report I'd read a week ago—seemed like a year—had mentioned a figure of eight thousand Japanese infantry having been sent to Korea. I'd seen none since the bombardment started. They weren't in the city. That made sense, too. Let the navy bomb the bejeesus out of the place first, and only when the fort was breached and those within destroyed would the ground troops take over. They'd be holed up somewhere safe until they were given the signal to go forth and finish the conquering.

This was no disorganised skirmish. The Japanese had learned well the lessons taught to them by their German military mentors. They had become competent conquerors. I, therefore, knew that soon the cannon fire would cease, and there'd be Japanese troops running amok everywhere. God knows what they'd do to civilians who got in their way. I had between now and when the cannon fire stopped to get out of there.

Inland routes out of the city were out of the question. There had to be Japanese troops garrisoned on the outskirts, waiting. If troops were billeted any closer, there'd be a risk of accidentally being hit by an errant cannonball. Seoul had ocean to the west and land on all other points of the compass. Troops poised to march in could be anywhere but the sea. My escape had to be by sea. Yes, the sea also contained the Japanese Navy, but it was a big place. Somehow, I needed to get myself onto a ship leaving Seoul.

Korean merchant ships would be confiscated by the Japanese as soon as they were victorious if they hadn't been already. A ray of hope pierced my increasingly pessimistic consciousness. Philo Norton McGiffin, captain of the *ZhenYuen*, which was hopefully still anchored where I had left her, north of here behind the island of Ganghwado near the mouth of the Han River, Seoul's waterway. Maybe the Japanese Navy hadn't gotten that far? Concentrating, as they were, on seizing the capital. Maybe that less-patronised little anchorage had not yet come under siege? There was a little rocky peninsula between the anchorage and the large bay called Incheon, from which I guessed the Japanese were firing. The *ZhenYuen* could still be there, unseen by the Japanese, by virtue of the rocky peninsula.

It was good to have a plan, woefully mediocre though it was.

Some cashed-up noble in the neighbourhood surely had a stable. I scurried along a shaded back lane, jumping up from time to time to see over the back walls of the residential compounds. I found one at last with four horses in their pens. I climbed a tree whose branches overhung the wall and got myself into the yard. I crouched against the inside of the wall behind a shrub and listened for two minutes.

Between the booms and thuds of distant artillery, I heard no sounds coming from the house. I crept to the pens. Three of the horses were jittery because of the noise, but one was calmly munching on a pile of hay in the corner of his pen. A stallion, as evidenced by his substantial stud tackle.

I crept over to the double gates, listening for sounds of anyone who might be about to challenge me. Hopefully, they were already away from here, fleeing for their lives. Or perhaps cowering in a basement. I lifted the latch and, as quietly as I could, opened the gates wide. Not bothering with a saddle, I slipped a bridle onto the stallion. I led him out of his pen, but his loud hoof-falls on the cobblestones brought a shout from the house.

I grabbed his mane and hauled myself onto his back. I gave him a sharp kick. He lurched, and I steered him to the open gates. He neighed and arched his back as we went through the gate, and I had to duck down flat, the top of the arch grazing my back and tearing my jacket. This horse had brains. He did not want me on his back.

We were through and out into the lane. Another kick in the ribs and we were galloping down the lane, the sound of shouts from the house fading from my hearing. It had been ages since I rode a horse bareback. I pinched my legs in tight and tried to keep from sliding too far forward, where I'd be placing my balls at serious risk of being crushed on the beast's neck.

We galloped the whole way, and it took an hour. South at first to get to the bridge over the Han River, upstream of the docks, where I saw boatmen hiding under the bridge. Then north on dusty roads through outlying villages, whose residents were standing in front of their houses looking anxiously across at the city, watching columns of smoke rising into the sky. I was grateful not to see any Japanese troops. They must have been further east. The stallion and I continued north and then west back to the coast. He continued to try to evict me by veering under low tree branches and arches, but I was wise to his game and remained aboard.

From his back, as we cantered along the ridgeline of the bluff, I almost swooned with relief when I saw the *ZhenYuen* still peacefully at anchor a mile off the shore. If it weren't for the distant sound of cannon, I could almost have imagined she was a pleasure boat out for a cruise. I unbridled the horse, slapped his arse, and he was away. I hoped he didn't end up in someone's soup.

I rubbed my own arse to try and get some feeling back into it. I scanned the beach and spied a half a dozen dinghies tied to the stone jetty, the jetty we'd arrived at only four days ago. Seemed like a month. I scrambled down the dune, untied the nearest one, jumped onto the middle thwart, and rowed with all my strength.

After a few minutes, when I was about five hundred yards from the shore, I heard the distant sound of a chain rattling through a hawser. I was facing away from the ship, but I didn't need to turn around to know that she was weighing anchor. Fear gripped my chest at the prospect of being marooned on the Korean peninsula. I looked over my shoulder and saw that she was still about four hundred yards away and that an outgoing tide had turned her bows shoreward, pointing at me. She'd have to manoeuvre around before she could head out to sea. I could still make it.

My arms and hands burning, I rowed like the devil. My ill-disciplined rowing technique left me saturated with seawater, which was cool against my sweat-drenched skin.

I rowed in a deranged frenzy, desperate to reach the ship. So deranged, in fact, that I slammed into her hull at full tilt, throwing me onto my back and cracking my skull on the forward thwart. I thought I was still a few hundred yards away, but her manoeuvring must have brought her closer to me as she was brought around.

I shook my aching head to clear it, raised myself to my knees, and hollered myself hoarse. A face appeared over the rail far above me, and a rope ladder was dropped, it too landing on my tender head. I scrambled up, leaving the dinghy to drift on its merry way.

The rope stung my blistered hands. Once on deck, I stood slumped, hands on knees, and tried to regain my breath. Between gasps for air, I wheezed, "McGiffin... Captain... knows me..."

Mention of McGiffin's name appeared to erase the suspicious expressions of the two Chinese sailors standing before me, one of whom was hauling the rope ladder back aboard. A European in officer's uniform arrived, and I told him who I was and that I was on his ship to escape the siege.

"Follow me", he said, and I staggered after him as he marched back the way he'd come. He led me up steep stairs and opened the door to the bridge. He stood aside to allow me to enter first, where a smiling McGiffin gave me a warm handshake, crushing my blistered fingers.

"Glad you're aboard, Swagger. Watched you in that dinghy from here and came to meet you. Time we got the hell out of here."

Now I understood why I'd crashed into the ship; she was coming to get me. Relief swept over me, and I had to lean on the instrument panel to keep from collapsing onto the steel floor. The relief wasn't just that I'd escaped and was now in the company of competent sailors but also that no news about my being fired from the IMCS, or that I was probably a fugitive from the police, had yet reached him. Or if it had, he didn't care.

The *ZhenYuen* turned about and headed west. I looked longingly to the western horizon, willing the Chinese coastline to come closer. We steamed west for some miles. Then McGiffin nodded to the helmsman, who looked a little anxious as he swung the wheel counter-clockwise. My heart sank. We were turning south. South was where the Japanese Navy were. The captain was taking us back to the fray, towards Incheon harbour and the siege. By this route, we'd come up behind the Japanese ships whose guns were obliterating Seoul. We were about to engage the enemy.

Chapter Twenty-Two

Relieved as I was to be out of a city under bombardment and safely aboard a sturdy ship steaming away from bomb-wracked Seoul, I'd have much preferred to side-step the battles in this undeclared Sino-Japanese war and get to Dongying to determine the fate of my opium. Failing that, I'd settle for some brandy, a little opium, and the attentions of a maiden skilled in the erotic arts. But it was not to be. I watched with rising trepidation from the bridge as the *ZhenYuen* steamed south instead of west and drew nearer to the Japanese warships.

I'd not yet given up completely on my opium shipment and hoped that this fighting would remain confined to Korea, for now, at least. If the Chinese were kicked out of Korea and the Japanese took over, Japan would have secured the food supplies it was so nervous about. Hopefully, they'd stop there, Heineken's mysterious master plan notwithstanding.

Wherever we went, I'd rather it was away from cannon fire, not toward it.

It took us an hour to steam around Ganghwado island, and I could see from my corner of the bridge the battle from behind. It was all but over. The Japanese ships hovered in place, their guns pointing landward, but firing had ceased. That could mean that there were now troops in the city, securing the victory.

The ship under me, the *ZhenYuen*, was a German-built 'ironclad'. She was well-armed but no match for a Japanese armada. McGiffin lamented the futility of engaging. "The Jap warships have gun turrets on both sides. Getting any closer would be suicide—they could load those guns and start firing at us in a trice. We hold station here, for now, out of range."

Fine with me.

He pointed out to his first mate another ship, to the south of us, billowing smoke and listing alarmingly, the deck on her port side already awash. She was flying both the white ensign of the British Navy and the Qing's navy flag.

McGiffin said to the first mate, "The *KowShing*. Leased from the Brits. She'll have aboard both British officers and Chinese crew in training."

The first mate did not need to be told what to do. He shouted some orders into the speaking tube, and the ship turned to starboard. I could feel the vibrations of the straining engines as they were pushed to full speed. I looked to where McGiffin had pointed and could see the ship he was referring to, and the black smoke billowing from both her funnels and the gaping tears in her hull. The *KowShing* was going down fast.

The bridge was silent for several minutes as we ploughed ahead. As we drew nearer, McGiffin said to nobody in particular, "This is what happens with an untrained crew. I've been telling them for years..."

The ship slipped beneath the surface, cutting off the trails of smoke. I heard and felt the engines powering down as we neared the spot where the *KowShing* had been only a few minutes before, at which point I heard them power up again in reverse, stopping us in the water. I looked down at the deck and saw our deck crews throwing rope ladders over the rail and lowering boats. McGiffin looked at me and nodded to port. I looked in that direction and saw that a Japanese ship had spotted us, perhaps the one that had sunk the *KowShing*, and began firing on us as the crew were trying to pull sailors out of the water. The Japanese shells, mercifully, fell short. McGiffin knew where to put our ship, so she was just out of range.

One well-aimed shell smacked us in the stern quarter, making the whole vessel shudder. "Superficial," McGiffin said in answer to the concerned look I gave him. But he nevertheless gave orders to get the rescue boats back aboard and pull up the rope ladders. "Can't save them all," he said, his jaw clenched, staring ahead.

Rescuing over, we turned and steamed west, away from the Japanese armada. I didn't know how many sailors we were able to rescue. McGiffin ordered me off the bridge and down to the infirmary to help tend the rescued wounded. I did as I was told.

From the bridge I took the steep stairs down two levels and walked along the dimly lit corridor towards the stern. Before I got near the infirmary, I had to slow my walk and try to step over and around the bodies of the wounded. Groaning sailors lined the corridor, forming a queue. Some were sitting, some were standing, and others were prostrate on the floor. All were wet, and I almost lost my footing on a pool of blood-stained salt water. When I reached the doorway to the infirmary itself a pretty nurse in a bloody uniform looked me up and down, decided I wasn't wounded but was here to help, thrust a wad of gauze into one of my hands and a bottle of some clear liquid into the other. "Sponge that disinfectant on the wounds of the men in the corridor." She turned her back on me and I went and carried out my orders. Groaning sailors groaned louder when the alcohol disinfectant hit their cuts and burns. The first man I splashed didn't look at me, and when I wiped the wound with gauze, small chunks of burnt skin came away, stuck to the fabric. The next few I simply poured the liquid on their wounds and let it drip onto the floor. The last sailor at the end of the corridor made no sound when I poured the alcohol onto his neck. He was pale and cold to the touch. He didn't need disinfectant.

It would take weeks to get to Dongying if indeed we would get anywhere near it. At least we were in the right sea; the Yellow Sea, with Dongying only four hundred miles due west, through the Bohai Strait. I was alive and not being bombed or shot at with cannon. I tried my best to forget my troubles and concentrate on helping the wounded with theirs. After I'd emptied the bottle, I stepped over bodies to get back to the infirmary to find out what I could do next.

Frustration at my lack of progress with any of my own problems was forced, mostly, out of my mind by the horrors of naval warfare and the ghastly injuries men sustained. The wounded weren't just in the infirmary, they were everywhere. Cabins, corridors, and even on the deck. The medic had arranged them in order of likelihood of survival, the ones nearest the infirmary being the ones most likely to live.

I felt guilty that I was still worried about my future and impatient to get after my opium, given the suffering I was witnessing. Being ankle deep in blood and viscera in the infirmary, attending to the troubles of others, almost made me forget my own.

Almost.

The next task the medic had in mind for me was ferrying dead bodies out of the infirmary and the corridors. A sailor and I carried the dead upstairs and laid them out on deck. There was a crew of four Chinese sailors sewing the corpses into calico sacks and slipping them over the side. I leaned over the rail to see the line of white cocoons trailing in our wake.

That task complete, I spent the rest of the evening in the corridor chatting to and comforting wounded sailors while they waited to take their turn under the surgeon's knife, wondering which limbs they'd be allowed to keep. I'd hold the hand of a wounded man, offering comforting platitudes, and when the medic called "Next!" I helped stretcher him onto the infirmary operating table, kicking amputated limbs out of the way, and trying not to slip over.

In the days that followed, snatching sleep in a corner from time to time, I helped tend wounded and sew the dead into calico shrouds that would cosset them on their journey to Davy Jones' Locker.

The workload eased after about forty-eight hours, and we were able to take breaks. I found sleep elusive, so I played mah-jong with the Chinese coal-shovelling lads in the boiler room. Somehow, they'd made this airless hovel into a cosy home. Coal dust coated every surface, and the air was hot and humid. Using steel pipe and canvas the lads had strung bunks along the rusty hull and constructed stools and a table from rough pine packing crates. The mah-jong tiles were also rough pine, rectangular, with their characters burned into the wood with a hot iron.

Though I tried to keep it a secret, they soon learned, somehow, that I spoke English and demanded quick lessons before each game began. Naturally, I taught them profanity first.

"You're putting smoke into my anus!" said Tang one evening, in response to a transparent attempt at a bluff by another player during a game. He was wearing only a loin cloth, as were they all, and his muscles and sinews were so pronounced under his dirty skin you could see the pulse in his neck and the heartbeat in his chest.

I told him, "It's 'blowing' and 'up my arse', Tang. Try it again."

He snorted. "It's a stupid expression. Why would I let someone get close enough to blow smoke up my arse? I always wear pants, anyway. It's not possible. Wouldn't I notice that someone was on his knees behind me?"

"You'd love it!" said Kim, the one who had tried to bluff him, and who had the most magnificent black and scarlet tattoo covering his whole torso, depicting a warrior slaying a dragon.

They all laughed uproariously, and despite myself, I laughed like a drain too.

Playing mah-jong in the gloomy bowels of the ship with these rowdy, illiterate, soot-covered blokes gave me comfort and a welcome distraction from blood, gore, suffering, and my own worries. Especially when the rice wine was poured from the unlabelled, four-gallon barrels.

But in the dead of night, alone in my cabin, my mind inexorably turned back to my own urgent needs. I pondered whether I could I get myself transferred to another ship. One that won't get sent into battle and might get me home sooner? Home. Where there *might* be a couple of opium bales with my name on them.

Ships need supplies. Maybe the *ZhenYuen* would get re-supplied at sea, and I could transfer to a supply ship? Or maybe she'll have to make for a port for supplies. Hopefully, not one under siege.

At night, through my porthole, looking over to the eastern horizon, there were no longer cannon muzzle flashes lighting up the sky. I guessed we were far enough away not to see them. I doubted the Japanese would be content with conquering only the Korean Peninsula. I assumed that was merely target number one.

Their partner in imperialism, the kaiser, had much more ambitious plans.

Chapter Twenty-Three

F our days after we'd steamed away from the Korean Peninsula, I pondered my plight standing at the starboard rail, watching the sun come up, trying to figure out how to convince McGiffin he needed supplies, and he should head for Dongying, where supplies are plentiful. I could make up a story about the ammunition having gotten sodden in the hold or one of the boilers being on its last legs.

Dumb ideas, there are supply officers for that kind of advice, and I wasn't about to commit any sabotage to get my way. I have some scruples. But I desperately needed to get to the mainland.

I watched the foaming water stream along the side of the hull. Aptly named, the Yellow Sea. Fine sand combined with silt suspended in the water crowded out the usual greens and blues of ocean water. I pulled my eyes upwards to the horizon, breaking the hypnotic spell of the torrent below. I felt impotent. Things affecting my life and my future were happening; aboard the *Matsushima*, if my opium and Jack's lists had been discovered, and within the IMCS if Dickinson was not dead. Machinations and manoeuvrings were also happening that could strike a heavy blow to China, militarily and thus economically.

And I could do nothing but watch the red sun detach itself from the flat, grey horizon.

The sunrise. Watched from the starboard rail. I realised with a start that that meant we were steaming north—a direction precisely perpendicular to the required heading to fetch Dongying. *Damn it!*

I raced up to the bridge to find McGiffin. When he saw me burst through the door, he knew what I'd ask him, so he spoke before I could. "Hold your horses there, sailor. I've been ordered to help defend the mouth of the Yalu River."

I groaned loudly and rolled my eyes. That was the border between China and Korea. If the Japanese are fighting there, they must intend to cross the river and march into China itself.

The *ZhenYuen* was going into battle. *Shit.*

I left the bridge crew to it and went downstairs to get some breakfast from the mess, grumbling and muttering to myself all the way. Twenty minutes later with a belly full of tasteless gruel, I moped back to my cabin and reclined on my bunk, where I stared at the ceiling, accumulating cigarette burns on my shirt.

The journey was swifter than I expected. I felt the engines slow in the late afternoon and went up to the bridge.

Again, we were late. The battle was all but over. Again, the only help we could offer was rescuing floating sailors. The non-floating sailors were beyond help. Having soundly thrashed the Chinese ships, the efficient Japanese warships had withdrawn to a position about a mile away, forming a defensive line across the wide mouth of the Yalu River. From the bridge windows I could see thick, forested bluffs on either side of the river mouth, and the Japanese Navy flotilla pointing their bows in our direction.

The British signals officer entered the bridge, saluted, and told McGiffin that the Japanese were flying flags that indicated that they would not fire upon any opponent's ship, so long as no opposing ship fired upon them. It was their way of saying we were allowed to rescue our sailors. Very sporting of them.

McGiffin asked the signals officer if the ship he could see steaming south-west was the *Matsushima*. I was immediately all ears.

He held up his binoculars and confirmed that the ship was indeed the *Matsushima*.

McGiffin squinted through the windows. "Is she signalling? I see flags going up."

"Yes, sir. Wait a moment." The signals officer watched intently, then he took the binoculars away from his eyes and consulted his thick, Japanese signal book. I was impressed that he had one. Maybe our side had spies too. "She's signalling the other members of the fleet, telling them that her destination is Lushun, and to await further orders from the captain of the *Kongō*."

I was jumping out of my skin to ask McGiffin if we could *please* pursue the *Matsushima*. Lushun, or what the Brits called Port Arthur, was the Chinese fortress stronghold just south of Dalian. If the *Matsushima* stayed in port in Lushun for a while, I might be able to find a way to get my bales off, take them to Dongying myself. If I could get there and retrieve my opium, I might be able to get aboard a smaller vessel, maybe a fishing boat, to take me the short distance across the Bohai strait to Dongying.

McGiffin looked at me, and he could tell I wanted to ask him something but guessed the wrong question. "The *Kongō* is the second biggest ironclad ship the Japs have, the biggest being the *Matsushima*. She won't fire on us unless we fire first. Now, go help the medic."

During the time I had been on the bridge, our ship had been manoeuvring towards the clutches of sailors in the water. We'd arrived at one such grouping, and I noticed with a shudder that there were fewer sailors in the water than I had seen only moments before when we were still a few hundred yards away. I wondered if death by drowning was any better or worse than being blown to bits. It was certainly better than slowly dying from burns.

I went down to deck level, where sailors plucked from the water were already accumulating on deck. Amid the loud wailing of injured men, I helped haul wet and wounded sailors over the netting that had been draped over the side of the ship and reached down to the water. Bodies were hauled aboard in various states of wholeness.

The next morning, after another twenty hours as medic's aide, I staggered to my cabin for some sleep. There was a Brit sailor sitting up in my bunk, drinking a cup of tea.

His name was Alexander Purvis, an engineer from the now sunken *ZhiYuan*, and he was in bad shape. He was too long for the bunk and his bare feet stuck out of the end. Blood was seeping through his head bandage and onto the pillow he was propped up on. His breathing was laboured and one of his sky-blue eyes was half closed. A purple and yellow bruise covered half his face. He needed my bunk more than I did.

We talked for hours. The same age as me, Purvis was a kindred spirit, a fellow stranger in a strange land. He regaled me, between coughs and wheezes and grimaces, with the story of how his ship had been severely damaged and burned, yet still, the plucky crew attempted to ram the *Matsushima*. Good for them. I could have tolerated the loss of my opium if it meant that Heineken and Takagi were swimming with the fishes.

The *ZhiYuan* sank before they reached the *Matsushima*, however, and Purvis had a hellish mad scramble to try to get out of the bowels of the ship and into the water without being trapped below decks.

We smoked some of my remaining opium together and talked. I asked him how long he'd been here in the east.

"Arrived in '86, by way of 'Frisco. Went aboard the *ZhiYuan* as Engineer when she was docked in Nagasaki, Japan."

"Wait, *August* '86?"

"Yeah, mate." He gave me his lopsided grin. "You're thinkin' of the 'Nagasaki Incident' as it's called, yeah?"

I was. It happened before I got to China, and the newspaper articles I read in Australia left me with more questions than answers. They read as if they had been judiciously censored. "I know a little, but it'd be good to hear the story from someone who was there."

"Yeah. I read a report in the papers a few weeks after, and they got it all totally arse about."

"So, what happened?"

"Well, we all drank rather a lot. You know the Japanese drink their rice wine hot?"

I nodded.

"My job was to train the Chinese sailors, see? And they're big on giving respect. I'd never been in any kind of 'respectable' profession, but here these little Chinese fellers were bowing to their teacher and giving that hand-and-fist thing."

"The *baoquan li*? Like this?" I held my open left hand against my closed right fist.

"That's the one, yeah. Well, this respect they were sendin' my way fair filled me with pride, I don't mind tellin' yer. They took their teacher out for drinks, they did. And, with this hot wine, we all got completely shitfaced. Them Chinese fellers sure can put it away."

I knew what he meant. We Australians had a reputation for hard drinking, but in my experience, most Chinese blokes could drink any man under the table. The women could put it away, too, when the opportunity arose.

"They spoke no English, and I no Chinese, but we got along like a house on fire. We were in a bar in the ladies-of-the-night district, see? When I sang the 'Spanish Ladies' song for their entertainment, like, we got kicked out of the bar and sprawled out over the street. I was busting for a leak and relieved meself against the wall of this tiny shack, you know, like a kiosk?"

I nodded. I knew what he meant. The little police box one sees on the streets of Japanese cities, called a *kōban*, that houses two or three policemen. A bad place to take a piss.

Moonlight from the porthole illuminated his face. "Well, I'd just got a good stream going when this Jap cop came out and began shouting his babble at me. My Chinese mates tried to calm him down, but I just kept on pissing, couldn't stop, you know? Anyhow, two more rozzers came out of this little kiosk and began pushing and shoving the Chinese. I finished, buttoned my fly, and by then, it had become an all-in brawl. Me and my twelve Chinese mates clobbered the Jap cops, maybe going a bit too far. Two of them crawled away when we were done, but one wasn't moving. He was dead. Then this rickshaw driver came up and started yelling at us. He got clobbered too. More locals came and joined the fray. At some point, I got knocked out and woke up hours later on the ship. We weren't allowed ashore again, and it took a full three days to get rid of my hangover."

All that the newspaper had said at the time was that a drunken brawl started by Chinese sailors had resulted in the death of a policeman and sparked a riot. China did not apologise.

I liked Alex's story better.

I left him for a few minutes and went to visit the quartermaster, from whom I bought a small bottle of a clear liqueur called baijiu. At 52 percent proof, a small bottle was plenty.

Back in the cabin, we drank and smoked, tobacco this time. I toasted the Beiyang fleet.

Alex said, "And here's to old Ding, a good admiral, hamstrung by a simpleton emperor."

We clinked glasses and drank. I knew Admiral Ding was in charge of the Beiyang fleet, which comprised about three-quarters of the Chinese Navy, but other than that, I had no idea what he was referring to.

He read the bemusement on my face, and his brow furrowed. "Admiral Ding is in charge of the whole Beiyang fleet, right? Chinese Navy's best and brightest. We Brits, and some Frenchies, training the Chinese crews. But the idiot emperor ordered Ding *not* to engage the Jap Navy, but instead to hide his precious ships in WeiHaiWei!"

"What? Jesus! Then what was your ship doing at the Yalu River?"

"Getting blown to bits and sunk, that's what. We were too slow, had some cheap coal aboard, and it took ages to get the boilers up to operating temperature. That brown stuff, not much more flammable than mud. The rest of the fleet left us behind while we struggled to get up a good head of steam."

He was building up some steam himself. "I mean, how the hell is a handful of Qing Navy ships meant to defend the bloody realm if the best bloody ships fuck off?"

I could easily believe that some Qing Manchu bureaucrat, from the safe distance of Beijing, could insist that an admiral hide his fleet for safekeeping. What're a few thousand sailors' lives worth? Less than the price of a ship, apparently.

I slopped some more baijiu into his glass, and we talked for another hour, about everything and yet nothing important. We talked about love, duty, war, and how scratchy woollen uniforms are in hot weather. About patriotism, revolution, and belly-button lint. I don't know who fell asleep first. I slept on the cabin floor.

In the morning, Alexander Purvis was not breathing, and I went off to get a shroud and a sewing kit.

His troubles were over. Mine, it seemed, had barely begun.

Chapter Twenty-Four

The late Alexander Purvis, the plucky engineer from the *ZhiYuan*, now rusting on the seabed, smiled benignly at me as I sewed him into his burial shroud. Alex too would soon be resting in peace in Neptune's embrace. I carried him over my shoulder from my cabin, up the stairs and onto the deck. The rising sun was in my face as I slipped him over the side. He went down with barely a splash, like an expertly executed dive from a high board. I watched his floating cocoon tumble in the ship's wake until it sank.

The weeks following Alex's death dragged by while I waited for my chance to get ashore and chase my loot. Frustratingly, no supply ships came to our aid, and we didn't touch land the entire time. The Japanese had officially declared war on the 1st of August 1894, though the fighting had been intense for weeks prior, and the *ZhenYuen* was a warship after all—we were expected to help. Captain McGiffin did his duty and thrust us into the fray time and again. Wherever there was naval action, we steamed right to it. But we were outnumbered and outgunned each time. Our hull sported dents from several hits but thankfully no holes. McGiffin was a dutiful and honourable man, but he was not suicidal. He kept us out of reach of the Japanese guns. We merely remained nearby to help with skirmishes and rescues.

I had just retired to my bunk one night when I was called up to the bridge. Captain McGiffin had had news for me. "You've probably noticed that we've been heading south for the last few days. We're bound for WeiHaiWei, where the rest of the Beiyang Fleet is hiding. Emperor's orders." He rolled his eyes.

He knew I'd been eager to get ashore. I'd pestered him about it often enough. "At last. When do you think we'll fetch up there?"

"Few days. But before we get there, we're to meet up with a hospital ship." He squinted at the chronometer on the bulkhead. "At oh-two-hundred. She's steaming to us out of Lushun. Thought you might like to get aboard her?"

Abso-bloody-lutely. The *Matsushima* had been said to be bound for Lushun, though that had been weeks ago. "With your permission, I'd like to get aboard that hospital ship and get to Lushun."

He grinned. "As you wish. Get yourself ready."

Within thirty minutes I was on deck with my knapsack, peering into the darkness, looking for a ship's lights. If there was even the slimmest chance that I was still the proud owner of the goods in the bowels of the *Matsushima*, and if she was still in port, I had to chase it. It was my entire net worth. The spy lists, if they were still there, also represented the remote possibility that I might be able to bargain my way back into the good graces of the Qing, and by extension, the IMCS.

Time was not on my side. The signals officer had been keeping me up to date with the news, and none of it was good. The Japanese had conquered the Korean Peninsula and from there began swarming down the Liaodong Peninsula, but I understood that they were still a long way from Dalian, which was twenty miles north of Lushun. I needed to get my business done and get out of there before the Japanese arrived.

The hospital ship hove into view through the gloom and came alongside. I eagerly boarded the ship via the wildly gyrating ship-to-ship gangplank, carrying one end of a stretcher holding a wounded sailor. Once the wounded were aboard, the gangplank was retrieved and we bore away to the west, bound for Lushun. I waved goodbye to the bridge of the *ZhenYuen*.

The voyage was uneventful. The hospital ship's crew were professionals and knew what they were doing. I was told to remain on deck, out of the way. I caught some sleep atop some folded canvas. Summer had turned to autumn during my meanderings in the Yellow

Sea, and I shivered in my torn IMCS blazer. I woke to see the predawn glow lighting up the eastern horizon and the ship nuzzling up to a wharf. I chatted with an orderly while the gangplank rattled its way to the ground. He gave me directions to Dalian, which amounted to simply, "When you get off the ship, turn right, go about twenty miles up the coast. You can't miss it."

I did as he said when I stepped onto the wharf and turned my collar up against the chilly autumnal breeze, which whipped around in turbulent gusts in the wide corridor between the ships and the weathered warehouse buildings. I saw no rickshaws or carriages or even oxcarts loitering in the vicinity. I'd be on foot from here. Red leaves swirled around me in mini tornadoes and landed in puddles. I was disappointed that the *Matsushima* wasn't within easy reach in Lushun, but that didn't mean she wasn't in the neighbourhood. Dalian, twenty miles to the north, had a large port of its own. The Japanese Army was said to be making its way down the peninsula. The *Matsushima* might be required to remain nearby and provide support for the land push, to flex the Japanese Navy's muscles and ready the ground for the imminent arrival of the victorious army.

I was trying to convince myself. I was just glad to be on land and to have something to do, some way in which I could exert some semblance of control over my life after weeks at sea feeling utterly impotent.

Lushun was known to Europeans as Port Arthur because a Brit surveyor sailing around the neighbourhood during the second opium war, looking for good port locations to swipe from the Chinese, chose to name the place after himself. Humility is overrated. It was near the tip of the Liaodong Peninsula, and the smugglers' port was around the other side, about five miles over the hilly isthmus.

I changed course. It occurred to me it wouldn't hurt to check-in at the smugglers' port on the way to Dalian. If my opium was salvageable, I'd need to retrieve it and arrange passage for it—and me—

to Dongying, or as close as I could get.

The road out of Lushun snaked uphill, then along a ridgeline, which gave me an excellent view of the fort to my left. There were no houses once I'd passed the last dock warehouse. The steep hills surrounding the port had dissuaded folks from building homes there—the little township of Lushun was apparently up in a plateau a few miles to the west. The sun had just breached the horizon and revealed the fort to be a formidable structure, as one would expect. The walls made a brown semicircle around China's most strategic deep-water harbour, with cannon facing the narrow entrance to bar the way in.

The Qing had hired the German firm Krupp to build it, who did so with typical Teutonic efficiency fourteen years ago. Initially, the Qing had ordered local Chinese contractors to construct the fort, but when the first rows of fortifications fell into the harbour, killing dozens of workers, the Qing wisely called in the professionals.

Remembering that event made the fort a rather forlorn sight. The civilisation that built the Great Wall, the Forbidden City, the world's longest and largest canal and innumerable forts and palaces, had, somewhere along the way, forgotten how to build simple fortifications and had had to hire foreigners. Must have been humiliating.

My route took me along the northern outskirts of the little township of Lushun, and I found myself passing through a simple residential district. Mud-brick houses interspersed with vacant lots lined each side of the road. The vacant lots were those little cooperative land plots where locals banded together to raise modest numbers of livestock and to cultivate vegetables and fruit, the distribution of which was handled by a committee of elders. It made me smile to see thriving agriculture in miniature. Peasants looking after each other.

It was still very early, and nobody was on the road. I could see smoke coming from the chimneys of the houses; people were here, just indoors. My stomach rumbled as the scents of breakfast noodles—shallots, honey, soy, pork broth and many aromas I couldn't place—met my nostrils. I drew level with the last house in the street, beyond which there was a high wooden arch apparently marking the Lushun village city limits. Beyond that, rural countryside stretched out on either side of the dusty road. I stopped and turned and walked towards the doorway of the last house, hoping to talk the occupants into selling me some breakfast.

When I was ten feet from the door, I heard screams and shrieking coming from inside the house. I stepped quickly to my left and vaulted the low stone wall adjoining the house. I crouched out of sight and peered over the top. The shrieking stopped as suddenly as it had started, and I watched six burly European men burst out of the door at which I had been about to knock.

I ducked, waited a few moments, then silently popped my head above the little wall. The men were dragging three limp Chinamen out of the house and toward the wooden archway spanning the road. They looked dead. I watched the Europeans strip the corpses, then re-dress them in clothes they pulled from a bag. They threw a rope over the arch and strung the corpses up by their necks. They left them dangling there, about eight feet off the ground.

Their job apparently done, the six hangmen ran away along the road, out of town, leaving the corpses swinging in the breeze. I watched as they left the road about three hundred yards further along and ran into the scrub, heading north.

I was aghast and confused. I couldn't figure it out.

There was still no one around, and I left my hiding place to take a closer look. The Chinese corpses were dressed in dusty Japanese soldiers' uniforms.

Extraordinary. And horrific. And mystifying.

I stared at the swaying corpses for some time, trying to nut out the significance of it all. I was so caught up with my own thoughts that I didn't notice the stampede of soldiers coming down the road until they were almost upon me. A group of around forty Chinese soldiers were coming down the road, sprinting toward me, terror written all over their faces. I retreated into the house the corpses had been dragged from and watched the soldiers run. As they entered the village, paying no heed to the swinging bodies as they passed under the arch, they ran carrying their flintlock carbine rifles in one hand and tearing off parts of their uniform with the other.

They could only be running from one thing: the Japanese Army.

Now I could hear the rumble, the sound of either a cattle stampede or of thousands of hooves and boots on the dusty ground. I heard rifle fire.

From the window of the house, I turned to look back into the village. People were coming out of their homes. They shouted at the fleeing soldiers, trying to find out what they were running from. They found out soon enough.

Six Japanese cavalry soldiers, riding ahead of the rest, arrived at the arch where the corpses were strung up. They stopped. The one on the tallest horse stared up for a moment, his face turned scarlet. He let out a hellish roar followed by a loud tirade I couldn't understand, spit and foam flying from his mouth, his rifle held in a white-knuckled grip. A hundred yards behind him, foot soldiers were marching to the village. The cavalryman turned his horse to face them and shouted something. The infantrymen broke into a run, brandishing their rifles and shouting with bared teeth.

It dawned on me what was happening. And what was about to happen. Seeing what they believed to be three of their comrades hanged, the Japanese were about to go berserk.

And they did.

I crawled away from my position by the window. If the soldiers knew I was there, they'd be in here like a shot. I ran through the house, cursing every creak of the floorboards. The back door had no handle, so I simply crashed through it, making an almighty racket. The Japanese would have heard that for sure. I bolted away from the house then skidded to a halt, kicking up a dust cloud. To my right I watched as dozens of Chinese were doing the same thing, running out of their back doors. They were fleeing in the same direction I was headed. I thought fast, my heart pounding. The Japanese would chase us down, shoot us in the back. I needed a different strategy. I heard what sounded like the door of 'my' house being kicked in. I scanned my surroundings. There was a shed propped against the house. I ran to it and jumped onto its timber roof. From there I scrambled onto the red tiles of the house's roof. I scurried up to the crown and lay flat on my face. As predicted, shots rang out, and I saw people who were running away into the fields, falling and skidding face-first in the dirt, then lying still.

I stayed right where I was. I smelled gun smoke and dust. Amid the cacophony of gunfire, shouting and screaming, I heard footsteps and breaking crockery. The sound was coming through the tiles. They were here. I dared not raise my head, but I did turn it to one side. Then I wished I hadn't. I'd heard the screaming, but now I could see some of the screamers. Women and children. The men were being summarily shot through the head, but the terrors awaiting the women were much, much worse. I watched as two soldiers held a young girl down while another smashed out her teeth with the butt of his rifle. Then they dropped their trousers and took turns humping her face while she tried to vomit.

I turned my face away. I put my fingers in my ears.

I counted to five hundred, humming the numbers, hoping to drown out the screaming and moaning. I pleaded with gods I didn't believe in, begging not to be found by the soldiers. After what felt like an eternity lying on the hot roof tiles, the noise of rifle fire and screaming subsided and gave way to wailing. I deduced that the soldiers had gone from house to house and had progressed down the road. I turned onto my back cautiously and sat up. I neither saw nor heard any Japanese soldiers in the immediate vicinity. I crept down from the roof, listening intently for male voices. I knew there'd be no Chinese men left alive here, so any male voices would have to be from some lingering Japanese. I heard none.

I sprinted due south, perpendicular to the road and to the trajectory of the wave of the Japanese shooting and slashing their way through the district. I heard a shout behind me. "Hey you. Stop!" Then two shots. I heard a bullet whiz past my ear and felt a sting in my arm. Fear of a painful death compelled me to ignore it and keep running. I ran until the sounds of firing, shouting, and screaming became distant. I reached a stream. I guessed that downstream it must feed into Lushun harbour, so I ran upstream, over the uneven and rocky bank, under willows and through prickly shrubs. I remembered that the Liaodong Peninsula was narrow this far south, maybe twenty miles across. I was running uphill, and the stream eventually became no more than a trickle. I left the now grassy bank and wheezed my way to the top of the nearest ridge. From there I looked west, and the sparkling waters of the Yellow Sea twinkled back at me. I could see, maybe eight miles north-west, a little cove; the smugglers' port.

From that distance, I couldn't make out any detail, merely topography. For want of a better idea, I began a scrambling descent of the ridge and headed north-west. I doubted that the little cove would have any smugglers still doing business there, what with the invasion and all, but at least my journey was putting some distance between me and marauding Japanese soldiers. I could hear artillery fire now, and I was sure the whole peninsula could hear it. Anyone with a boat would have had enough sense to cast off and head out to sea. If the Japanese had gotten this far south, then the peninsula was all but conquered. I hurried my pace, realising that I was in a desperate race to get off the peninsula before there was nowhere to hide. The Japanese never took prisoners. Transporting prisoners slowed an army's progress. For practicality alone, it made sense to the Japanese to kill wounded or surrendered opponents, then forge ahead. After plundering and raping, of course. If captured, the best I could hope for was a bullet to the head. The worst was unimaginable.

I ran downhill toward the cove, hoping against hope for some kind of sanctuary.

Chapter Twenty-Five

As I expected, the little ramshackle port in Yangtou Bay was deserted and the discarded mooring tackle and fishing nets told me it had been vacated in a hurry. The door to the small shack at the foot of the jetty hung loose and was swinging from its one remaining hinge. The locals knew what was good for them; flee before the Japanese conquered the whole peninsula. My vain hopes of sanctuary dashed, I sat under the forlorn jetty with a third of its planks missing, out of the sun and hopefully hidden from view.

As my heart rate slowed after all the running, the pain in my arm increased. I gingerly took my jacket off, the inside pocket still bulging with Spratt's papers. I took off my shirt and washed the wound on my upper arm with salt water. It was a gash from a bullet, though not a hole. There was no bullet lodged in the flesh, thankfully. Damned painful, though. I had forgotten how much flesh wounds hurt; like someone was holding a red-hot poker against the skin, then sprinkling chilli powder on the wound.

I grimaced and took stock of my situation, which consumed no time at all. I was in a battle zone with no friends or even allies, and the little grain of hope I had had—that I might be able to retrieve my opium from the hold of the *Matsushima*—was gone too. If I lived through this, I'd still have nothing. And be a fugitive from the Japanese, the Chinese, and the foreigners. Marvellous.

I started to shiver and sweat at the same time. Shock, I guess. I'd never before seen such savagery. Humans torn limb from limb or disembowelled and dismembered while still alive. Never heard the haunting screams of a child being raped. I could hear it still, above the sound of my teeth chattering. My mind presented me with snapshots of what I'd seen; a man on the ground, propped up against the back wall of his house with his bowels draped over his legs, a child with her hands cut off. I stared up at the sun through a crack in the jetty, hoping to burn the images from my brain.

I could hear rifle shots and cannon fire, and the sound was getting nearer. I turned my eyes away from the sun and waited for them to adjust, when I spied a discarded dinghy wedged under the jetty. I entered the water, remaining under the jetty and hopefully out of sight, and waded to the dinghy. I looked over the painted wooden gunwale. It had one oar, a wooden bucket, and about a foot of water in the bottom. I slithered quietly over the side, baled some water out, and started sculling for all I was worth.

I was about three hundred yards off the shore when I looked back and saw the first few soldiers scurry over the scrubby dunes and tumble down to the beach. I put down the oar, crouched and slipped over the side and into the water. I grabbed the little rope dangling off the bow and began to swim slowly, pulling the little boat along with me. I kept the dinghy between me and the shore, hoping that all the Japanese could see was a stray dinghy drifting away. No shots arrived in my direction, and I swam for as long as I could manage, taking short rests of drifting, holding on to the gunnel to keep my head above water. Eventually, the beach was far enough away, the figures on the beach barely discernible, for me to risk climbing back into the dinghy and taking up the oar. The sun was only a few hours away from setting and thus behind me, hopefully making me even harder to see from the beach.

I relaxed a little and drifted for a while, between bouts of sculling and bailing out the leaky dinghy. The massacre told me I'd underestimated how dangerous the Japanese were. I reflected on how easily the Japanese were pushing into China, like a hot knife through butter. The Qing had tried to modernise their military with the help of some French military 'experts'. But not only did the Qing have to go to war with the Frogs to avoid losing more territory in the far south of China, the Frogs also recently got clobbered in a war with the Prussians—the war that effectively united Germany, under Prussian rule. The Japanese wisely chose to get themselves German military advisors to modernise their military. The Qing chose the French losers to help with theirs. Maybe they came cheap? The Germans had been helping the Japanese modernise their military since that general in the Prussian Army, Jacob Meckel, had become a foreign advisor to the newly restored Meiji government in Tokyo.

I was pretty sure now that the European men I watched dress and string up those villagers' corpses must have been German. But why turn an invasion into a massacre? Why goad the Japanese into an even more savage rampage than they were planning already? Whose orders were those Europeans working under? Heineken's? He had been aboard the *Matsushima,* and she had been bound for Lushun when I'd last seen her three months ago. Ergo, he'd been in this part of the world. Doing what?

The Japanese advance seemed inexorable, but I couldn't figure out why anybody needed to make it worse. Why would Germany want a routine incursion to turn into a slaughterhouse? The international community, rapacious and corrupt as it was, would condemn Japan for such an atrocity, surely?

It didn't make sense.

Or maybe....

A nebulous idea was trying to congeal in my exhausted brain as the dinghy bobbed on the wavelets. I knew the German kaiser was bitter about being late to the colonisation party and was desperate to catch up to his grandmother, Queen Victoria, who appeared to own half the globe. I also knew that the Russians had been eyeing off the Liaodong Peninsula for ages. They had no year-round port in the east, Vladivostok being frozen six months of the year. Could the kaiser and his cousin Tzar Nicholas have some kind of colonial catch-up plan? One that necessitated a massacre and the inevitable international condemnation that would follow? Goad the Japanese into doing the invasion part, then take it from them later? Could they be hoping for some kind of post-war treaty that clipped Japan's wings and paved the way for the Russians to swipe a chunk of Manchuria? This chunk, with its deep-water port at Lushun?

Double-games and geo-political contortions made me dizzy. That and hunger. Maybe I'd lost more blood than I'd thought.

Now that I was a mile or two offshore, an island hove into view, several miles to the north. To the west and south, I could see a grey smudge of smoke on the horizon. I couldn't be sure it was the coal smoke from the funnels of Japanese warships, but I couldn't take the chance. I turned the dinghy and sculled toward the island.

How had the Japanese become so strong so fast?

Assuming Heineken had found the spy list by now, in the 'tea' bales, that would mean I'd inadvertently furnished him with not only a list of double-agents hidden among the Qing—that he presumably knew all about anyway, he being one of them, but also the names of spies among the Japanese and perhaps even the Germans that Spratt had compiled. I had no idea how long the list may have been or whose names were on it. But the more I thought about it, the more complicit I felt. Inadvertent or not, I'd probably given the villains what they needed.

I slowly began to confront reality. I'd managed to shove an uncomfortable feeling down deep, but it came back up now and punched me in the guts.

My carelessness almost certainly got Okori Masamoto killed. I mustn't have shaken off my tail as well as I thought. And I'd helped the Japanese-German war effort. I'd given up the names of some of their enemies within their own ranks. There was blood on my hands, and the shrieks of the Chinese rang in my ears. If the Japanese-German plot, whatever it was, succeeded, I was partly to blame. I'd helped them discover the identities of the moles in their midst.

I tried to stop chastising myself, my fatigue and growing despair fanned the flames of guilt. As I got closer to the little island, the sun set, and I worried that I wouldn't be able to find it in the dark. I needn't have, I could see a fire on the beach. I headed that way. I hoped the locals were friendly.

Chapter Twenty-Six

I sculled the leaky dinghy, its transom creaking much more loudly than it had hours earlier when I commandeered it. Aching muscles, blistered hands and exhaustion helped keep horrific memories of the atrocities I'd witnessed at bay. My bullet graze was bleeding more than it should.

I sculled and rested, off and on, through a hazy sunset and into the night. By the time my dinghy nudged the sand, a waxing moon had risen in the east, but it was not yet high enough to provide much light. I stepped out of the dinghy into a foot of water, peered into the darkness, but saw nothing but vague shapes of trees and dunes. There was no sign of the fire I had seen earlier. It was either out, or I had missed the beach I'd been aiming for. I dragged the dinghy up the sand and into the scrub. I flipped it over, crawled under it, and slept like the dead.

I woke with a start when the dinghy was abruptly lifted, and suspicious faces stared down at me through the morning sun. Two muscular men pulled me upright, pinned my arms behind my back and marched me inland. They ignored my questions, were gruff but not violent. From that, I deduced that while they didn't consider me a threat, they yet regarded me with the same suspicion they'd regard anyone they didn't know. Understandable, these were dangerous times. When we came to a small clearing, they threw me to the ground near the trunk of a tree and tied me to it. There were a dozen or so people scattered around the clearing, and there was a campfire with steaming pots strung over it. My stomach rumbled loudly.

They eyed me warily. Time to do some fast-talking before their imaginations ran away with them. "I have escaped the murderous Japanese savages, and I come here seeking sanctuary." I gave a short, heavily sanitised history of who I was, and the tension on their faces appeared to ease. "I sculled that dinghy all the way from Shuangdao Bay, my apologies if one of you is the real owner of it."

One anxious young man came forward and asked, "Did you pass through Shuangdao village? Have the Japanese been there?"

Other faces looked at me eagerly. I guessed most of the boat-owners from the smugglers' port of Shuangdao Bay lived in Shuangdao village. "No. I came up from the south-east through scrubland. But I can tell you that as I was sculling out of the bay, Japanese soldiers were coming down the dunes. I fear that the whole peninsula is now overrun with the bastards."

It wasn't what they wanted to hear. My audience cast their eyes downward with the dread of imagining the likely fate of their loved ones back on shore. The ones they'd had to leave behind.

Someone silently untied me, and I was beckoned to come to the fire. Steaming bowls were passed around. I was given a bowl of noodles with fish, and we all ate in silence.

My bowl empty, a man handed me a pipe. I drew deeply but, sadly, it was only tobacco. Eating over, conversation haltingly began. They were a mixture of smugglers and fishermen who had escaped Shuangdao Bay with little more than their boats and the shirts on their backs. I counted nine men and five women, no children. They'd stashed their five boats in a hidden cove on the western side of the island. This island was known as Shedao Island and had no permanent human population. It was, however, often used as a place to hide from pesky customs collectors. Like those of the IMCS. Despite the fact that my uniform blazer was drying on a tree branch, they appeared to bear me no grudge. Their old enmity with customs men paled into insignificance in the face of the new, infinitely more savage Japanese Army and Navy.

The dread I saw on their faces didn't last. As talk flowed, the downcast demeanour of dejection slowly gave way and was gradually replaced with sombre indignation. I gave lip service to Japanese hatred myself to cement my place as an ally among them. Not much of a stretch for me. A couple of them, younger men, were determined to get themselves to the mainland and join in the fighting, defend their homeland. "We can't rely on the Qing," a man spat. They even implored me to join them in the righteous cause. Their elder brethren scoffed and admonished them for such suicidal notions, and the young men brooded and stared into the flames.

They let me lick my wounds for a few days on the island. One man even offered me a smoke of some particularly pungent opium. I still had a little of my own left, but it was drying on a rock in the sun.

It didn't taste the same. As we sat around the campfire one afternoon passing the pipe, talk flowed, mostly about the injustices the Chinese people were suffering. European powers swanning about like they owned the place and swiping chunks of land so that they *did* own the place and even fighting wars for the right to take bites out of China. And now the Japanese swarming through the kingdom on a murderous rampage. What next?

I was surprised, however, to hear my new friends empathising with the Qing Dynasty rulers. Campfire conversation moved in the direction of the efforts the Qing had made to improve the lot of average folks, and how best to support the government in their hour of need. Extraordinary. I'd assumed they'd feel abandoned and resentful. But no, despite their ineffectiveness against foreign invaders, these simple folk still held the Qing in reverence as the rightful rulers of the Middle Kingdom, still believed that the Qing had the Mandate of Heaven, and they were counting on them to prevail.

But I knew that the Imperial Court would have to sideline the Empress Dowager Cixi first. I had learned on the hospital ship that while I'd been at sea, she had retaken the reins of power after her token 'retirement' when the emperor had come of age a few years ago, and was now well and truly back in the saddle. She'd treated herself to a lavish sixtieth birthday party as the Japanese took over Korea and began slashing their way through Manchuria.

I kept these thoughts to myself. The depraved despot was still popular among the people, I'd been told. This region, the Liaodong Peninsula, must be predominantly populated with Manchus, descendants of the Mongol hordes that invaded China a few hundred years ago. The Mongols had swept down from the north, ousted the ethnically Han Ming Dynasty, and declared their divine right to rule the Middle Kingdom. Persecution of the Han, the original majority, had abated in the nineteenth century, but old enmities die hard in China. They have long memories. There were innumerable Han secret societies dedicated to the overthrow of the Manchu 'invaders' and 'usurpers' and 'oppressors'—the Qing.

Despite what I perceived to be their misinformed position regarding the Qing government, I had begun to share some of their anger at the foreign invaders, not just the Japanese. The Chinese had been getting it from all sides for almost a century. The more these folks shared their food and histories with me, the more I began to share their grievances.

I'm not Chinese myself, only half, on my mother's side. Thus, it wasn't really my fight because this country was not my home. But their strong feelings were entirely justified, and I silently wished them luck in their coming fight. They'd need it.

The peasantry had always been the backbone of China. The little people. I liked them and generally found them better company than people higher up the social status ladder. I'd attended the occasional lavish soiree thrown by the IMCS top brass but could usually be found in the kitchens sharing a smoke and a drink with the 'help'. These hardy fisherfolk on the island were welcoming me as one of them, almost. Despite my former career, I certainly now shared their lowly status, anyway. I was little people too.

A plump and cheerful woman dragged a log up to the campfire and sat down next to me. She accepted the opium pipe as it was handed to her and drew deeply. She exhaled the sweet and sour smoke at me. "You want me to wash and mend your fancy jacket?" She meant my filthy and tattered IMCS blazer, and I said I'd like that very much. The gabardine had dried, but the salt remained. Salt in clothes attracts moisture from the air, so the blazer gave off a musty stench. It smelled like old cheese. I took Jack's soggy sheaf of papers out of the inside pocket and laid them on a rock to dry, then took off the jacket and handed it to the woman. She took another deep drag on the pipe, then got up and left the circle.

One of the men handed the pipe to me and noticed the telegram on top of the pile of papers. He said, "That translation is wrong."

I turned to him, the pipe halfway to my mouth. "What?"

"Those German words. They don't mean the same as the other writing."

"What?" I blinked at him for a few moments. "Wait. You read German? *And* English?" Astonishing.

"Yep", It really says; 'Make use of the Society of the Elder Brethren—'"

"Hatchet Men." The man to my left cut in.

"Right, yes. Hatchet Men. The second part of the telegram there says, 'of whom there are many placed in the Court.'"

My mouth still hung open, and I looked from one man to the other.

The first man said, the hint of a smile tugging at his lips, "I teach languages, or used to, many years ago." He took the pipe I'd forgotten to toke on and puffed away while he waited for me to finish absorbing his surprising revelation. He handed the pipe to the next fellow and explained to me that he had been a high school teacher of languages on the Kowloon peninsula in the '50s. "When the Brits took the peninsula next to Honkers by force in 1860, I fled and wound up in Dalian. I'd grabbed enough of my savings before fleeing to buy a small fishing boat when I got here. I met a girl, and we've been a fishing family for the last thirty years." He turned his face away, and I saw that he was looking at the woman who was darning my blazer, sitting cross-legged about twelve feet away. She smiled warmly at him, a smile that told me she regretted not a minute of their simple life together.

She called out proudly, "We have four boats, now. And a beautiful boy."

The man turned back to me and introduced his son, sitting next to him, and smiled at the heir to the fishing empire. Then his face quickly darkened. "No fishing business now, obviously—the Japanese'll have it."

I tried to lighten the mood. I swept my arm around to embrace the peaceful island setting. "Well, there are worse places to retire to."

He shot me a look that showed as much contempt as politeness allowed, and which told me what he thought of my attitude. "An engine with no load will destroy itself. It needs to be doing some kind of work, overcoming resistance, to prevent it from exploding."

Gawd, if China's value was measured in her quantity of philosophers, she would rule the world...

The son broke the tension. He spoke of how he wanted to get himself armed and take on the Japanese, single-handed, if need be, such was his thirst for vengeance. The Japanese had stolen his inheritance.

I had a fleeting vision myself of heroically murdering Japanese soldiers and winning the adulation of the Chinese people and the love of a beautiful noblewoman. Opium will do that to a man's mind. And this particular batch had crept up on me. It didn't taste especially strong, and I had consequently drawn all the deeper. Now I'd lost feeling in the tips of my fingers, and my feet were tingling. The urge to lie down was almost overwhelming.

But the wild and egocentric fantasy of fighting heroically against the invaders was not entirely without merit. If the Chinese fended off the Japanese, and I helped in some noteworthy way, maybe I could endear myself to the Qing. Get some well-paid job in the system, one with ample opportunity for graft. Maybe even redeem myself in the eyes of Robert Hart, overlord of the IMCS and influential personage at the Court of the Qing.

It wasn't as if I had I had anything else to do. My life, as I knew it in China, was over.

I thought of Mistral. God, I hoped old Ting was taking care of her in the stables. She needs a daily run, or she'll get frustrated and kick the stable to splinters. Did she miss me? Would I ever see her again? The idea of her ending up in someone's meat locker made me shudder.

Maudlin. Opium will do that too. It'll amplify emotions that are already there, no matter how deeply one buries them. Getting high was probably a bad idea right now. I knew what I needed to do, and I needed to do it sober. Take control of my fate.

The pipe came around to me again, and I took the deepest drag I had all evening.

Chapter Twenty-Seven

I was an engine with no load. I needed to get back to the mainland, preferably Dongying, but nearby would do. I was penniless and without status. If Dickinson and Möllendorff survived the siege of Seoul, I was also a wanted man, a fugitive from justice. And stuck on an island.

I awoke the next morning in the same place I'd fallen asleep; curled up on my side next to the fire, which was now only ash. When I closed my eyes, sunlight pierced my eyelids and the only image my opium-hungover brain would serve up, over and over, was to get back to Mistral. With her, I could ride away. Just away. During my jovial evening under the stars with the fisherfolk with whom I was marooned on this little island in the Yellow Sea, I had toyed with the idea that when I got back to Mistral, somehow, we could ride south to try to find a job with the Frogs in the slice of Chinese territory they'd recently stolen. I knew a little of their language. Maybe I could be an interpreter for them. My Cantonese was rusty, but I'd pick it up soon enough. It shared characters with Mandarin, so I'd only need to master the patois.

I had noticed one of the smugglers getting antsy too. He was a solitary and quiet man, and on the occasions when he joined the rest of us around the campfire, he politely eschewed the pipe. Instead, he'd stare at the sky, pointing out cloud shapes and telling us what kind of wind they foretold.

I went looking for him that morning. I left the clearing and followed the sandy path to the beach, dodging prickly bushes and swatting away sand flies. I found him at the beach, standing knee-deep in the water, staring at the horizon.

"Longing to get home?"

He turned and gave a weak smile. "I *am* home. Look." He pointed down at his feet in the water. "Being on land too long makes me uneasy. Doesn't move right."

A true seafarer. I'd heard of communities that spent their entire existence on the water. It looked like I'd met one of their number. "And you've lost your boat? Your home?"

"What? No. It's over there." He pointed along the beach to where there were five boats pulled up, aground in shallow water. They were resting on their shallow keels and canted over at different angles. These were working boats with scarred and barnacled hulls. Gulls squawked from the rigging and scanned the ground for prey.

"Ah. Why not sail away then? Get back to your life?"

"No crew. Can't sail without crew. No engine. Nearly wrecked her getting here by myself."

"Can you show her to me?"

"He exhaled and grunted and waded off through the shallows toward the boats on the beach. I followed. When we reached his boat, he climbed over the gunnel in one deft motion, displaying an athleticism I was surprised he possessed. When I tried to do the same, I didn't make it and he had to give me his hand to pull me up. He puffed out his chest with pride as he pointed out the woven bamboo junk sail furled on deck, the loosely stayed mast, the miles of rope, and he was particularly proud of his shiny brass anchor windlass at the bow. "Real time-saver, that." I thought he was going to blow it a kiss.

He took two steps aft and sat on the cabin top, apparently pleased to have someone to whom he could brag about his pride and joy. "This little boat has no engine, as I think I mentioned. Unlike the bigger fishing boats with their antique steam power plants. Some would consider me to be only small time in the smuggling game because I'm just starting out in the trade. But you know what? This boat was going cheap, and her small size means she's often ignored by the customs boats."

I looked over the raw teak decks, the glassless cabin windows, and the uncoiled ropes, which looked like some kind of giant noodle spillage. I could see his point. This dishevelled vessel wouldn't attract a second glance from the captain of one of our customs patrol boats.

"I make a comfortable living smuggling counterfeit wine. The wine is grown and bottled just outside Dalian, and me and my cousin put convincing French or Italian labels on the bottles and sell them to foreigners on the mainland. The higher-ups, the foreign toffs, can spot a fake a mile off, but ordinary foreign soldiers don't know the difference. Come."

Because they're illiterate, no doubt. I followed him down the companionway into the diminutive cabin. "See here, nine hundred bottles."

My eyes slowly adjusted to the gloom, and I could make out the brown glass bottles in the hold, stacked neatly and secured with rope. "How is the wine?" I think I might have even licked my lips.

"Disgusting. Make you blind, you drink enough of it."

Thus, making it irresistible to thirsty European privates far from home. I sat on the only bench, and he turned and fiddled with a little brass hob. He got a flame going and placed a silver pot on the ring. I rolled two tobacco cigarettes and waited. His pot began to steam, and he poured hot water into two chipped ceramic mugs and handed one to me. I'll never understand the Chinese compulsion to drink plain hot water, no matter the season. I handed him one of the cigarettes I'd rolled. He held a chopstick to the flame, then used that to light us both.

"So, you had to leave Shuangdao Bay in a hurry. No time to gather crew or your cousin."

He nodded. "I fear for him. I hope he was able to stay out of the way of the Japanese." He went on to explain that his two regular crew members had been away in Lushun when the Japanese arrived, and he'd had to get underway alone and flee. He presumed his crew was dead. Everyone in Lushun must be, he supposed. I agreed. He'd barely made it to the island without crew and had had to run the boat up onto the beach because he couldn't handle the mooring tackle and steer at the same time.

After a moment of looking at the floor, maybe mourning the lives lost in Lushun, he composed himself. "I need to get her to Yantai, about a hundred miles south of here. Although the Japanese Navy will be patrolling the Yellow Sea, the infantry won't have gotten anywhere near that part of Shandong yet, if they ever will."

Yantai was only two hundred miles from Dongying. And the man needed crew.

I sipped my hot water and drew on my cigarette, scrutinising the man's face and ruminating. Thinking even further ahead, I realised that making friends with a small-scale smuggler who could slip past officials unmolested was an excellent investment. He might be persuaded to bring over a bale or two of Bengali Gold from time to time...

"I'll be your crew!" How hard could it be?

Chapter Twenty-Eight

I squinted at the glare as I looked back at the little island that the fisherfolk had fled to when they learned the Japanese were on a killing spree all along the peninsula. Looking down at the water flowing past the hull, it seemed we were moving at little more than strolling pace. Nonetheless, in what seemed like only a few minutes, the island started sinking into the horizon as the boat, the skipper and I moved in a tiny arc over the little sphere we all live on.

As it turns out, crewing on a smuggler's junk was extremely hard. Hauling that damn sail up with the rough hemp rope left me with aching muscles and blistered and bloody hands. With its woven panels lashed to stout bamboo battens, it weighed a ton. And I had no help. The skipper remained at the tiller.

But I was on the tranquil sea once again. I was getting to like it.

He had told me his name, but I preferred to call him 'skipper'. He had accepted my offer to sign on as his only crew member with a large dose of scepticism, but I assured him I was an agile, diligent, and industrious worker who carried out orders without question. I even said it with a straight face.

No one on the island had needed a tide chart to know that the best time to have the boat pushed off the shallow bottom was just after midday, and everyone turned out to shove the stout little junk into deeper water. Farewells were hollered, and I stood waving at the bow in my newly mended IMCS blazer as we bobbed away from the shore, until a shouted order from the skipper to haul the sail aloft had me hurrying to the mast and grabbing the halyard.

Our progress was slow. Skipper estimated four days' sailing, minimum, to get to Yantai. For most of the journey, we were out of sight of land and often shrouded in the ghostly mists that prevail throughout China, especially in autumn. The mists that Chinese painters so loved to depict enhanced the aura of the Middle Kingdom as being the Mystical East.

Between bouts of strenuous activity there were long stretches of idleness, a routine I was getting used to. I rested my hands, arms, and back and chatted with the skipper, cooked meals, or slept below deck. The skipper was content to snatch sleep in little bursts of about thirty minutes at a time, an ability that impressed me. He'd nod off, still holding the tiller in his armpit, and the boat would track straight and true while he rested.

Despite there being a couple of hundred bottles of cheap wine lashed into the hold, I resisted the urge to escape into oblivion. The skipper was a good man, and I enjoyed his company, but if he found me unconsciously drunk, I had no doubt he'd pitch me over the side.

The antagonism towards China's plunderers I had come to share with my new fishermen friends on the island had not subsided as the opium left my bloodstream, as I'd thought it would. The skipper and I had many hours to talk over the plight of his much-ravaged country while watching navy ships on the horizon and tracking their courses, changing ours if skipper thought our courses would converge.

He mentioned that at one time, he was a leading light in the KoLaoHui, Liaodong chapter. China is so festooned with secret societies that most of them end up fighting each other. The KoLaoHui had gotten further than most, however, before their inevitable demise. Their aim was to kick out all foreigners and murder the emperor and his family. Simple. They appeared to have no explicit plan as to how to run the country afterwards. "We even enlisted the help of Charles Mason, your colleague at Customs. I met him, you know? I was the courier that handed him the money."

It seemed every Chinaman knew all about the Mason Affair. It would haunt the IMCS until hell froze over. Mason's collusion with the KoLaoHui to buy arms for them, and his subsequent capture and slap on the wrist by the Brit court, still rankled. The bad blood between the Qing and the IMCS persisted, despite Robert Hart's most respectful apologies. Behind closed doors, rumour had it, Hart had roundly berated the British consul for not handing over Mason for execution by the Qing. I'd heard it came to blows, the diminutive Irishman Hart soundly thrashing the pampered consul.

"Don't worry," the skipper said, "I bear you no grudge, customs man. I know how much we need the revenue, and I know how much Robert Hart loves this country."

In addition to providing the Qing with one-third of national income, Hart had also been asked by the Qing many times to broker more favourable deals with the foreigners, and Hart gave such negotiations everything he had, trying desperately to stem the tide of foreign powers stealing Chinese territory and resources. His efforts hadn't gone unnoticed by the Qing, nor indeed by more educated Chinese.

"I was with them up until about two years ago, in Kiangsi province."

I felt my eyebrows shoot up involuntarily. "The KoLaoHui? Really? That would mean you were with them during the time of the great escape."

"You know your history."

I did. Two years earlier, in '92, some KoLaoHui rebels were captured in Kiangsi province. Two were put to death, and the others were imprisoned to await trial. About a thousand members of the society rose, liberated their companions, and bore them away. They were chased by the local militia, and in the resulting skirmishes, lives were lost on both sides. But the KoLaoHui, now that they were in actual rebellion, didn't know what to do next. For want of a better idea, they elected a King and two Princes, and made a stand in the mountains, from which they made occasional sorties into neighbouring towns. I didn't know what happened after that, but I'd heard no mention of them since, not in the papers nor in IMCS memos.

"Are you still determined to kill all foreigners and the Qing?" I needed to know if I had to sleep with one eye open.

"Revolution's a younger man's game. I'm not so hot-headed these days." He stared wistfully at the horizon.

"You were lucky you didn't get caught up in the arrests and executions. I heard that they'd found almost all the KoLaoHui and beaten them to death."

"'*Bastinado*', they called it." He gave a little shiver after he said it, as did I. Although it was a Spanish word, it yet described one of the more horrible ways to die. It was beating the condemned man with bamboo until he was dead. Usually took several sessions over the course of a day for a man to finally expire.

"By the time our hideout in the hills was found and attacked, I was already halfway to Manchuria. My comrades in the south got rounded up and murdered, but I was well out of reach by then."

"With the KoLaoHui extinct, do you still hope to someday rid China of foreigners and restore the Han to the throne?"

"Who says they're extinct?" That took me by surprise. Everyone knew they were dead and buried. "But yes, I drifted away, and keep myself to myself these days. No more revolutionary secret societies for me. As far as having foreigners infesting our country and filthy Mongols on the throne..., ahh, what's to be done? The horse has bolted. The situation is what it is." Now I understood why he'd been so aloof on the island. He was Han, while the others were Manchu. "And now the Japs! Best just to live a good life in whatever way you can. A righteous life."

I wished I could share his attitude. I asked him, "The name KoLaoHui is Cantonese, isn't it? What does it translate as?"

"We liked being called the Hatchet Men. Had a nice ring to it, don't you think? Militant and brave. But the literal English translation is the 'Society of the Elder Brethren.'"

Somewhere in my crowded brain, a penny dropped, loudly echoing around in my dense skull.

Didn't that fisherman by the fireside mention something like that? I was descending into a delightful opium abyss at the time, but yes! He had said my handwritten translation under the German text of Jack's telegram was wrong. I never did get around to finding a dictionary and translating it properly. He'd said it translated as 'Make use of the Society of the Elder Brethren, of whom there are many placed at Court'.

More frenzied brain activity ensued while I furrowed my brow and squinted. Synapses did whatever synapses do. *Ah-ha!* The correct translation of the telegram brought a revelation. Suddenly I felt taller. I made the Mason Affair connection: *That* must be the plan. My jaw dropped and I stared into space.

The Germans and Japanese had spies in the Qing Court, Jack and Okori had listed them. But they were not just double agents, they were triple agents. The lists contained the names of agents of a reincarnated KoLaoHui—The Society of the Elder Brethren, the Hatchet Men, 'of whom there are many placed at Court'. Hence Jack keeping the German telegram, along with the Mason article. *Well, well, well.* The plot to assassinate the Qing royal family has been revived.

An alliance with the KoLaoHui would give the Germans and Japanese access to their spies in the Imperial Court. With the help of the KoLaoHui, the Japanese and Germans must be planning to conquer the country and murder Cixi and those loyal to her, including the emperor. Thus, paving the way to having enough power to plunder the coffers. The audacity of the scoundrels. They'd grant themselves rights to build railroads, mine minerals, and approve massive loans from European banks, in which they undoubtedly held stocks. All this loot going to themselves and their cronies: Germans, Japanese, Russians, even some perfidious Brits.

Wait. No, not murder the emperor, only Cixi and those loyal to her. Keep the emperor as a puppet. He's certainly suggestible enough. Word had it he was a sickly fellow, always suffering from one ailment or another, and that he was only interested in his hobbies, leaving the fate of his people to the gods. If I were a conquering Japanese, I'd leave him in place and pull the strings from the sidelines.

It's all about plunder. China, one of the last asset-rich places on earth to conquer, and the shoguns and the kaiser—and his relatives—had a plan to do it, making their underlings rich in the process. I almost swooned at the audacious brilliance of it.

If they succeed, Cixi had only herself to blame. She'd been fiddling while China burned, renovating the Summer Palace with funds reserved for the navy and having a lavish birthday party. Should I somehow get word to the emperor and motivate him to re-deploy the military to where it could do more to try and stop the Japanese advance? Or at least slow it? Get the damn Chinese Navy out of hiding in WeiHaiWei, for a start?

Oof, that'd be a scheme way beyond my meagre resources. I looked around at the empty ocean as we bobbed like a cork on the waves. The horizon was flat and grey and clear all around. I was a long way from the levers of power. But I had to do something. I wanted revenge. That bastard Heineken ruined my life. Frustrating his plans was going to be my new mission in life, purely out of spite.

As I began to picture the plot in my imagination, tectonic plates of motivation were rearranging themselves in my mind. I wasn't the only one who deserved some revenge. Some measure of justice. The simple hedonistic life I had been pursuing so earnestly was never going to be sustainable long-term, not with a country in such a flux and beset by vultures. Things never stay the same, and power always tries to wallop the powerless and take what their labours have produced.

I thought about Captain McGiffin, the Pennsylvanian farm boy who couldn't get into the US Navy and chose to make China his home. He'd gone native, loved the Chinese people. He was risking his life defending them. He was one of them, albeit with a bigger nose.

My fate *was* inextricably tied to Other People's Problems, and I would have to help them and get help from them. I was not an island, much as I had tried to be. I could no longer be the impartial customs man, observing the travails of this country as a dispassionate spectator. This was now my home. Today, I was a Chinaman, and my country needed me. I'd chosen a side. There were wrongs to be righted. Plans to be crafted.

And eyes to be spat in.

An action plan started to take shape in my mind as the skipper looked askance at me, like a flummoxed Labrador. I guess the acrobatics my brain had been doing showed on my face. Yes, I was a penniless fugitive bobbing about in the middle of nowhere, but I was not entirely powerless. In fact, I might be the only human on earth who saw and understood the whole devious plot. That knowledge came with a burden. An obligation to act. For China and for my old mate, Jack Spratt.

Someone had to fight for these people. I wish it wasn't me, but who else was going to?

I felt an energy surge through me and felt more clear-headed than I'd felt in ages. I was going to nail the bastards.

The skipper handed me a cigarette that I had not seen him roll. He smirked and squinted as the smoke from his own cigarette, dangling from his lips, curled up into his eyes. "Something momentous has just happened in that thick skull of yours. I could hear the gears grinding from here. I reckon you've decided to do something unfeasibly stupid when we get to Yantai. Good luck with it, whatever it is. Try not to get murdered."

Chapter Twenty-Nine

It took the better part of a fortnight to get back to Dongying, during which my eagerness to implement my plan remained undiminished.

The skipper and I had bobbed our ambling way across the Yellow Sea, making slow but inexorable progress to our destination port of Yantai. The sun and moon rose and set, the days got a little shorter as autumn progressed, my stomach flattened, my calluses grew, my muscles hardened, and my determination to thwart the plot I'd figured out deepened.

The skipper had schooled me on what he perceived were scandalous deficiencies in my knowledge of history. I'd never understood why the Han-Manchu animosity hadn't diminished over time. The decaying Ming Dynasty was put out of its misery by invading Mongols, like shooting a horse with a broken leg. That was two hundred and fifty years ago, and all the current rulers, the Qing and all the officials, were Manchu, descended from the Mongols. They looked different, in as much as they could grow beards, which few Han could manage. They sported the cue—a long-plaited tail down their back—and shaved a few inches of their hairline back from their foreheads. Many Han Chinese had adopted the cue, too, but were still forbidden from entering government service, thus perpetuating a rift that should have waned centuries ago.

I had been a good crew for the skipper, once I'd learned the ropes, literally. He was Han and warmed to me even more when he learned that the Chinese half of my parentage was also Han. In fact, mother maintained that she was at the end of a lengthy line of nobles whose lands had been stolen by marauding Manchu invaders. She'd bring that up any time I was deemed to have been disrespectful, which was often. But it was so many generations ago that I thought she really should have gotten over it. I mean, when it comes to theft of lands, if both the perpetrators and the victims are long dead, then the prospect of justice died with them, surely? One has to deal with what's in front of one.

One overcast and chilly morning the skipper had tied the mooring lines of the plucky little junk at an out of the way jetty just outside of Yantai, and we'd bidden each other a fond farewell. He surprised me by giving me wages, a little bag of silver coin taels for my work as crew. I hadn't expected it, but it was gratefully received.

An exhausting combination of bone-jarring ox carts and walking left me, after four days, exhausted, smelly, and bedraggled on the outskirts of Dongying. I clambered out of an ox cart on a hill overlooking the town, grunted thanks to the driver, and looked down at the only town I could call home. A lowering sun was at my back and an evening mist was mixing with the red dust that overhung the city. The locals would be preparing their dinner. Families would be herding their children, maybe dunking them in a bath if they owned one. They'd sit down to eat and talk. I wished I could join them. Pretend for a while.

I found an inn on the outskirts of town. The lobby had a dozen people coming or going. They looked to be travellers and traders, refreshing themselves either for their foray into Dongying's markets or their journey home. I paid for one night, used the bathhouse and got myself fed, washed, and rested, ready for the onerous task ahead.

Dawn found me awake, and I dressed and breakfasted, then stood on the balcony of the inn with coffee and cigarette, surveying the scene from the slightly elevated position the inn enjoyed. The few leaves remaining on the trees were a dark red. I hadn't been in town for three months. An autumnal chill was in the air, and a thin fog was descending on the city.

The innkeeper sidled up to the wooden railing next to me. "Looks peaceful enough from here."

I sipped my coffee. "You think the Japanese'll get this far south?" All the talk in the dining room the night before had been about the Japanese invasion.

"They only want Korea and Lushun, for food and a strategic port. They'll stop there, no doubt."

"No doubt." I drew on my cigarette. He couldn't be more wrong. I knew that their ambition was no less than the conquest of the whole country, and they had devious and powerful helpers.

I wished that this could have been a cheerful homecoming, a return to my old life. An easy job, guilt-free sex, recreational opium use, and weekend getaways with my equine companion.

This homecoming was going to be nothing of the sort. I was going to have to tread *very* carefully in Dongying. There were so many people to avoid. I'd have to keep clear of police. They'd have to have been alerted to my fugitive-from-justice status by now. Avoid the IMCS, obviously. But what most worried me was the network of spies and watchers my opium dealer maintained. They could be anyone, and I'd have to have eyes in the back of my head to spot them on my tail.

I finished my coffee, and on my way to the counter to pay my bill, I snuck into the laundry, stole some dirty peasant clothes, and shoved them into my salt-stained knapsack. I paid my bill and left. In the dark and damp alley next to the inn, I changed into the peasant clothes, shoving my regular clothes into the knapsack. They might still come in handy, especially the IMCS blazer, darned and bloodstained though it was.

I stooped and kept my head down in that meek way coolies do and walked into town along the main road, confident that my disguise would keep my identity secret. I passed a stall and bought a conical hat with the last of the coins the skipper had given me, just for an extra measure of anonymity. I should have saved my money.

Cash would have been more useful than my transparently ineffective disguise. I got recognised almost immediately.

Chapter Thirty

I took a circuitous route to Customs House through narrow slate lanes shaded into gloominess by overhanging mulberry trees, whose leaves would not fall until late winter. Even the back alleys were abuzz with industrious locals. My coolie disguise seemed to be working, as evidenced by passers-by having no compunction about jostling me aside if I was in their way. I arrived at the iron-framed, wooden back gate of Customs House by lunchtime.

I waited, lurking across the lane from the gate as inconspicuously as I could. I pulled my collar up around my ears as a chill wind funnelled through the lane. Presently, as I'd hoped, old Mrs. Lee came lumbering down the lane, pulling her reluctant mule, who was strapped to a rickety cart. She was the lunch lady. Each working day she and her mule carted huge steaming pots of noodles around the diplomatic quarter for the Chinese workers. Not the diplomatic staff, obviously. They took their long lunches in local restaurants, as I had. The cleaners, stable hands, maintenance workers, and any other coolies took their meals from Mrs. Lee, who asked only one copper coin for the service.

The gate opened after she'd knocked, and I slipped inside behind her cart, ducking straight to my right and the stable building. A couple of the workers glanced at me, but in the usual Chinese style, they remained nonchalant, minding their own business, waiting for Mrs. Lee to begin slopping noodles into tin bowls.

Once inside the timber structure, I hurried to Mistral's pen. My heart sank. Her pen was occupied by a morose and docile black gelding.

"Hey, you!"

I spun around. Old Ting, the stable master, was pointing at me and striding toward me with his manure shovel aimed like a spear. I took off my conical hat. "Mr. Ting. It's me."

The shovel hit the cobblestone floor with a clang. "Mr. Swagger! Where have you been?" He half smiled, but his eyes nervously darted left and right, as if he was worried someone might be watching.

In a loud whisper, I said, "Quiet, I'm on a secret mission. No one can know that I'm here. Where is she?" I jerked my head toward Mistral's pen.

He stared at me for a few moments with one raised eyebrow. I knew what he was thinking: secret mission, my arse. But he was trying to figure out a way of saying it that didn't make me lose face. Even old Ting would have heard the news that Swageman of the IMCS was persona non grata. He failed to find a way to express this, gave up trying, and his eyebrows levelled up.

"We didn't know where you were. We didn't know when you were coming back. *If* you were coming back. I couldn't stop them..."

"Keep your voice down. Couldn't stop what?"

"Taken by a big boss. Don't ask me who, I wasn't here when it happened." He looked downcast and submissive, maybe thinking he was about to get a beating, which had happened before when he incurred the displeasure of a haughty foreigner. Not me, I'd never had anything but friendly relations with him. He looked up with hope in his eyes. "But I know where she is kept! I have seen her coming out of the back gate of a house over on Victoria Street."

"Which one?"

"I can't say. The numbers are on the front of the house, not the back gate. The back gate is on a lane with no name. I can tell you, though, that the house must be only four or five houses east of the place where Victoria Street ends, at Fleet Street." He made a T shape with his hands.

I knew where he was talking about. The streets had been renamed by Londoners, who had commandeered the neighbourhood as increasing numbers of foreigners came to the area.

The migration had begun in earnest when European powers realised that China couldn't stop them, not anymore.

His eagerness to please was touching. I'd always liked him, mainly because he treated Mistral so well. "Okay. Thank you. I'll look for her when it's dark." There was more I needed to know. "Like I said, no one can know that I'm here. Tell me what you've heard about me. Don't soften the news to spare my feelings, give it to me straight, please." I added this last to be sure I got the full story. Without that waiver, Ting would most likely have given me an inoffensive version, as manners required.

"Not much to tell, really. No one came and gave me any news officially, but when I asked my boss, Mr. Clifford, where Mistral had gone, he only said, 'Swageman won't be coming back. His nag has been reassigned. If you see him, have him arrested'. Mr. Swageman, what has happened?"

Clifford was your traditional haughty Brit bureaucrat; licked the boots of his superiors, kicked the arses of his underlings. He'd not have bothered expending much energy on explaining things to a coolie as far beneath him as old Ting.

I told Ting some of the story, just enough to leave him with the impression that I was on a secret mission to sabotage the Japanese, and that for now, even my colleagues must continue to believe that I had gone rogue. I may have embellished my tale with some thrilling heroics.

We parted with him, promising to keep the fact of my being in Dongying to himself. With my conical hat back on my noggin, I headed to Victoria Street.

On my way, I killed some time in a bustling workers' café. I figured that the cover of darkness would aid my ambition of separating Mistral from her new owners. After lingering over my dinner of prawn and garlic dumplings dipped in malt vinegar, I deemed it dark enough outside to set out for Victoria Street. It was around nine o'clock, and on my way there, I was struck anew by the contrast in lifestyles between the citizenry and the foreigners. Thanks to my peasant disguise, I seemed to have been imbued with a fresh perspective. I didn't feel like the superior, uniformed foreigner, striding around on important official business, and thus I began to notice things I hadn't before.

One side of Victoria Street had a ramshackle collection of homely huts cobbled together with discarded timber and sacking, with cooking smells pervading and noisy families with their naked children running about playing games with whatever debris they could find. Workers were coming from, or going to, long shifts of toil. There was an air of warmth and gaiety. People smiled at each other. On the other side of the street, large, walled compounds housed the foreigners in sombre and foreboding detachment.

In the nameless back lane that paralleled Victoria Street, I counted back from the corner of Fleet Street. When I reached the wall of the fourth house, I jumped on the spot to try to see over the wall, looking for a stable. I didn't see one at the fourth house and repeated the process at the fifth. No stables.

At the sixth house, when I jumped, I espied a glimpse of a structure that would serve as a place to house a horse. A few more vertical leaps and I could see that it was raw timber nailed onto a frame with overlapping planks and open at one end. It had a simple thatched roof and looked like it could house three or four horses. I crept along the wall, saying "Mistral" in a loud whisper. At the farthest corner, I received a neigh in reply. She was here!

There was a back gate in the wall, but when I silently tried the latch, it wouldn't move, locked from the inside. I went away and fossicked around in the lane until I found a few suitable packing crates. I quietly stacked them up into a rickety set of steps and scaled the wall which, mercifully, had no broken glass embedded into the mortar on top. I jumped to the ground and crouched against the wall, listening. I heard the clanging of dinner dishes being washed and the subdued voices of the washers. There was no sign that anyone was enjoying an after-dinner cognac and cigar in the courtyard. There was just enough of a chill in the air to keep such activities indoors.

I crouched low and crept across twenty feet of the courtyard to the stable. She neighed and grunted when I was close. "Shh, shh, girl!" I whispered through watery eyes while I hugged and stroked her neck, which she usually hated but put up with this time. I kept her between me and the house, hoping that was enough concealment. I held her for a few more moments then broke off. I looked around. She was in a small stable on her own that looked as if it had been only recently constructed just for her. There was something new about her. Her blonde mane and tail were plaited. Pink ribbon was woven through the plaits. She was all prettied up. There was a polished saddle slung over the low wall, and even in the dim light cast from the house, I could see that it was *pink*. Good grief. That had to mean she was now the recreational plaything of some rich lady.

I heard the unmistakable sound of a footfall crushing an autumn leaf. Mistral began to stamp a foreleg, her usual method of demanding to be let loose. I hid behind her and stroked her flank to keep her quiet. I heard the sound of a key in a lock and saw the back gate slowly open, as if whoever was opening the gate did not want to alert the occupants of the house. A furtive face emerged through the gate into the light cast from the house.

Well, well, well. It was Mrs. Dickinson. I knew her face from the handful of times I'd met her at IMCS functions. It was a face I had admired. She had very pale blue eyes and haughtily high cheekbones, yet she was open and engaging with people she was introduced to, no matter their status. She had a quick and sardonic wit that made me immediately jealous. Dickinson didn't deserve her. Unlike many of the wives of foreigners stationed in China, she did not have that air of resigned timeserving, making the most of the distractions, waiting patiently until their return to their homeland. 'Camping' some of them whimsically called it. Not Cynthia Dickinson: she was determined to have a fulfilling time wherever life took her.

Right now, she seemed to be finding fulfilment of a more familiar type. I watched her look around, fail to see me, then turn and kiss a man behind her in the gateway. I could only see the top of his head as the two of them locked lips. It was a long and lingering kiss that made me wish I was him, and I watched enviously as the man's hands artfully massaged her buttocks.

When they disengaged, and he lifted his head, I saw that he was *not* her husband. Mrs. Dickinson was having a bit on the side. Ha! This was delicious, indeed. I wanted to shout, "You enjoy yourself, darling, your idiot husband never deserved you." My old nemesis had been cuckolded. Not man enough to keep his wife satisfied. I'd rub his nose in *that* if I ever got the chance.

Unless... could he be dead? Could Mrs. Dickinson be a grieving widow? Another, even more delicious, prospect. I doubted it, though. If a widow, why a furtive kiss at the back gate? Why not take him to the boudoir and do unspeakable things with him? Or with me?

My imagination was running away with me, as usual. It had been too long since I had enjoyed the attentions of a woman, and the images my mind was serving up to me, of Cynthia in the throes of shuddering ecstasy, were not helping right now. I shook my head to clear them.

She closed the gate on her lover and went to the back door of the house. Alistair Dickinson himself greeted her at the door. *Damn. Not dead. Shame.* He'd escaped Seoul and got back to his old life. Must have confiscated Mistral for his wife or daughter. One of the spoils of his part in my disgraced exit from the IMCS.

They went inside, and the house went quiet.

Back to business. How to get Mistral out undetected? She had resumed stamping her foreleg. I came out from behind her and stood beside her. I held her foreleg still and stroked her flank. She stamped her other foreleg.

I had already decided that getting to Beijing to talk to the emperor was my plan. I had no idea how, I just knew the ultimate goal: expose the plot, and have the conspirators executed. Simple.

But now that I had Mistral back, at least I had transport—swift and exhilarating transport. I just needed to get my other ducks in a row.

Mistral went still and turned a big brown eye at me. She snorted. She knew; she always knew. It dawned on her that I was going to be leaving her in situ, right at the moment the thought came into my head that I must leave her here, for the time being, and come and get her later for the trip to Beijing. She neighed and kicked her back legs, hitting the wooden back wall of her pen. Worried the noise would bring someone out from the house, I kissed her on the cheek, and she neighed again, much more loudly.

There was a barrel a few feet outside the pen. I used it to scale the stable wall and jump onto the top of the outer wall. I then jumped to the ground outside, Mistral's protestations ringing in my ears and piercing my heart.

I needed to find a peaceful spot to nut out a plan.

And quickly.

Chapter Thirty-One

Blindfolded and tied to a chair in a stifling room wasn't the ideal thinking space I'd had in mind.

As soon as my feet had hit the ground outside the walls of Dickinson's compound, a sharp blow cracked me in the back of my head, and everything went dark. I came to slowly with what felt like an anvil resting on top of my head and felt the lashings on my wrists and ankles. I was completely immobilised. I heard footsteps coming toward me, and my blindfold was suddenly torn from my eyes. My opium dealer glowered at me, then punched me in the face. Blood ran into one eye, and I could see through the other eye that we were in a dark and mouldy basement. A solitary oil lamp on a hook on the wall gave him a looming shadow on the opposite wall, and the small window high on the far wall gave me a glimpse of the stars in the night sky.

"Your package arrived, two bales. Bales of *tea*! Were you trying to be funny, posh man?" Another blow to the face caught me on the cheekbone this time, then an open-handed slap. I tasted blood in my mouth.

So, Heineken must have found my opium and swapped it for actual tea, a *figurative* slap in my face. I spat out some blood. "Were there any papers in the bales?"

My dealer threw a piece of paper at me that fluttered onto my lap, face up. It read: 'Thanks for this, from Prussia with love.'

Hilarious.

I consoled myself with images of mashing Heineken's jowly face in. Then slitting his throat and watching his blood spurt.

Three men came in through the door, one brandishing secateurs, while my dealer took two steps back. "We will not kill you, but we will teach you a lesson. One you'll remember every time you try to open a jar."

Oh, God. My thumbs.

Secateurs man moved to a position behind me and held his weapon open around my thumb at the second knuckle. Giving up any pretence at bravery, and hoping to explain myself, on the off chance it could help, I breathlessly explained The Plot. "Using the KoLaoHui and other double-agents, a Japanese-German cabal is going to conquer your country, murder Cixi and those loyal to her, keep the emperor as a puppet, plunder the coffers, grant rights for railroads, mining, big loans from European banks, etcetera to their cronies; Japanese, Germans, Russians, Brits, everyone. It's what the whole Japanese invasion is about. Nations from all points of the compass plundering the country. Millions will be murdered, millions more subjugated under the boot of imperialism..." My rant petered out pathetically. Then I realised that it might help to mention something more: "One of the Germans swapped out my opium, your opium, for tea. He was trying to neutralise me. Get you to do his dirty work for him. If you take that bait, he's duped you. I sent you eight bales," I lied. "But he's somehow switched them for two bales of tea to incite you to kill me. One bale even had a list of spies, which is why I asked about papers..."

The room went quiet as I ran out of words. My dealer flicked his eyes toward secateurs man. Inspiration struck me like a bolt of lightning. I blurted out, "And they manipulated the price of silver! They have contacts in the US Treasury. It was all part of the scheme. To weaken China by sending her broke. So the Japanese could march in." I was counting on the likelihood that he'd taken a serious personal loss when the silver price crashed last year. I certainly did. Obviously, I was distorting and embellishing the story, and he knew it. But when trying to save one's skin, truth is an acceptable casualty. Throughout my frantic, barely coherent babble, my dealer had remained aloof, cocking an eyebrow, his mouth a mixture of grimace and grin.

"If you don't believe me, find the paperwork in my jacket in the knapsack. The evidence is all there."

One man grabbed my knapsack from the floor and emptied the contents onto the dirt. He looked at my dealer, who said, "Bring it," and walked out through the door. The men followed, one carrying my things under his arm, and the one with the secateurs looking crestfallen.

I was alone in the room. I tested the strength of my bonds with my numb fingers and mercifully still-attached thumbs. There was no give in the ropes.

They left me alone for hours. The window showed me some light as daybreak arrived, and a narrow sliver of sunshine streamed through. That told me that the window faced east, a fact collected, but unlikely to be of any use. The square of sunlight slowly moved across the floor until it vanished. Noon. The door opened, and my dealer and his men entered. He placed a chair in front of me and sat astride it, backwards, facing me. He scrunched up his nose at my stench. I'd emptied my bladder during the night and could feel my urine squelching between my toes in my boots.

His eyes bore into mine for what seemed like an hour but was undoubtedly less than a minute. "My own spies have suspected something for some time—"

"What spies? Which *something*?"

"Don't interrupt. My interpreter here," he jerked his thumb at one of his men, "confirms that the papers indicate that your friend Spratt was chasing down some kind of conspiracy."

I interrupted anyway, despite the warning. "The stockholder list, the German telegram referring to the KoLaoHui. And you already know that the Germans and Russians are in cahoots. Their damn leaders are cousins!"

"Settle down, settle down. The question is, what were you planning to do about it?"

What indeed? Describing my plan as in its larval stage would be to elevate it considerably. "Set the evidence before the emperor so he can foil The Plot. The KoLaoHui are Han, hate the Manchu and want them slaughtered and Han rule returned to the Middle Kingdom..." I paused because I suddenly realised that I might have accidentally insulted him. I tentatively asked, "Which are you?"

"I'm Manchu! Those Han dogs, the Hatchet Men, can rot in hell!"

Phew. It was good to have struck a nerve. I didn't mention my own Han ancestry. I continued while I was making progress. Secateurs man was hovering in the doorway. "Besides, how will your businesses fare under Jap/German rule? Maybe they'd turn a blind eye, so long as they received a big slice of the drug dealing and prostitution—"

One of the men piped up. "And protection, and—" My dealer shot him a look, and he shut up.

Again, my dealer gave me the silent treatment. I kept quiet and let him think and tried to keep a determined and righteous expression on my face. Minutes passed.

He stood up, walked around behind me, and untied my bonds. I rubbed my wrists to try to return blood to them and stop the tingling.

He and his men walked out of the room, leaving me alone again. I stood and stretched, not sure what to do next.

"You coming?" came a disembodied voice from the corridor beyond the door. I followed. The corridor ended at a staircase, at the top of which was a spacious kitchen. The middle of the room was dominated by a stained and scarred table with four stools on either side. A steaming pot sat on a flame on a hob in the far corner of the room, with a stooped henchman carefully stirring. A grubby window on the far wall looked out onto a walled garden. I could see small rows of cabbage plants and a creeper covering the slate wall, which looked to my untrained eye to be passionfruit. I heard a scraping noise and saw that my dealer had kicked a stool out from under the table. He nodded at it, and I sat.

Over the course of a working men's lunch, I saw a very different side of my ruthless, pitiless dealer. I learned to my great surprise and relief that he was the most patriotic Chinaman I'd ever met. He vociferously supported the Qing, dismissing their foibles and reiterating several times that they enjoyed the Mandate of Heaven. He praised the way they honoured their ancestors and said that if the "congenitally retarded Han morons" couldn't see what was best for them, then they deserved to be subjugated and killed, in that order. He railed at the treachery of the KoLaoHui, spittle flying and from his mouth.

It was strong stuff, and I kept my own thoughts to myself, agreeing enthusiastically with my dealer's opinions while we scooped noodles and hunks of pork into our mouths.

Silence fell around the lunch table while he inhaled his lunch. With a mouthful of masticated noodles and meat, he said, "Here's what I'll do, you mad fucker. I will help you. When it's all over, if you're still alive, you and I will have a serious talk about how you will atone for your sins against me."

Apart from wiping his food from my face, I didn't move a muscle.

"This," he pulled my wad of papers from his pocket and slammed it on the table. "This stuff may or may not induce a Manchu official to take you seriously. It's not exactly a dossier. It's a collection of papers that Spratt compiled that indicates the *possibility* of some plot."

"It might yet motivate an investigation if we got it in front of the right official—"

"Shut up. I'm way ahead of you. Here's what's going to happen."

And he told me. He reasoned that The Plot and its evidence, weak as it was, would be better received if it came from a man of status, an IMCS man, even a former one, though that inconvenient fact would remain concealed.

Of course, my dealer knew all about my misadventures in Seoul. His grapevine was the very model of information efficiency. Better than the telegraph. "My men in Beijing supply a very important personage with substances for enlightenment. Have you heard of Concubine Zhen? Also known as Pearl?"

"You're joking!"

He laughed, and his men, hearing him laugh, obediently joined in. They stopped when he stopped, except for one. My dealer shot him another look, and he shut his mouth. "Not only Pearl, but also her cousin, who is an influential eunuch at Court. He can't get enough of my product, and by way of payment has arranged several lucrative jobs for other, distant 'relatives' of mine."

Bribery and nepotism were legitimate managerial systems as old as time itself. I had no doubt that the 'relatives' were either working directly for my dealer or were sufficiently bribable or blackmailable to ensure that he could both continue and expand his empire. I was even more impressed than before. I felt like the rankest amateur at graft in his presence.

He took a piece of paper from his pocket and handed it to me. It was a signed letter of introduction to Concubine Zhen, also known as Pearl. I was soon to meet royalty. I looked at my dealer in surprise.

He laughed again. "Yes, posh man, customs man, you're about to meet someone rather special."

The meal finished, and they all got up from the table. "Follow me," he said, and we walked out of the room into the yard. It was good to be outdoors, and I turned my face to the sun.

We were in the garden, which I could now see was longer than it looked through the window. I blinked in the bright sunlight.

When the delicious sun-blindness abated, I saw Mistral, saddled up and ready to go. His men must have sprung her from Dickinson's.

My new best friend, my saviour, had reunited me with my real best friend. I manfully held back tears.

Even with all this help from my militantly patriotic drug dealer and pimp, would I be able to get into the Forbidden City to see a high official? The place is quite literally a fortress. China's most impenetrable. At nearly two hundred acres it was a city unto itself. Few Westerners had seen beyond the thirty-foot walls, which themselves were surrounded by a deep moat. I'd studied a map of the area years earlier and noticed that here was a city that was well prepared for any kind of siege. There were three sets of city walls with gates and garrisoned troops stationed all over the place. Beijing was well equipped to keep enemies out, and I worried that if I was able to get in, I may never come out. I tried to bury my trepidation deep down. I would just have to trust that the dealer's people, including Pearl, were as influential as he claimed. I had my doubts.

Chapter Thirty-Two

It took Mistral and me five days to ride to Beijing, which literally translates as the "North Capital," Nanjing being the "South Capital." It was good to be moving through the landscape with my best friend, and I was very tempted to keep going past Beijing and not stop until we were far away from our troubles. Alas, troubles have a way of finding one.

We approached from the south, traversing the rural flatlands cultivated mostly with wheat. It was a common fallacy that Asian peoples lived on rice and noodles, but the further north one went, the more flour-based delights awaited. The main trunk road to Beijing was as straight as an arrow for four hundred miles, and paralleled the Grand Canal, China's most impressive engineering feat. I'd never seen it and took a deliberate detour to have a gander. I expected to be impressed, but really, it was just a wide canal, dead straight, all the way to both the northern and southern horizons. Huge steam barges, three hundred feet long, chugged northwards, laden with coal, timber, wheat, or other mysterious goods under canvas covers. Empty barges headed south. I imagined Beijing was some kind of giant hungry dragon, demanding to be constantly fed.

Back riding along the major trunk road, my mouth had watered when the scent of baozi, steamed buns with a filling, met my nostrils. We stopped and ate like pigs.

As we cantered northwards, fields gradually gave way to houses. Further, villages became larger and denser, and we eventually arrived at the southern gate of Beijing's outer wall. I climbed down and walked Mistral through, passing under the imposing granite arch in company with traders of every hue, their goods loaded precariously atop carts or simply carried on their stooped backs.

The road inside the gate continued due north, as dictated by long-dead Feng Shui prophets, with the Temple of Agriculture to our left, the Temple of Heaven to our right—they looked the same to me—and directly ahead, the Forbidden City, which was the compound just inside the Imperial City walls. This city had been invaded so often it sported no less than four sets of walls.

My first contact was to be Consort Zhen, also known as Pearl, the objective being to enlist her help with the plan. My dealer had said he'd laid the groundwork and arranged the introduction, but I still needed to sweet-talk her. Pearl's mother was Lady Zhao, and her father was the vice minister of revenue. She was just eighteen years old and had only recently been elevated to the status of emperor's consort, of which there were dozens, after serving a mandatory term as a concubine, which numbered in the hundreds.

As we approached the wall to the inner city, I espied a suitable inn that had stables on one side. I settled Mistral in the stables and then checked myself in and ordered a dinner of dumplings and steamed buns to eat in my room, leaving my travelling clothes with the proprietress for laundering. My room had a balcony facing north from which I could see over the canal on the other side of the street and beyond that the wall of the inner city. On the other side of the wall was the thirteen-hundred-acre foreign legation, the area where the Qing designated that all foreign diplomats and trading companies must conduct their business. Foreigners were allowed to live outside the legation, but their work had to be performed inside the fortified walls. Soldiers patrolled the ramparts. The IMCS was the only entity exempt from this Qing edict, primarily because it was not technically a foreign entity; it was a Chinese government department staffed by foreigners. Robert Hart himself lived in Beijing, his home about nine miles east of my inn, just inside the outer wall.

Morning found me scrubbed, fed, and appropriately dressed. My dealer had supplied me with a new blazer, one with gold buttons and epaulettes. He didn't say how he came by it, and I didn't ask. I left Mistral munching hay in the inn's stables and set off on foot for the Zhao family compound. Consorts are greatly restricted in their movements outside the Concubine housing in the Forbidden City, but they are allowed to visit their family from time to time.

I found the street, just off the main road, and presented myself at the circular gate. A servant wearing what the Brits call a morning suit answered my knock and ushered me inside the compound, through a large and fragrant courtyard whose trees exuded a ghostly majesty now that they were denuded of leaves. Inside and to the left of the shiny red door of the dwelling, I was shown into what the Brits would call a withdrawing room and told to wait.

A small Chinese man strode proudly into the room, dressed for all the world as if he was off to the races at Royal Ascot; morning suit with grey topcoat and a paisley cravat tucked into the high collar of a silk shirt. He puffed out his chest and thrust his hand out. "Delighted to meet you, Mister Swageman." The petite dandy had a falsetto voice, like his balls had never dropped.

"Delighted to meet you too, Mister...?" His answer was not forthcoming, and we stared at each other for half a minute. There was something off about him.

Only when he threw his head back and burst into a high-pitched giggle did I notice the lipstick.

"Got you! Ha! I'm Consort Zhen, but please call me Pearl." Her outstretched hand was pale and delicate, now that I looked at it. I stepped forward, still confused, and we shook hands. Tea was brought into the room by a smiling servant, apparently in on the joke, and we sat side by side on a brocaded yellow settee.

"Sorry for teasing you. I prefer men's clothes, so much more comfortable, especially as the weather cools. And especially the shoes! Have you seen the type of shoes one is supposed to wear at Court? Crippling!"

"I can only imagine."

"My feet were never bound. Barbaric practice. Horrid. Thank heavens Daddy forbade it. He's thoroughly modern, you know."

She prattled on about herself until our tea went cold. She told me she often wore simpler men's clothes to go wandering anonymously among the common folk, and that Empress Dowager Cixi indulged her whimsical pastimes. She had a refreshing candour. She explained that Cixi appreciated her talents, and the empress hired top artisans to teach her to paint and play musical instruments. That said, apparently, Cixi was somewhat wary of her because Pearl had also urged the Guangxu emperor to be 'strong and independent', and to 'cut the umbilical cord', as it were, and encouraged his attempts to introduce political reforms and the teaching of foreign languages. Pearl's love of photography saw her inviting foreigners into the Forbidden City to teach her about the art, also an unprecedented development in the rarefied confines of the palace walls.

She asked me no questions. Either she knew everything about me already or didn't care to.

A light lunch was brought into the room, and that signalled the end of frivolous chatter. We moved onto more serious matters.

Even while we did so, she continued in her disconcertingly insouciant manner, giggling from time to time, treating me to the visage of mouthfuls of partially chewed food in her mouth. She explained all the court protocols and hierarchy and said she had already arranged for suitable clothing and credentials to be supplied to me and her men. She and her chaperone would accompany us to the meeting.

"We're meeting a Manchu Official," she said, as soup dribbled alluringly down her chin, wetting her now loosened cravat. "Who, though several rungs down the ladder from the emperor himself, yet holds some influence at the Grand Council. My consort status grants me no special rights to meet with any Manchu Officials, but with the help of my cousin Zhirui, head eunuch to the emperor, and your

IMCS credentials"—assuming that it was not yet known that I was persona non grata at the IMCS— "I'm confident we'll be welcomed and listened to."

Her confidence was not contagious. It probably wasn't going to be a meeting with anyone who could get my information directly to the top man, the big cheese, Emperor Guangzu, but it was a start. "I hope my arguments will be compelling enough to make it all the way up the chain to the emperor."

"I hope so too." She giggled, crumbs falling onto her chest. She was excited to be part of the plot. It was a grand adventure.

I wished that I shared her enthusiasm. We were talking about the formidable Forbidden City. One hundred and eighty acres of royals, noble Manchus, and well-armed guards of every stripe.

She called for the lunch things to be cleared, and when the servant had retreated, she picked up my tobacco pouch from the table and deftly rolled two fat cigarettes, handing one to me. She scootched closer on the settee to light mine with my matches. We puffed in silence for a minute, then, cigarette dangling precariously from her lips, she slid closer still, raised one trousered leg, and straddled me. With her head higher than mine, she spoke, and ash fluttered onto my nose. "Now, I need you to defile me. Strenuously and mercilessly."

So I did.

Her Consort training soon had me forgetting all about plots and intrigues and schemes, and we abandoned ourselves to sweaty ecstasy. She was no innocent. She had skills. I gave a silent nod of appreciation to her teachers at the Consort Sex Academy, or whatever they called it.

Chapter Thirty-Three

A small team of men had been put together. Whether the men were gathered from the ranks of my dealer's Beijing henchmen, or whether they had been cobbled together from Pearl's own contacts, was not made clear to me. Neither were the precise details of their role.

I had staggered from Pearl's family compound around midnight, taken a rickshaw to my inn, and fallen into bed. In the morning, the proprietress had knocked on my door and asked me to come downstairs. There were five burly men in the breakfast room, scaring the guests and waiting to meet with me. The dining area of the inn was on the ground floor, just off to the left from the lobby. There were no menus. You simply sat down and a waitress in an apron brought bowls of salty noodles and pots of tea.

Burly and battle scarred, the faces of the five men seated opposite me testified to the many skirmishes in which they'd fought or probably started. "You should see the other guy," one of them said when he caught me staring at a crescent-shaped scar that pulled his right eye downwards. Another was missing an entire nostril, and yet another had had his smile widened, with one-inch cuts in each corner of his mouth.

Though I wouldn't want to bump into any of these men in a darkened alley, I found them to be amiable enough. The largest of them appeared to be their spokesperson, like a mastiff among Dobermans. When we all introduced ourselves, he said his name was Zhiqiang. That was comforting; it meant 'strong-willed' in Mandarin.

I cleared my throat. "Gentlemen, here's the plan—"

"The consort has told us what she wants us for. What we need to know from you is, are you actually serious?" Zhiqiang tilted his head and gave me a pitying look, like I was a simpleton.

"Very. Look, we're not going to storm the place. We're just having an informal meeting with an official. Chances are that you won't be needed for anything other than giving the appearance that I am important enough to have a contingent of personal bodyguards. It's about saving face. Just try to look intimidating." That should be no effort at all for these blokes.

He eyed me from under his heavy brows. "They won't allow us any weapons. We'll get searched at the gate."

Another of them piped up. "They never search the boots. That's where my dagger will be." He brandished a fearsome six-inch blade, held it up to the light to admire it.

"Put it away," said Zhiqiang. Some of the inn's guests were staring at us over the rims of their breakfast bowls.

"None of you should need any weapons. If everything goes to plan."

"If..." Zhiqiang said. The word hung in the air for a minute. I slurped my coffee and winced, my jaw still tender from the previous evening's exertion with Pearl. The silence was broken when another of the men said, "What I don't understand is why we don't let them kill Cixi. I mean, she's the problem, right? Kill the bitch, I say."

Another agreed. "Yeah, but what about the emperor? Guangzu himself? I hear he's a sickly brat, interested only in his cats. He's never even been outside the province."

I knew I wouldn't be able to explain the labyrinthine geopolitical scheme I was hoping to foil, so I didn't bother. "You're right, but Cixi's death is only a small part of the plan. We're not going in there to save her neck; we're going in there to try to prevent this country from being dominated by an unholy cabal of Japanese and Germans."

He didn't look convinced. Zhiqiang turned to him. "Have you forgotten your time with the KoLaoHui? What a bunch of self-righteous idiots they were? That was their plan ten years ago, and they died for their stupid, ill-formed ideals."

The men stayed quiet. So, one of our number was a former member of the Hatchett Men. I'd have to keep an eye on him. If he reached for his boot at any time, I'd have to be ready.

Zhiqiang turned back to me. "I'm told you have convincing evidence that you believe will motivate this Manchu official to take the matter to the emperor. Is this Manchu even able to get an audience with the emperor? And, er, can I see the evidence?"

"The evidence is compelling," I lied, "but no, you can't see it. And Consort Pearl assures me that the official is lofty enough to insist on an audience with his highness."

"I don't like it. We'll do as the consort asks, but we will not commit suicide for her. If things get ugly, we're gone."

"Fair enough."

I kept to myself my own reservations about just how convincing the Manchu would find the sheaf of water-stained and blurry papers I was calling 'evidence'.

Zhiqiang said, "The consort told me that she has made your appointment. It is for ten o'clock tomorrow morning. We will meet two hundred yards west of the western gate at nine-thirty."

"Very good."

He stood up, and his men did the same. I shook his calloused, four-fingered hand, and they left. I took stock. Suddenly I had a team under my command, of sorts, which was a new experience for me. And they looked like they could handle themselves, like they were no strangers to violence.

I had to assume there would be a cohort of undiscovered double agents secreted throughout the palace complex. Whether they were answerable to Heineken, Takagi, or some other cog of the cabal machinery, I had no idea. But I *did* know that if we failed to get the message all the way through to the emperor, through the opaque bureaucratic layers of officials, we'd not just be merely disappointed. When the spies at court found out what we were up to, we'd be either arrested and then executed for treason or simply done away with in a quiet dungeon. I didn't like either of those two options, but I was about to find out there was a third.

Chapter Thirty-Four

So it was that our rag-tag mercenary team presented itself, scrubbed and respectfully dressed, at the western gate, the 'tradesman's entrance', of the Forbidden City the next morning.

The IMCS had no special uniform for meeting dignitaries, but I was glad the blazer my dealer had supplied was crisp and new. Pearl's paisley cravat adorned my neck and smelled of lavender. It was nice to be looking dapper again.

My five comrades had scrubbed up rather well too. They were all dressed in identical navy-blue tunics with brass buttons and knee-high leather boots, the customary though informal uniform worn by mercenaries hired to guard noblemen. Some noblemen dressed their guards in more embellished outfits, to convey, hopefully, higher status. But that impressed no one, least of all guards of the Forbidden City, loftiest of the lofty among the warrior classes.

My men carried some discreetly concealed small weapons but weren't able to hide any long swords under their tunics. We'd have to make do without them.

Sartorial splendour was Consort Pearl's modus operandi too. She was resplendent in the finest of British male aristocratic dandy's duds. She wore a silk three-piece suit of deep scarlet, the colour of blood, with a golden waistcoat and a black tie tied in a fat Windsor knot. Forbidden City guards were used to seeing her elegantly clothed as a man and concealed their smirks well. She was accompanied by her dowdy chaperone, Miss Hu, who wore a shapeless dress of beige brocade. Pearl was aboard Mistral, enjoying the additional stature it gave her, and it meant she towered over all of us, could look down with condescension upon her underlings. It suited her.

We'd rendezvoused at the appointed hour and walked together across the bridge over the moat and presented ourselves to the guards standing straight-backed under the massive stone arch of the western gate. Pearl's short conversation with a guard resulted in us being ushered straight through and into the hallowed interior of the palace complex. We men were directed to one roped-off waiting area to the right of the gate while the women and Mistral were politely herded to an identical roped-off area to the left. Imperial consort or not, there were extremely strict rules about where women could and could not be within the Forbidden City. Women were confined to clearly defined routes and buildings. The huge courtyards were off-limits to the fairer sex, whatever gender's attire they sported.

A relieved sigh involuntarily escaped my lips at having made it inside the walls of the Forbidden City. So far, so good. I watched as a regally robed man met with Pearl and her chaperone, twenty feet from where we stood. Cousin Zhirui, no doubt, high-status eunuch of the Imperial Court. Eunuchs were officially prohibited from leaving the Forbidden City, though a little bribery of palace guards meant that many could be found in the seedier parts of Beijing. Not only drinking establishments but also brothels. Rumour had it that while every eunuch had been castrated, usually at a young age, some of the surgical procedures were more thorough than others. A fat bribe to one of the official doctors that performs the procedure, and a boy might find himself with a convincing scar and a much-reduced scrotum, yet with the plums still intact inside the smaller sack. It was also rumoured that one such not-quite-castrated eunuch, Li Lianying, was Cixi's lover, servicing the dowager vigorously whenever the whimsical notion overcame her.

Zhirui finished talking with his cousin Pearl, and they were led away by calm but alert guards along the inside of the wall. Mistral flinched and stood her ground when a guard tried to pull her along by the reins. Pearl patted Mistral's flank and whispered in her ear, and she relaxed, allowing the guard to guide her. Zhirui came over to our little group and whispered in the ear of one of the eight guards watching over us in the roped-off pen. I scanned the scene. Directly opposite the gate was a courtyard about the size of two tennis courts. The paving stones were light grey granite. The inside walls of the complex had a row of single-story buildings looking rather like stores but were probably administrative offices.

The whispered conversation finished, Zhirui walked over to me and shook my hand. "Welcome, Mister Swageman. Cousin Pearl has told me a great deal about you." He winked at me. Surely Pearl wouldn't have mentioned our breathless horizontal exercise?

I thanked him for his warm welcome. Looking over his shoulder, I noticed that the guard that Zhirui had whispered to was looking intently to his right, and I followed his gaze. He was looking at Pearl aboard Mistral, with Mrs. Hu and their contingent of guards, as they turned the corner of a building and went out of sight.

The guard looked back at Zhirui, who looked back at him and nodded. Without a word being spoken, all eight guards surrounded us and drew their swords, their polished points glinting in the sun. My heart sank and my jaw went slack. *Oh, fuck.*

The head guard said, "Don't even think about it," as three of our number reached for their boots, where their daggers resided. I heard Mistral neigh loudly somewhere out of sight. That sound always carried far, as nature intended.

Zhirui, hands on hips and scowling at us, barked another order to the guard. "Strip them of their weapons. Then you know where to take them." He spun around so fast it took his heavy robe a second to spin with him. He strode in the direction that they had taken Pearl and her cohort.

Thus, at sword point, we were marched in the opposite direction, across the courtyard. I felt like such a fool. I avoided looking at any of my men. A sexy consort, an 'influential' eunuch cousin, an unnamed Manchu official—all organised by a criminal drug dealer and pimp four hundred miles away. Of *course* we were captured. And being sent to painful incarceration and probable execution.

It had all seemed so plausible as it tumbled out of their mouths. My dealer blithely confident of his contacts and influence, Pearl's feisty and haughty demeanour exuding a contagious certainty that all would go as planned.

Swagger, you numbskull. Our band of guards and prisoners turned at the end of the courtyard, rounded the corner of a building and entered a narrow lane between the building and a small temple. Our head guard stopped and turned back to face me and my men. He exhaled loudly. His formerly hunched shoulders relaxed. The guards flanking us relaxed too. The hairs on the back of my neck stood on end.

"Stand right there and don't move a muscle," said the head guard. We did as we were told. The other guards stood much less rigidly than before, but their swords remained aimed at our necks. The head guard opened a door in the building, poked his head through it, checking it for something, then said, "In here."

He went in first, and the guards herded us through, one of them closing the door behind us. We were in a spacious food storage area, and the smell of baked goods assailed my nostrils. The head guard sheathed his sword. "We are Kansu Braves. We don't take orders from eunuchs," he spat on the floor. "Such a creature is not a man!"

I'd heard that there were numerous guard factions in the Forbidden City, each set with loyalties to different masters.

"You! Customs man. Follow me."

The circle of swords parted just enough for me to walk through. I followed the guard, wondering what was happening. I was mystified but cautiously optimistic; we weren't going wherever Zhirui had ordered the guard to take us, and that had to be a good thing.

He walked ahead of me, unconcerned that he was presenting me with his unguarded back. He didn't regard me as a threat, or he was confident that even if I attacked him from the rear, he'd be able to deal with me. Looking at the size of him, I was confident he could deal with me too.

It was only then that I noticed his black turban and a necklace of blue and brown beads. *Of course!* The Kansu Braves, as he had just said. Now I remembered. The Royal Muslim Guards.

The Chinese military, though slowly changing, was still a mixed bag of platoons with shifting loyalties to one general or another, depending on who paid best, meaning which general shared the proceeds of corruption evenly versus which general kept too much for himself.

The contingent of guards whose specific role was to defend the Forbidden City was the elite Wuwei Corps, the most modern and best-trained arm of the Chinese military, and they had recently incorporated into their ranks the Muslim soldiers from Kansu province, whose courage was said to be rooted in their belief that a noble death guaranteed an afterlife of hashish and nubile virgins. The Kansu Braves were the division within the Wuwei Corps, whose only job was to defend the emperor and his family. The Kansu Brave I was following turned and faced me. "A mutual friend has told me who you are and why you are here."

"Who?" *I have a friend who knows a Muslim warrior? News to me.*

Wait. They liked their hashish. Could my dealer have used his legendary grapevine? Made provision for the likely contingency that our arrival at the Forbidden City might not go as smoothly as hoped by sending some quality marijuana their way?

"Names are of no importance. Just assure me. You are here to frustrate the invaders from the eastern islands?"

Did he mean Japan? Did it matter? If an affirmative answer would get me on his good side, then he shall have one. "Oh, yes. I hear the invaders are being particularly bloodthirsty with the women of your faith." I made that part up.

He spat again. "The likes of the half-man Zhirui and the effeminate tutor, Weng; they are the problem. I have watched them entertain the islanders lavishly, bowing to their every wish."

Grand Tutor Weng was the emperor's almost constant companion and had been more of a father to him than his own late father had ever been. The emperor did nothing without consulting Weng first.

I said, "I heard it was Weng who cut spending on the military and kept the emperor in the dark about everything. No wonder the Japanese are having such an easy time invading."

He closed his eyes and exhaled slowly, the scent of peppermint on his breath. After almost a minute of silent contemplation, he opened his eyes. "It's Cixi you want. Don't believe everything you've heard about her. She holds the power and wields it with skill, not Weng or the idiot boy, Guangzu."

I frowned and stared back at his inscrutable face, the tip of his red beard pointing at my nose. Only moments earlier I had despaired, abandoning the plan, and shifted my strategy to one of swift and thrilling escape. But this man was telling me that the Forbidden City was not finished with me yet.

Chapter Thirty-Five

O ur mission was over. We needed to re-group, get out of the Forbidden City, and re-strategize. Court intrigues and mysterious loyalties were a labyrinth I did not yet know the way through. Despite what the Kansu Brave was telling me, we couldn't just modify the plan on the fly. We had to get out.

I doubted Pearl was in any danger, given her status, so I decided that all I needed to do was get myself and my team out and think things through before trying again. I was just about to tell my new Muslim best friend to smuggle us back out of one of the gates and to tell Pearl the plan was postponed, when a door behind the Kansu Brave flung open, and a breathless man in heavy white robes stood in the doorway, one hand on the handle, his wispy beard waving in a breeze.

The Kansu Brave spun around. "Grand Tutor Weng!"

So, *this* was the man who held the boy-emperor in hypnotic thrall. Weng shouted over his shoulder to unseen men outside. "There they are, seize them!"

He stood aside, and a dozen men ran into the room. I turned and sprinted back to where my men were waiting, the sound of running feet close behind me. The guards had heard the ruckus, and one word that I didn't understand from their leader was enough to send them charging into the fray. They ignored my men and turned to face the new enemy.

My own men grabbed anything they could find in the bakehouse with which to defend themselves, lumps of wood, pans, a length of stovepipe, and ran to the melee. I grabbed two rolling pins off a bench and faced the fight, feeling inadequately armed with a rolling pin in each hand.

It was a sizeable room, but not large enough for twenty men fighting each other. They collided and got in each other's way. It looked more like a rugby scrum than a battle. Swords clashed, and men grunted or cried out in agony as blades found their mark and makeshift bludgeons landed on skulls and boots connected with balls. I could tell that my men and the Kansu Braves had tacitly joined forces and were fighting Weng's personal guards together. I stood on a crate and whacked someone's head. Then, over the top of the fighting, I saw Weng on the other side of the scrum, retreating through the door whence he'd come.

Someone must have thrown a bag of flour because suddenly the room went white, and I could see nothing. I brushed flour from my eyes, and the big Kansu Brave's face loomed right in front of mine like he'd mistaken me for one of Weng's men. He was wide-eyed and grimacing. He shouted above the din, "Just go! Do what you came to do!"

I hesitated. I hated to leave my team behind. But the Kansu Brave spun me around and, with a boot in my back, propelled me out of the door we had come through earlier. I landed on my front like I'd been thrown out of an inn. A cloud of flour dust followed and enveloped me.

I stood up on the granite paving stones and, hoping my men could fend for themselves, and for want of a better idea, I ran in the direction of the palace building itself.

I sprinted north toward the palace, using any laneway I could find between buildings. I whizzed past the surprised and frightened faces of the handful of people I encountered. I was still covered in flour and must have looked like a wild and blurry ghost. They were presumably workers, cooks, cleaners, royal bottom wipers. I didn't know or care.

I estimated I was still about a quarter mile from the palace complex when I saw Grand Tutor Weng slipping through a narrow arch about two hundred yards ahead. He was striding swiftly, and there were no guards with him. I quickened my pace. I wasn't sure what I would do when I caught up with him, but I knew I could rattle some facts from him if I could get him alone.

I reached the arch, and I could see him now only fifty yards ahead of me. He stopped at a door in a building on his right. With his hand on the handle, he looked around and saw me running toward him. In my breathless run, it was gratifyingly to see the wide-eyed fear on his face. He rushed through the door, closing it behind him. I reached the door about five seconds later and tried the iron handle. It was unlocked, thankfully, and I entered the red brick building.

I was in a dim corridor lined with shiny red lacquered walls and a high vaulted ceiling, and doors on each side spaced about twenty feet apart. Of Weng, there was no sign. The corridor was long, and though it was possible he'd made it all the way to the end before I arrived, I felt it more likely that he'd slipped into one of the side rooms. I closed the door and listened, but all I heard was my pounding heart.

I cautiously opened the first door on my left and peered around the door jamb. Wham! A sharp blow to the back of my still-bruised skull, and everything went black.

For what seemed the longest time, I was at the bottom of a deep and warm well, comfortably resting on my back. I could see kindly faces far above, peering down at me over the shiny brickwork, beckoning me to return. Without any effort on my part, I levitated up the well toward the faces. When I reached them, cool and refreshing water splashed into my face from somewhere.

I woke some indeterminate time later and found myself with water dripping from my chin and a grinning face with untamed nose hair close to mine. A second later, I noticed that I was in an opulently decorated room tied to an ornate, mahogany chair.

Again.

My head throbbed, my ears rang, and my vision was blurred. My vision cleared enough to see Heineken, Tyler, Weng, and the Japanese Admiral Takagi, brandy snifters in hands, staring at me.

Heineken spoke first. "Ah, our tenacious ex-customs minion is awake."

Chapter Thirty-Six

As one or two of my faculties returned, I could stare back at my captors. That Grand Tutor Weng was present told me something I had not been entirely sure of before: that he was in on the cabal. He was more than just one of the Manchus at court; he was the most influential man in the emperor's inner circle. Could that mean the emperor was in on it too? Selling out his country because running it was beyond him? Governing his people just too much effort?

I said, "You're under arrest, Heineken, for the murder of Jack Spratt."

Heineken chuckled. "It might surprise you to know that Spratt's murderer was the very man the police arrested and executed. Indeed, I can be certain because I hired him myself. Through an intermediary, obviously, whose family has been well compensated for his execution. Spratt was on the right track, and it was decided to nip the Spratt problem in the bud."

They'd have searched me while I was unconscious, and I was glad I'd had the presence of mind earlier to hide my papers under Mistral's saddle.

Thoughts of how best to extricate myself from the situation were temporarily crowded out by plain old curiosity. One of the papers, my 'evidence', was about the KoLaoHui, and how there was a member of the 'Elder Brethren in the Court'. I gambled on the probability that Weng was that particular hatchet man and might not have realised that his co-conspirators planned to sideline him when they had achieved their aims.

I thus hoped to sow some discord in the group and rattle Heineken when I said, "And your KoLaoHui spies here at court? Will they be just as expendable as Spratt? There won't be any room in the German-Japanese coalition-run China when the dust settles, surely?"

Heineken, despite himself, shot a glance Weng's way before quickly returning his gaze to me. "Your futile plan to expose our objectives would never get any traction. Did you think you'd find a sympathetic ear here at the palace? True, the KoLaoHui are clueless pawns. We are grateful for their help, but when we take over China, they will be pushed aside, executed if they get too—" he turned to Tyler. "*Kriegerisch*?"

"Belligerent."

"Belligerent, yes."

Damn. I'd guessed wrong. Weng looked unphased. He mustn't be KoLaoHui himself. I tried another tack. I turned to stare at Weng. "You know, the kaiser was late to the colonisation party and jealous of his grandma Victoria's colonial coverage of the globe, so he and the tzar are trying to acquire and carve up territories to plunder. Why are you doing the bidding of the European aristocracy? You must know they'll cast you aside when they have what they want. It's not a club that accepts new members from outside the circle." I shifted my gaze to Takagi, hoping he too would see that non-Europeans would not be among the winners when the spoils were handed out.

Heineken put a cigar in his mouth, and Weng lighted it for him. He swirled his brandy around in his snifter, then took a sip. "Too much of the globe carries the British Union Flag. It's time the balance shifted back to where it belongs. Sharing China's riches and territory with Japan will make Germany strong, strong enough to take some of fat queen Vicky's territory away from her. She doesn't deserve it. Look at India. They had an uprising and just about won back their independence. We would never allow that level of sedition in one of our colonies. We'd crush such a peasant uprising with a brutality that would make your eyes water. No, the Brits don't value what they have, as can be expected of a country with a woman in charge. Maybe we'll even take the British Isles themselves!" He chuckled again, and the others joined in. Heineken, and presumably the kaiser, certainly didn't want for ambition.

Takagi chimed in, helping his friend educate the idiot tied to the chair. "China is rich in coal and metals. Its backward superstitions mean that much of those riches remain under the soil. Unearthing them and dividing them will bring forth a new industrial age for Japan and her ally, Germany."

"Hence the need for railroads," I replied, then turned my eyes to Heineken. "Which of your family members is on the board of Barings? Is it Ernst?"

"My father, actually."

"And do your comrades here know that your father's bank owns a controlling stake in Rocky Mountain Railroad? Can we assume that it will be the successful bidder for contracts to build railroads here?"

Takagi looked at his boots, but Heineken apparently saw no shame in making money. The crafty baron said, "Indeed! The miraculous resurrection of that company will send the stock price in a most favourable direction. Spratt would have profited too if only he'd lived."

Fury boiled up in me, and my muscles strained against my bonds. I took some long, deep breaths and tried to bring my heart rate back down. A grandfather clock chimed the half-hour in the silence of the room.

Heineken's eyes bore into mine as he basked in my discomfort. "Perhaps you see something distasteful about profiting from the conflict? No, of course, you don't. That would be hypocritical. Why, I vividly recall pouring your opium over the side of the *Matsushima* and having it replaced with tea. You're in no position to act righteous. You're as corrupt as the next fellow!"

I sat and seethed, not knowing what to say to that.

Weng saved me when he butted in defensively, "China's traditional ways will never change, even in the face of foreign industrial superiority. The emperor knows that only with a collaboration between China, Japan, Germany, and Russia can we hope to modernise China the right way."

"By killing his mother?" Before he could answer, I forged ahead. "He only knows what you tell him. Tell me, Weng old cock, was it you that ordered Admiral Ding not to engage the Japanese? To hide the Beiyang Navy in WeiHaiWei, for 'safety'? For later seizure by the victorious Japanese, thus enabling Takagi here to double the size of the Japanese Navy? Will the emperor thank you for thus donating the Chinese Navy to the enemy?"

I left that hanging, thinking fast. Weng's words told me a few things. Any attempt by me to expose the German-Japanese-KoLaoHui conspiracy to the emperor would have fallen flat. If I had gotten to the emperor, Weng would have easily explained away my claims as the ravings of a deranged traitor, and the boy would believe it like he did everything his surrogate father told him. Besides, given that The Plot involved the murder of Cixi and those loyal to her, the emperor would probably be delighted to support it. It was she, after all, who denied him his divine right to rule. The Empress Dowager was the usurper, and Weng would have made sure that the boy Guangxu would approve of getting rid of her.

Weng didn't answer me, Heineken did. "The Chinese don't deserve those ships! We Germans built most of them, and the Qing haven't even paid them off. Their crews are lazy peasant conscripts, too stupid and undisciplined to even try to learn how to operate their equipment. They deserve what's coming to them—"

"Do they just? You're not just doing your duty for kaiser and country. This is personal for you, isn't it? You *hate* the Yellow Peril. And by that, I mean *all* Asian peoples. Your own race is superior in every way to them. Tell me I'm wrong." The kaiser himself had said so many times. I was hoping to drive a bigoted wedge between Heineken and Takagi and Weng. "What happened? Did a Chinaman piss in your soup? Fuck your wife? Did a Chinese servant spank you as a child?"

"Come now, Phillip. You won't succeed in goading me into saying something to offend my friends here." Heineken indicated the others with a magnanimous wave of his hand and received deferential nods from Weng and Takagi.

He had used my first name, getting surprisingly familiar and chummy. *They want something of me. Why else would I be alive?*

My papers. My evidence. They *did* have something damning in them. Something that would expose them. To whom? And what? Which of the documents I had optimistically been calling 'evidence' were they after?

For the first time since I awoke in the chair, Tyler spoke to me. "C'mon Swageman. We know you have it. Where is it?"

I ignored him and spoke to Weng and Takagi, the only Asians, apart from me, in the room. "Besides, are you gentlemen aware that this man's," I nodded in Heineken's direction, "Kaiser *coined* the term 'Yellow Peril'? He thinks you are savage primates, simpletons to a man. Existing for no other purpose than to be used as slaves."

I got no reaction. Takagi sipped his brandy and puffed on his cigar. Weng turned and spoke to Tyler. "You searched him, didn't you? Thoroughly?"

"Yes, of *course*, I did. Thoroughly." Tyler was miffed at the very suggestion. He turned back to me. "Your only chance of getting out of here alive is to hand over the names."

Ah. *That's* what they wanted. He must have been talking about the names of double agents in their midst. I'd presumed that there had been a list of such names in the bales of opium, as Jack's note in the engagement ring box had said. But Tyler had just told me that these men didn't have the names at all. The list must not have been in the bales. Now it made sense. There'd been a question tugging at the back of my mind ever since Seoul: why did Heineken even want me on the team? Because killing Spratt had not yielded the list of names. He needed me, Jack's oldest friend, to ferret the list out of its hiding place.

But if they hadn't found it in the opium bales, where could it be? I didn't have it. What could Jack have done with it? Unless, maybe, there never was a list. Maybe Jack was bluffing Okori. Why? To get *his* list of names?

Either way, I appeared to have a bargaining chip.

"Do you expect me to believe that if I hand over the list, you'll untie me, hand me a glass of brandy, and light me a cigar?"

Takagi turned to Heineken. "Told you. Let me bring my man in here. He's waiting in the corridor, and he has his tools with him. We'll soon get what we want. No one can hold out for long when my man is working on him."

I shivered. That was a terrifying escalation. I'd seen what determined Japanese soldiers could do when they were in a savage mood. I had no doubt that Takagi's pet torturer waiting in the corridor had exotic and inventive ways of delivering intolerable pain and suffering. I didn't think I'd stand up for long against his methods, whatever they were. I didn't have the information they wanted, but I'd be forced to make something up.

Heineken kept his eyes on me but answered Takagi. "There's no need for that, Admiral. Not yet. Phillip here knows what's good for him. Don't you, my boy?"

"You fellers are coming at this arse about. You have to open with payment. We should be haggling over a price, not threatening each other. C'mon, tell me. What's the information worth to you? Untie me, and let's start the negotiations afresh."

Tyler scowled, as did Takagi, but Weng merely stared at me, unable to figure me out. Heineken smirked and stifled a chuckle.

I needed to live long enough to escape from here and figure out my next move. I crossed my legs and noticed for the first time that they weren't bound. Only my torso and arms were tied to the chair.

Heineken went back to the earlier conversation topic and continued to bang on about lazy and venal Chinese, present company excluded, of course. I wasn't listening because I heard what sounded like hoof clomps coming from outside the open window to my left. Could it be? A long, loud, and throaty neigh confirmed it. Mistral. I'd know that sound anywhere.

Was she wandering about the Forbidden City untethered? Surely not, she'd have to be led by someone. Could it have been a coincidence that she neighed right outside the window of the very room where her owner was held captive? More pertinently, could I dive for the window? Did my captives have firearms concealed among their clothes? Could they put down their cigars and snifters long enough to lunge after me?

There were two guards stationed at the door on the far side of the room, long swords on their hips, but no firearms that I could see. A silk curtain covering the window wafted gently inwards on a breeze, almost beckoning me. I'm not normally prone to trust in fate, or even other people, come to that. But my future with these bigoted megalomaniacs would end badly for me, probably in the form of a painful death. There may be torture for information or simply amusement.

I had to take a leap. And hope that my friends and allies had my back, somehow. After all, I was trying to defend their country, my country. Didn't I deserve their help in my time of need?

Amid the sound of laughter—someone must have made a joke—I stood up, and the chair came with me, tied to my torso and arms. I sprinted in that awkward, crouched position straight to the curtained window, vaulted the ledge, twisted, and fell backward into the air. While falling, I heard the scuffle of boots on floorboards, someone shouting, and the sound of glasses crashing.

I landed hard on my back, though not as hard as I'd expected. On my back, my eyes were turned skyward, and I watched as one, then two, then three heads poked out of the window above. Broken chair parts were still tied to me, but I got free enough to kneel upright.

I looked around. I was in the back of a hay cart. The soft hay had broken my fall a little, though I still hurt all over. A fat and bloody mahogany splinter poked out of my hip. In front of me was Pearl, smiling back at me over her shoulder, in the driver's seat of the cart, with Mistral harnessed to the front.

She turned back to the reins and gave them a twitch, but Mistral was already on the case. Her hind leg muscles tensed and sprung her immediately into a gallop. I almost fell out the back of the open cart as I watched the faces of my former captors. Weng's was agape, Takagi scowled, and Heineken mashed his cigar to tatters between clenched teeth.

Their shock and discomfiture gave me a warm feeling of gratification, which was immediately replaced by the realisation that I was now a fugitive in one of the most fortified and heavily guarded places on Earth.

Chapter Thirty-Seven

I hoped that my former captors hadn't recognised Pearl. They could make her life very difficult indeed for aiding and abetting a fugitive. As in deathly difficult. She wore a felt hat whose broad brim was blowing back in the breeze made by our desperate flight, as she bounced about on the cart's driver's seat. I hoped she'd kept her face hidden.

As we galloped away from the shouts emanating from the window, I untied my bonds from the broken remains of the chair. That's when I noticed my shoulder in excruciating pain; it was dislocated. I took a deep breath and flung my torso against the back of the driver's seat to jam it back into place.

"Argh!"

Pearl, startled, looked back at me, her face blurred by the jostling of the cart now travelling at speed. The contraption was not made for speeds such as this. I hoped it would hold together for as long as it took us to get to—

"Where are we going?"

"You're welcome!" She shot back at me.

"Sorry. Thanks for the rescue. How did you—" I thought better of it. "Never mind. Where are we going?"

Pearl steered Mistral around a corner, the cart fishtailing behind. We raced along a lane, then around two more small buildings. She yanked on the reins and Mistral skidded to a halt. I tumbled forward, over the bench seat, past Pearl, and fell in a crumpled heap under Mistral's arse. I rolled over and stood up while Pearl unhitched Mistral from the cart. I yanked the splinter out of my hip. I held on to the side of the cart, waiting for dizziness to subside.

Pearl hissed, "Come on!"

Still in her Savile Row three-piece suit, her shirt having come untucked, billowing out behind her, she ran, leading Mistral by the bridle. I tried to keep up. We were switching back and forth through more narrow lanes, Mistral having to duck under several arches. Pearl looked like she knew exactly where she was going, and I was glad to be with someone who lived in the Forbidden City. We all three slipped and skidded around corners on the shiny paving stones like children running on polished floorboards in their socks. One last corner and we slid to a stop ten yards from a building with a pair of large double doors and a uniformed guard stationed in front of them.

He raised what looked like a ceremonial spear and pointed it at us. "What is your business here?"

Pearl said, "Just returning one of the horses to the stable. Stand aside."

"That nag's not one of ours. I think you're thieves."

"Thieves returning their loot?" I asked, one eyebrow raised.

Pearl feigned indignation. "How dare you! Don't you know who I am?" She removed her hat, strode right up to the man, and stood only a foot away from him, her hands on her hips. She was gorgeous when she was defiant. The top of her head was level with the man's chest.

I sidled closer as casually as I could, as did Mistral. I kept a close eye on his spear.

Recognition spread across his face as he looked down at the angry face staring up at him. "Consort Zhen! I apologise for my rudeness, but I have orders to prevent anyone but the master wrangler from entering the stables." Then his eyes narrowed. "Come to think of it, women aren't allowed anywhere near this area." He pulled something from his tunic and put it to his mouth and blew. A shrill and piercing note came from the device. A whistle. He was summoning more guards.

Pearl tried to reach up and grab the guard's arm, but he swivelled away from her grasp and blew harder, the noise loudly echoing off the walls of the surrounding buildings.

Mistral had casually sidled up closer to them both, and I swelled with pride as she opened her mouth wide and chomped down hard on the guard's shoulder. He screamed and dropped the whistle, and I rushed forward and gave him three hard punches in quick succession to his face and head. He fell silently to the ground, unconscious.

Maybe he was wearing cotton and Mistral was just hungry. Or maybe she was smarter than I gave her credit for.

"Open the other side, quick!" Pearl said, and we opened both doors all the way on their creaky iron hinges. All three of us ducked inside, me dragging the guard and pocketing his whistle, Pearl leading Mistral, and we closed the doors behind us. I found a rake and a shovel, and I slid both of their handles through the rings on the inside of the doors.

The unmistakable scent of hay, manure, and horse flesh met my nostrils. We were in a stable, with a dozen pens down each side, most of them empty, I counted only five horses as we passed their pens, one of whom became very excited when he saw Mistral. Or perhaps it was her scent. Must have been a stallion.

We walked to the end, opened the last pen, and went inside.

"We'll be safe here. For a little while anyway." Pearl noticed the blood covering my trousers. "Oh, you're hurt!" She knelt before me and deftly undid my belt and pulled my trousers and underpants all the way down to my ankles. Fond memories floated into my mind, but now was definitely not the time. Unaware that my mind had gone directly to an inappropriate place, as it did so often, she said, "It's still bleeding. Wait."

She stood up, reached into her own trousers, and pulled out a wad of pink fabric. Without embarrassment, she said, "You pounded me so hard the other night my period arrived early. Here, this is cotton, infused with PaoJiang oil. It's an herb that stops bleeding. See? I've worn it all day, and it's only a little pink. I'm down to a trickle. Hold it here." She held the wad to my hip, and I put my hand there to hold it. It gave off a sweet fragrance, like lemon ginger tea, while my blood mixed with hers, turning the cotton wad a deep red. We stood facing each other in silence for a minute. I heard the occasional shout and the sound of running feet outside the stable's timber walls, but no one had tried to get inside through the doors we'd barricaded.

We couldn't stay here for long, there'd have to be hundreds of palace guards out searching for us by now. I hoped that they'd assume we'd abandoned the horse and were fleeing toward one of the gates. They wouldn't know that Mistral was no ordinary beast of burden. Thus, I hoped that it didn't occur to anyone to come looking for us in a stable. But they'd get around to this building eventually, just to be thorough. I didn't know how many stables there were in the vast Forbidden City complex, but I felt sure it wouldn't take long for them to search them all.

I took stock. I'd failed to expose The Plot to anyone that might be convinced to do anything about it. Who would that be anyway? I'd only succeeded in exposing The Plot to its own architects. What an exercise in futility. And I was hiding in the best-guarded place in the eastern hemisphere, perhaps the world.

The words of that Kansu Brave came back to me. *"It's Cixi you want."*

I still didn't know what he meant. The Empress Dowager Cixi had only returned to power a few weeks before. Surely she couldn't have usurped the emperor entirely in such a brief time? Then again, she had been in charge for decades before her retirement only a few years ago. Maybe she was already every bit the dictator she had been?

And even though I didn't have the double-agent list that my former captors thought I had, I could still spin the yarn and just hope that the empress found it convincing. If the rumours were true that she was paranoid on the subject of plots against her, she might just take my story seriously.

I was right here, in the Forbidden City. Where she lived. I'd come this far; I couldn't give up now. I owed something to Jack, to Alex Purvis, and to the Chinese people. My people.

I was not at all comfortable with having a depraved despot as my last hope, but I was out of options. I had to tell Cixi the plot. She'd either execute me or believe me. Maybe both.

"Pearl. At dusk, I'm going to swim the lake to Pu'An Palace on Jade Island, Cixi's home, and sneak into her chambers, somehow."

Her eyes went wide. She pleaded, "Don't be so stupid! Please, Swagger, that's suicide! Her guards will kill you on sight!"

"I'll find a way. You should go. Try to get out of the Forbidden City. Leave and never come back."

"Now you *are* being silly. I can sneak back to my chambers from here. They're just on the other side of that back wall. A quick change of clothes and no one will be any the wiser."

"Seriously, Pearl. You were seen in that suit. Entering the gates earlier and helping me to escape. The guards will know it was you who helped me."

She flung her hat defiantly across the room, and it landed at a jaunty angle on the head of the stallion. "Bah! No guards are allowed in a consort's chambers, only eunuchs! I can brazen it out with them; they're easy to boss around. With this suit disposed of and me back in my demure robes, no one will dare contradict my story. Don't worry about me, Swagger. Go and do whatever idiotic thing your delusions compel you to do. I'll weep dutifully at your execution."

She spun on her heel and took a step toward the back wall. Then she stopped, turned to face me, and flung herself at me. We hugged in silence for a few moments, then without another word she disengaged, turned, and walked away, wiping something from her eye. I had something in my eye too. Dust, probably.

She reached the back wall, fondled one of the timber planks, and a concealed half-door opened. She went through it, and it sprung closed, blending seamlessly with the planks and slats.

I waited with Mistral in the quiet pen and retrieved my precious papers from under her saddle. I was going to have to leave her here. If I was successful, I'd be allowed to come back and retrieve her. If I wasn't, I'd be dead, and she'd be as well treated here as anywhere.

Chapter Thirty-Eight

I slipped into the warm water at dusk and breast-stroked my way quietly from the carved stone shore. It had been a long wait, hiding in the stable with Mistral all afternoon. At the sound of every footfall or shout I'd heard outside, I froze. But to my surprise, no one tried to enter. And when I ventured out, it was mealtime, and I encountered nobody.

Keeping only my eyes and nose above the water, I approached the embankment of the island upon which sat the Cixi's residence. To my left I saw the famous nineteen arch bridge. It had its usual complement of guards on the landward end, but they were leaning casually on their spears and smoking. Good, they weren't on the lookout for swimmers in the lake. I hoped that my pursuers would have assumed that I was trying to escape the Forbidden City. I couldn't possibly be stupid enough to try to get to see the Empress Dowager. That would be madness.

And it was. It was widely known that she executed those who displeased her even a little. That she'd stolen three million taels from the navy modernisation budget to renovate the Summer Palace and had herself a lavish party to celebrate her sixtieth birthday while the Japanese were slaughtering their way through Manchuria. Depraved despot though she was, she'd surely have something to say about an assassination plot against her, if she believed me. And if I could get past her guard contingent.

For better or worse (probably worse), I was going to try to talk to the genuine power in China and do my very best not to get executed.

I scrambled out of the water and over the embankment near the rear of the palace building. I crawled to the trunk of a tree and crouched, listening for any sign that my presence had been detected. I counted off three minutes while I decided on my next move. I crept to the next tree, then the next. They were the ever-present willows that surrounded every man-made lake I'd seen in China. I arrived at the base of one of the biggest ones. I climbed, careful not to break any of the smaller branches, lest the sound brought trouble my way. Looking up, I reckoned that one of the higher branches would afford me a decent view of the second-floor windows. There was a balcony protruding from the second floor, and a glow from inside illuminated the upper branches of the tree.

I reached the branch I had been aiming for and sat astride it, my legs dangling free. I could now see that the balcony had an insect screen running its full length, which made it impossible to see inside clearly. I could make out some shapes moving through the spacious room beyond as they passed between me and the interior lights, but little more. I needed to get closer.

I inched my way along the branch and with each movement, the branch sagged. I stood up on the branch and held myself steady with a smaller branch above. Then I heard a loud crack.

The branch I was on fell away from my feet, and the one I held on to above sagged low, then whipped back sharply, pulling me up like a slingshot. At the apex of the upswing, I lost my grip on the branch and let out an undignified yelp. I was flung upward, propelled through the screen, and smacked face-first into the balcony ceiling. Then I was weightless for a split second before gravity sent me smashing onto the balcony's hard stone floor.

I was on my back and watched stars twinkle at the edges of my vision. The inevitable pain arrived, and it was excruciating. I tried to move, but my limbs were reluctant, as if they weren't mine anymore. I felt sure that I'd broken all of my... well, everything.

As starry tunnel vision gradually gave way to normal vision, the image of a jowly, powdered face loomed over me with an expression of detached curiosity.

Jack Spratt's voice came, unbidden, into my thoughts. "Close enough for ya?" he had once chided me, while I was clinging desperately to a sapling on the vertical face of a cliff, a valley floor three hundred yards below. We had gone exploring the sacred mountain of TaiShan in Shandong, during a long weekend shortly after we had first arrived in China. I had wanted to see over the edge. Just a little closer...

I'd hoped to reconnoitre the interior of the residence from a tree branch, maybe even get a glimpse of the Empress Dowager herself, then retreat and strategize. Now I was close enough to count her chins.

She and I stared at each other; I think she was as dumbstruck as I was. A squeal from somewhere on my left broke the spell. I turned my head, pain shot through my neck, and I saw a servant having apoplexy at the sight that met his eyes. He held a pipe and looked like a terrified statue. It was evening, so I presumed this was the after-dinner tobacco. I could do with a smoke myself, right about now.

Another man rushed onto the balcony, summoned by the servant's squeal. Even in my dazed, recumbent state, I recognised him. Earl Li Hongzhang, Cixi's former chief advisor back before she retired. I understood he'd been majorly sidelined in recent times, exiled to frozen Harbin. The bejewelled hilt of his sword sparkled in the lamplight. I felt the skin on my neck burn.

Earl Li stared sternly at me for a moment, hand on hilt, legs apart in a fighting stance, ready to strike. I braced myself. Then his features suddenly softened. He threw his head back and laughed like a drain.

When his guffaw subsided, he said, "Well, well, well. If it isn't plucky Swageman of the IMCS. I began to wonder what had become of you. We all thought you were dead."

I must have been dreaming, surely. I'd knocked myself unconscious and was having one of those surreal dreams where people who are supposed to kill me end up making me a cup of tea instead. I shook my head and remembered that Earl Li and Robert Hart, my erstwhile boss, were known to be firm friends.

I wasn't yet able to speak, something was wrong with my mouth, but I was able to sit up onto my elbows and scooch backwards a little until I was awkwardly sitting on the floor with my back leaning against the balcony wall. I tried again to speak, and after a sharp cough, some hoarse words came out. "You know who I am?"

"Oh yes," said the Earl, "Robert asked me to keep a lookout for you. Give you sanctuary if you resurfaced. He said you might have discovered something of interest to me. To us." He indicated Cixi, who was now reclining in her elaborate lounge chair, the pipe held to her lips by the servant.

Robert Hart? Taking an interest in little old me?

I reached into my inside pocket and pulled out the sodden sheaf of papers. I tried to hand them to him, but I dropped them before he could reach them. The wet pile hit the ground with a slap.

Earl Li picked them up and began separating and leafing through them, passing each one to Cixi after he'd read it. When he got to the empty envelopes, the ones Jack had posted to himself in Seoul, the stamps fell off and fluttered to the ground next to my legs, the glue having given up the fight after repeated dunkings. I looked at the stamps honouring the Korean royal family. To fit everyone in the stamps were unusually large.

I looked up at Earl Li. Something was wrong. He was staring intently at the envelopes, his mouth wide and his eyebrows so high they made deep wrinkles in his forehead. After what seemed like minutes, he closed his mouth and turned to me. "Thank you. This is what we needed."

He handed the envelopes to Cixi. She looked at them and gave the Earl a satisfied nod before handing them back to him. He turned back to me. "There may be more agents working against us, but these names are a start. Dealing with them will go a long way to helping us win the fight."

"Names?"

"Here, under the stamps." He held the envelopes up and I could see that where the stamps had been there were a dozen names in Jack's tiny scrawl. Two envelopes, two lists. Not in opium bales. Under stamps. *Jack, you ingenious bugger.*

The Earl gathered the papers and the envelopes and put the bundle in his pocket. "Now, Mister Swageman, is there anything else we should know?"

I took a deep breath and told them everything I knew. Both the earl and the Empress Dowager listened without interruption. I told them about Heineken, Admiral Takagi, Grand Tutor Weng, and the eunuch Zhirui. About how they were furthering the aims of their combined superiors for the subjugation of the Middle Kingdom. I explained the elaborate plan to have the emperor rubber stamp all of Weng's suggestions. That Weng would thus implement directions from the Germans and Japanese.

I spoke of how Weng had convinced the emperor to order the Beiyang Fleet to hide in WeiHaiWei, so the Japanese could scoop it up and thus augment their own navy with the German-built warships.

I told them that Heineken and Takagi, and probably loads of subordinates I didn't know the names of, had tricked the remnants of the KoLaoHui and their sympathisers into helping them.

The objective? Kill Cixi and her supporters, leave the emperor in place and nominally in charge, and run the place for the benefit of the kaiser, the tzar and the shoguns, and anyone else not Chinese.

I finished with, "Your Majesty, if the traitors succeed, China, as you know it, will cease to exist."

It was an unthinkable breach of court protocol to speak directly with Cixi. Most every man she needed to communicate with had to have discussions with her through a screen. That's why I told the whole story in a rush, before I was dragged away for breaches of protocol and a long list of other crimes.

Cixi and Earl Li looked at each other for a few moments. The earl opened his mouth to speak but was interrupted by a loud commotion. It came from the room behind the balcony doorway in which Li was standing.

Li turned and stood inside the doorway, facing the intruders. I leaned over and could see that it was Weng, Takagi and Heineken, and four of their guards.

Seeing me, Weng shouted, "There's the traitor!"

His guards took a step forward but hesitated when they saw Earl Li striding up to Weng.

Li slapped Weng in the face, hard. Weng squealed and held his face in his hand, like a jilted lover. To Takagi he said, "Did you really think the kaiser would help bring back the old days of the shogunate? Oust the Meiji emperor?" There was a pause, then Li threw his head back and laughed, while Takagi's face turned a shade of red so dark, I thought his eyes would pop out.

Heineken didn't move, and the guards remained still in the presence of Li. I looked at Cixi and she wore a sly grin as she reached up and pulled on a tasselled string hanging at her shoulder.

While the group in the room eyed each other like roosters in a cockpit, I heard the pounding of boots somewhere. A dozen men burst into the room, carrying rifles. I recognised the turbans, the beards, and the beaded necklaces. The Kansu Braves. I praised Allah.

Without a word, except for some grunted protests by Weng and Heineken, the Braves held the arms of what were now prisoners high behind their backs, in an immobilising hold, and frog-marched them out of the room.

Chapter Thirty-Nine

I was still sitting on the balcony floor, leaning forward, tense at the events concluding inside the room. Was there a guard on his way to take me to the dungeons for some bastinado?

As the sound of the protestations and footfalls of the prisoners and guards receded down the hall, Earl Li came back to the balcony with no guards in tow. A wave of relief and exhaustion swept over me. I slumped back against the balcony wall.

I would live through this, and the people that could do something about The Plot seemed to have it in hand. I hoped so. Because I was spent, I could do no more.

I looked at Cixi's stockinged legs. She had remained seated and my position on the floor gave me an excellent view of her knees. I had broken just about every rule of protocol in the book. I looked up at her face. She was looking at Li. An unwanted thought came into my head. Sometimes messengers get shot. People have been beaten to death for less serious breaches of Imperial protocol.

Li looked down at me. "I lost track of you when you fled from the *ZhenYuen* off the coast of Dalian. McGiffin had been keeping me informed of your progress, like the good ex-Pinkertons man he is. Tyler too, when he had the chance."

Tyler? But he's one of them, isn't he?

Li read my face. "Oh yes, he's one of mine. Embedded with Heineken for the last year or so. That reminds me, do you have any thoughts on what is to be done about Cuifang?"

"Who, Anee? What about her?"

"Surely you want some measure of revenge for the murder of your friend? Though I'd prefer to leave her in place. She could lead us to some powerful people within the Japanese hierarchy. She moves easily in those circles. Beauty has its uses."

In my punch-drunk state, it took me a second to glean his meaning. Li had just implicated Anee in Jack's murder. That was a turnup for the books. I wouldn't have spotted that in a million years. But then, I have it on reliable authority that I have something of a blind spot when it comes to the fairer sex. Still, I had a hard time believing she was evil. Perhaps she was being blackmailed?

Not expecting an answer from me about Anee, Li continued. "As to you, why didn't you come to me sooner? Why all this storming of the palace business?"

How was I to know who ruled the roost? How could I know who could or would be interested in saving the kingdom from being invaded and plundered? The Imperial Court had always been a seething hotbed of switching loyalties, private agendas, and vested interests. "Well, I wasn't sure who was really in charge, I mean..." I stumbled there, not quite sure how to put it. "Um... I couldn't be sure that my claims would meet with a sympathetic ear, if you know what I mean."

"You believe the rumours about our empress?"

Uh oh. The answer was a resounding 'yes', but I was trying hard not to say it. These were treacherous waters. I had to take care, lest I lose my head. "Hell no, but—"

"Let me set you straight on a few things. Firstly, you've heard how the restoration of the Summer Palace cost tens of millions of taels. Funds diverted from the project to modernise the navy. Yes?"

"Oh, well, maybe some poorly written newspaper articles—"

"You might be interested to know that the empress here used three million of her own money, saved from her Imperial Court stipend. That was augmented with some three million from the navy modernisation project. None of the principal, mind you, just the interest the funds earned in a foreign bank. Rothschilds, wasn't it?" This last to Cixi, who nodded. "The principal remained intact, and is there still, waiting to be consumed in buying ships, training sailors, etc. Thus, there was no reduction in the funds available to the navy.

It was the empress herself, against advice from the court, who set the navy, ten years ago, on the path to modernisation. But the simpleton emperor cut the funding, on Weng's advice, and let the whole thing slide. The money is still there today, untouched."

That was hard to swallow. Everyone knew how Cixi craved only comfort for herself. "Why not tell that kind of thing to the newspapers? Surely, they must—"

"Secondly," Li cut me off. He was on a roll. "It was widely reported that the empress was ignoring the Japanese threat, concentrating instead on her birthday celebrations, 'fiddling while Rome burned', as one columnist put it. Did the papers also report that she tried to cancel the entire thing? No, that isn't sensational enough! Doesn't fit their portrayal of their head of state. She was persuaded, by the court, to hold only a small ceremony, to keep the public from panicking."

Who would have panicked? Not me. It was true, though, that the Chinese might have regarded the absence of celebrations for an important milestone birthday as portentous. The peasantry might have taken it as a sign that their rulers were anxious. That might have given them pause.

Li's lecture wasn't finished. "It's outrageous! Some, in the press, have even accused the Empress of doing too little to prepare for war with the Japanese. Well, of course! She was barred from participation by her emperor! She was deliberately excluded from all court meetings and all news to her was blocked. She was retired, you remember, and thus prevented from receiving any information about anything! When the empress was finally able to regain these lines of communication, after the emperor had messed things up so thoroughly, it was too late. The Japanese advance was well underway. By then the emperor's neglect of the military proved to have made defeat inevitable."

I ventured some input. "The public seems to believe—"

"What? What do they believe? That the emperor is a 'tragic hero' who did his best in impossible circumstances? Eh? Bah!"

I kept quiet. He'd keep going and only interrupt me if I spoke up. I just had to wait.

"He's a pampered child who banishes anyone who dares tell him the truth. He wants only to hear pleasant news about his kingdom. He knows nothing about wielding power, hampered by an effete tutor who is equally ill-equipped to deal with such grand matters."

"The true source of these rumours is the press. The *Japanese-owned* press. Did you know that eighty percent of all newspapers circulating in China are foreign-owned?" I didn't. "I have advised the empress many times to close down the Japanese-owned newspapers, but she is too kind to execute those who slander her."

He shot her a submissive grin and bowed his head a little. She mirrored the expression and the movement, and they both went back to looking at me.

"She knows about it, of course. The empress is wise in the ways of modern diplomacy. But I have ventured the opinion that this viewpoint is too generous and benign. I'd burn the presses to the ground if given the chance. She only cares about the health of the country and of her people. She is a statesman par excellence." He paused for a few breaths.

I waited to hear more, but no more came. He'd finished. Finally.

He called for some tea and tobacco. He went into the room and came out with two cushions. Placing them on the floor facing Cixi, he sat down on one and indicated that I should do the same. I wasn't at all sure that I could. As I tried to stand, my shoulder and hip sent bolts of pain into my back, and I grunted loudly. I gave up trying to stand and rolled onto my hands and knees, crawling to the cushion. I sat on it, cross-legged, like a kindergarten student at the feet of the teacher. Pearl's bloody sponge fell off my hip and onto the floor.

A servant brought in a tray with a teapot, cups, and two pipes stuffed with tobacco, then poured some tea and withdrew. We sipped and smoked in silence for several minutes, Cixi holding her own pipe this time.

All this talk of how everyone had got it wrong and Cixi was diligently working solely in China's best interests, struck me as plausible but unlikely. I'd have to keep my own counsel on that score. If Earl Li was right, then, statesman or not, Cixi was doing a terrible job of publicity. I recalled being forced to read P.T. Barnum's autobiography while in high school. Barnum had a lot to say on the topic of publicity, much of it going against the grain of general thinking on the topic. I wondered if I'd be able to get translated copies of the book for both Li and Cixi.

Hoping to change the topic, I turned to Li. "What now? What will happen to Heineken and the others? Weng. What will happen to him? The emperor would surely have something to say if his tutor and mentor is tortured to death, though it's nothing less than he deserves. And if it does happen, can I watch?"

"Alas, Grand Tutor Weng will have to be left in place, but his wings will be severely clipped." Li smiled. I suspected he had elaborate and devious plans for the tutor. Plans that he relished.

Cixi had said nothing directly to me since I landed on my arse on the balcony. I thought nothing of it, given that protocol dictated that no man could speak directly to her, nor she to them. I looked up at her. Through a waft of tobacco smoke, she astonished me by talking directly to me, with a piercing intensity to her eyes, and somehow making her pixie voice sonorous. "My very good friend Robert Hart will be pleased with your diligence."

Well, if she can talk directly to me, then I can talk directly back. Politely, though. "Alas, your majesty, I've been fired, by one who is not part of this conspiracy, but an utter fucking bastard, nonetheless."

I heard a sharp intake of breath from Li.

She gave a chuckle and to my astonishment, little smoke rings came out of the royal throat. She said, "I'll have a word with Robert..."

Chapter Forty

Earl Li arranged for me to be fed and washed, my wounds tended to, and gave me a comfortable bed for the night, with two well-trained female companions. He told me he had taken similar care of Mistral, and I wondered if he was referring to that stallion.

I woke the next morning stiff and sore and alone, not sure where I was. I stared at the ceiling, willing my body to heal itself. A servant entered the room with coffee and a steaming bowl of salty porridge. I sat up, grimaced a few times, and sipped the coffee while listening to birds twitter outside the window.

I remained trepidatious about the progress of the Japanese. Executed conspirators aside, they were still a formidable military force. How far into China could they invade? Could diplomatic manoeuvrings halt or even slow their progress? How much territory would China have to concede?

More importantly, much more, what about me? Did I have a future in this country? I seemed to have powerful new friends. Cixi and Earl Li might well be able to convince Robert Hart to re-employ me. But after my adventures, could I be satisfied with a mundane job as a mid-level functionary of the IMCS? And would a position I might be given have any opportunities for graft?

I no longer felt like an impartial visitor to this country, dispassionately watching foreign powers snatching territories from her beleaguered owners, the Chinese people. For I was one of them. I knew that now.

I finished my coffee and the filling porridge then rolled over and went back to sleep, thinking, Well, *Que sera sera*.

Four peaceful days later, I was well enough to walk without help. Earl Li himself escorted me to the Forbidden City south gate, the big one that important people came through. We strolled and talked, and I voiced my concerns about China's future.

Li said, "It will be turbulent, that's a certainty. Those craving wealth and power will always exploit the weaknesses of the powerless. Kick 'em while they're down to get ahead."

He went on to explain how the Russians also planned to betray the Japanese; they had already begun diplomatic talks with other foreign powers to swipe the Liaodong Peninsula from the Japanese. The war was not yet officially over, and the Japanese had expended a great deal of time, men and munitions turning that peninsula into a bloodbath. The Russians wanted it and were busy doing behind-the-scenes manoeuvring to get it, leveraging off the outrage the international community expressed over what had now become known as the 'Port Arthur Massacre.'

It seemed to me, however, that Europeans simply could not countenance the notion that any of the Yellow Peril be allowed to grow strong, be they Japanese or Chinese. They had invited no Chinese representatives to the diplomatic talks.

I said, "The kaiser, with his withered arm and rampant bigotry, won't settle for anything less than a substantial colony in a resource-rich area of China's east coast."

"I know. I know." Li looked a little downcast. "We'll just have to watch and act as best we can. You know, Kaiser Wilhelm was only helping the Japanese to conquer China so that the Russians could then usurp the Japanese and take over again. That was the plan all along. Thus would Kaiser Bill and his Cousin Nick the tzar become the largest empire the world has ever seen. The two are playing catch-up, hoping to outdo their grandmother, Queen Victoria. It's a game of aristocratic chess, with the Middle Kingdom the field."

"And the Japanese as pawns. That must rankle. Have you advised the emperor? Has he any idea of the forces lined up against him?"

"No. Cixi knows, but the emperor is frail and sickly, and rather stupid. Always has been. Those that deliver unwelcome news to him are quietly sidelined. Some are exiled. That's why I shielded him from the worst of the war news. I only gave Cixi the whole rotten truth."

We walked in silence for a few minutes. Winter was coming, and the trees had shed all of their leaves, which crunched underfoot. I said, "If the Qing decide to approve railroad construction, be sure and exclude a company called Rocky Mountain Railroad. Oh, and keep away from Barings Bank, they're dodgy too."

He patted me on the shoulder like an indulgent uncle. "Yes, Phillip, we're way ahead of you there."

We parted at the gate where Mistral was waiting for me, all brushed and shiny, and sporting a stylish black saddle. I was surprised and delighted to see that standing next to her and holding her reins was that Kansu Brave who had saved my life.

Using English, which surprised me even more, he said, "She's a spirited one, this girl. A magnificent specimen. If I were you, I wouldn't leave her in the hands of these monkeys." He pointed to the regular palace guards at the gate, only a few yards away. He didn't want them to take offence. There were quite enough rivalries amongst the guard contingents at the palace, hence his use of my native tongue.

He leaned closer and spoke conspiratorially into my ear. "Got him in one stroke." He grinned proudly.

"Who?"

"The Jap. Yesterday morning at dawn. Earl Li didn't think I could do it. We made a wager. I sharpened my sword all night and practiced on a cow carcass."

Admiral Takagi. The Kansu Brave was talking about his execution. "You got him in one stroke, you say?"

"His head came clean off. I wish you'd seen it. Wiped the smile off that bastard's face, I can tell you. His head rolled all over the floor while blood from his neck spurted six feet into the air. I won five taels."

"Congratulations. If I am ever under your blade, make it quick, won't you?"

He laughed loudly and slapped me on the back hard enough to dislocate my shoulder again. "Keep your nose clean so the situation will never arise."

He handed me the reins, and we embraced for a full minute. We shook hands, and I walked away, leading Mistral, southwards under the gate and into the bustling and dusty maelstrom that is our northern capital, Beijing.

Epilogue

Some weeks later I was in a classroom, of all places. Foolishly, I had volunteered to give some classes to Chinese peasants. It was a program run by the IMCS, sponsored by Hart with Cixi's blessing. It was adult literacy in Mandarin Chinese. Astonishingly, the national literacy rate in China was barely thirteen percent, and it was believed that a people who could read would be better equipped to prosper. I believed that it was also hoped that literate peasants would be less likely to believe every rumour that circulated. Perhaps Cixi was finally learning the value of good public relations. An informed populace might better understand what their leaders were up to. The good and the bad.

In the classroom, I kept such thoughts to myself. I just hoped that some education might make the peasants a little harder to exploit.

The Dongying locals treated me embarrassingly well with gifts and compliments and invitations to delicious meals. Teachers enjoy high status in China. Naturally, I still felt like an imposter. What do I know about teaching? But at least I felt Chinese.

The conspirators were executed or exiled. Except for Heineken, who fled to Hong Kong, then to Germany to bask in the embrace of the kaiser's empire-building machine. The Plot was exposed and stopped, but Kaiser Bill wouldn't give up so easily; I was certain we'd feel the sting of his colonial ambitions again, and soon.

I had been re-hired and promoted at the IMCS, thanks to Cixi and Hart. I even got to meet the diminutive Irishman himself at his Beijing home. I was treated to one of his extraordinary parties, where he entertained guests with a brass band that he led himself. I hate brass band music almost as much as I hate opera, but the food, wine and company were excellent. I was invited to what was described as an 'after-party' by the wife of a senior British diplomat, but when we arrived at the house, the diplomat turned out to be away on business, and the only attendees at this 'party' were the woman and myself. A fine time was had by both.

Much later, once I'd returned to Dongying (by train, no less) I was gratified to learn that Dickinson had been transferred to Harbin in the frozen north. A fitting exile. Cynthia Dickinson stayed in Dongying, claiming that the cold would give her rheumatism. I should go and visit her to console her in her loneliness.

I read in a newspaper an account of the massacre at Lushun. The article condemned the Japanese for fabricating the reports of strung-up Japanese soldiers to justify their slaughter. I smiled and doubted the truth would ever come out. That Germans had done the deed that incited the atrocity, motivating the Japanese to cut their murderous swathe through Manchuria, which served the German agenda perfectly. The international condemnation led to the peninsula being taken away from the Japanese and given to the Russians, as predicted. I had to admire the cleverness of the strategy. The kaiser and the tzar played a long game and got exactly what they wanted.

With the help of some foreign troops, the Chinese Army had miraculously learned to shoot straight and stop the Japanese advance, though not repel it. The Japanese remained entrenched in Manchuria, holding firm. The diplomatic manoeuvrings Earl Li had spoken of had already begun. Yes, the Russians got the Liaodong Peninsula, but the Japanese were allowed to keep Korea. And they knew how to hold a grudge; they'd try to get back what they believed to be theirs somehow. I could feel it. The Liaodong Peninsula had such a useful deep-water port in Lushun that I felt sure that foreigners would fight over it for decades.

A wry smile spread across my face when I learned that even before the talks concluded the Russians had put it about that they'd be delighted to allow some extensive railroad building to get underway. And maybe even some mining.

At an international diplomatic level, the fact that China might have an objection to chunks of its coastline being traded between one imperial power and another, was neither here nor there. Again, no Chinese were invited to the talks. China would continue to shrink for the foreseeable future, the only arguments being between the looters as to who got which chunk.

Dongying was the same, but different. It was Christmas, an event about which the Chinese cared not a jot, and neither did I. It snowed yesterday and the city looked stunning in white. I looked at the snow falling in the twilight outside the classroom window. I needed to wrap up my class. We were running overtime, again. I guess I talk too much.

I had an appointment with Consort Pearl, visiting from Beijing. The appointment was to be in soft hay, in the loft above the swanky stables where Mistal languished in equine luxury.

I ended the class and dismissed the students. A lean and athletic man hung back and approached me when the others had left. He asked for a quiet word. He told me he and his buddies engaged in a special kind of exercise and would I like to join them. He said that the exercise was based on a kind of fighting. He called it Yihequan, which I knew translated as 'Righteous and Harmonious Fists'. In my mind, I scoffed at the grandiose name. But I was a little out of shape, and if Pearl chose to make more frequent visits to Dongying, as I hoped, then I was going to need more physical endurance. I told him I'd be interested in joining him and his buddies in some callisthenics.

Thus it was that I accidentally joined the Boxers. And didn't *that* complicate my life?

But that's a story for another time.

Historical Note

I may have taken some liberties...

The old cliché about history being written by the victors is true here too. The many English language history texts I consulted on this period of China's past are unapologetic about imperialism and colonialism. The term 'scramble for concessions' was used often in these texts and is much more benign than a more accurate description; conquer, invade, and occupy chunks of another country, for profit. Many of the British newspaper reports of the time quoted only British officials, the journalists being mostly unable to understand the local lingo. Thus the victors portrayed events in China as victories for their respective empires. Colonel Claude MacDonald, Her Majesty's Minister in China, was well known for his sexist and bigoted opinions, and is quoted widely in historical texts. This could be why the Empress Dowager Cixi is still described on Wikipedia as a depraved despot who was anti reform. Some recent documents unearthed in Europe and Japan indicate that she was anything but. She had officials looking into turning China into a constitutional monarchy, modelled along the lines of the British system.

For the Chinese, on the other hand, the period from the first Opium War of 1842 to the end of World War Two (when the Japanese were finally kicked out of China after fifty years of occupation) is known as China's 'century of humiliation'. China shrank during this period, and to this day she is yet to recover much of her lost territory.

In addition to English language texts, I consulted some translated texts from Chinese scholars, and while the tone was more condemnatory of the imperialists, the events weren't as different as I'd expected. Dates and places lined up perfectly, and there was a merciful absence of revisionism or propaganda. Naturally, they portray foreign invaders as, well, foreign invaders, a position I find it hard to argue with. I also ran my story past a Chinese scholar friend to make sure I hadn't messed up too many names of people and places.

The only liberties I've taken with history are ones of time compression. For the narrative to be compelling, I needed to have some historical events happen in quick succession, though they may have occurred months apart. Events like the Sino-Japanese war or the Boxer Uprising were a slow burn, unfolding over many months or even years. Rather than have our hero cooling his heels in his office or in an opium den for months, I decided to bend time a little to keep the action going.

While I study history, I'm on the lookout for characters that can play a role in the story. I'm keeping my eyes peeled for friends, lovers, victims, mentors, villains, etc... Then as I write the narrative some of the characters change, often for the worse. If a historical figure morphs into a bastard during the writing, I change his or her name to avoid having any descendants coming after me. If I portray them more or less as they were, they retain their real name. For example, Count Von Waldersee was as much of a deluded brutal scumbag as he is portrayed herein, determined to become known to history as the 'Conqueror of the Chinese', regarding all Asians as 'Heathen Yellow Savages'. If his descendants come after me, I say bring it on.

I have a mailing list, if you're interested in hearing about upcoming books from me. The signup page is on my website. I promise not to spam you with crap verbiage:

https://www.matthewwaiteauthor.com/

Coming soon...
Swagger Book Two: Righteous Fist
Chapter One

I t hurt when I breathed. One of my ribs was probably cracked.

My assigned opponent had kicked me in the sternum, and I'd gone down like a sack of rice, gasping in the sand. I rolled to one side and sat on my haunches, spitting sand and taking shallow breaths. I hadn't realized that calisthenics was a contact sport. I'd come to the beach at dawn for an exercise class. The first red flag should have been the class's title: "The Righteous and Harmonious Fists," "Yihequan" in Chinese. The righteous foot that had buried itself in my chest told my oxygen-starved brain that I might be in the wrong place.

But I *was* in the right place. Yantai was lovely in the Spring, and my workload was modest. Here on the beach, with the bustling city just over the dunes to the west, I could see the Yi river languidly pour its silt-laden golden water into Moon Bay, which opened out to become the Bohai Sea. Sadly, the river water had recently been made toxic by a mining accident upstream. Corrupt Manchu officials had been blamed for allowing toxic metals to leech into the river. The river still looked pretty, but I resolved not to eat river fish for a while.

An offshore breeze brought the bitter lemon scent of flowering Mulberry trees just beyond the grassy dune. Salt-stained fishing junks rested on logs on the sand, ready to be hauled into the water come sunset. I watched a group of women sitting on the beach, mending nets and gossiping. The breeze also brought the smell of wheat noodles with pork and boiled cabbage. Breakfast beckoned.

The pain in my chest eased, and I looked up at my assigned opponent, a pig of a man named Hao Zhang, and he was still scowling triumphantly down at me with his one eye while I tried to figure out if I'd been on the receiving end of genuine malice, or merely over-enthusiastic sparring. I wasn't aware of having wronged the man in any way, but I had to concede to myself that I may have. I was a Customs Inspector at the Chinese Imperial Maritime Customs Service or IMCS for short. I put a lot of noses out of joint in that job. Nobody likes the taxman. Perhaps he was an importer who didn't know that all he needed to do to gain a partial exemption from import tariffs was to discretely hand me the occasional envelope of cash. Baksheesh was a tradition as old as China, and I saw no reason to opt out of the custom.

Or perhaps he was the father or husband of that gorgeous and enthusiastic waitress that I spent the previous evening with.

The class's instructor, Fang, came over, shouldered Hao Zhang aside, and helped me up. Hao Zhang slunk away. "You alright there, teacher?" In addition to my customs duties, I did a little literacy tutoring in the evenings, hence the instructor calling me 'teacher.' My Chinese is excellent, having been well schooled by my Chinese mother. My father is British, and I was raised in the remote north of Australia. In the genetic soup from which I had sprung, I was blessed with my father's height of six -foot-one, and my mother's Chinese features of black hair and dark brown eyes. Both mother and father had an aristocratic demeanor and were most insistent that I learn English and Mandarin thoroughly enough to be able to speak both like a native. Just how they came to find themselves exiled in Darwin was a mystery, they fobbed me off whenever I tried to prize the history out of them.

Shandong was proudly agricultural, the breadbasket of the nation, but its people were mostly illiterate. It was 1899, on the cusp of a new century, and the Qing Dynasty government wanted China to enter it with something higher than a thirteen percent literacy rate. To that end, the IMCS had been asked to hold classes for the local peasants, and I'd drawn the short straw, being the only person on staff fluent enough. Hence the 'teacher' moniker.

"Yeah, Fang. I'm okay," I wheezed. "I didn't realize this class was going to be so rough."

"The coming struggle will be merciless. We all need to be ready."

"I won't be participating in any coming struggle, old mate. I'm just here for the exercise." Revolutionary talk was nothing new. People spoke of imminent uprisings all the time. Shandong people, in particular, had a reputation for being pugnacious. Starting an uprising here would be as easy as lighting a match.

Fang squinted up at me and raised his hand to sheild his eyes from the rising sun. "Maybe you'll have no choice but to participate."

"You've got me mixed up with someone else," I said, gathering up my jacket and brushing the sand off it. "I love it here, but I'm not a permanent fixture. My bosses will move me on sooner or later. Speaking of moving on, it's breakfast time." Fang smiled and gave me the baoquan li, the fist-and-palm salute, and bowed slightly. I did the same, turned, and walked in the direction of the noodle scent that had been getting stronger.

I'd gone only a few steps up the scrubby dune when a strong hand clasped around my upper arm. Fearing further fisticuff I spun around with my other arm raised, and my feet ready to deliver a high kick. But I needn't have done so, I'd been stopped by a woman holding a fishing net. She let my arm go and was now wringing her hands. Her brow was furrowed. "Mister teacher, my sons are missing." Now I recognized her from one of my classes. She'd invited me to her home for dinner to thank me for teaching her sons to read Mandarin characters. We had a lavish family dinner in their modest shack near the beach. The man of the house was a successful fisherman with two boats. When the sons inherited the business, they'd have a boat each. We'd eaten lobster, crab, mussels, and octopus, all washed down with one of Shandong's most lethal plum wines.

Her name finally came to me. "Mrs. Song, what's happened?"

"Liu and Fu snuck out after supper last night. Their beds have not been slept in. My husband had to cast off the boats this morning without them. He's out fishing with the crew. Can you help me find the boys?"

"I'm sorry, Mrs. Song, I can't. My duties. But they are almost men, and they have only been missing for one night. Please don't worry. I'm sure they'll be back soon." The boys would come back. There were half a dozen places in town where a man of any age could imbibe booze and opium and spend the night in the arms of skilled and alluring women. Such an evening's entertainment didn't come cheap, but there was much to recommend it. If I could afford it, I'd be doing that every night. Mrs. Song's sons would be sleeping off a hangover in one of the dens and would stagger home when the proprietor kicked them out. She looked unconvinced. "Look. If they haven't come home by supper time tonight, come and find me, and we'll start a search. Fair enough?"

She nodded, but her brow remained furrowed. I gave her my most empathetic smile and left her there on the sand.

I walked through the little grove of Mulberry trees on the fringes of the beach, grateful for the shade. Beyond the grove I sauntered along the boulevard that would take me to my breakfast meeting. It was lined with carefully manicured Ginko trees that were said to have been planted by Confucius himself, whose birthplace was only a few hundred miles from here. I knew Ginko trees were long-lived, but I was skeptical that these ones could have been planted two and a half thousand years ago. The Chinese love a good legend, no matter how thinly it stretches the truth. I liked that about them. It was a shame the Ginko trees gave off a stench that was like a soldier's socks.

The day was only an hour old, and Yantai was already a hive of activity, with everyone on the streets carrying or hauling goods of some kind, wearing rough cotton tunics of every shade of brown.

I handed a coin to a man hauling a cart of fish. He nodded and took the coin. I jumped up onto his cart and enjoyed the slow ride. Yantai was prosperous enough to have smooth, slate-paved roads in the town, for which my arse was grateful. The same slate covered the walls and roofs of the two-story buildings which lined the street. Businesses on the ground floor, dwellings above, and laundry hung from bamboo poles wedged into the upper story window frames. No smoke emanated from chimneys, spring was well underway, and it felt as if we were in for a hot summer.

We passed a larger building that loomed over the rest of the street; Customs House. It was made from the same slate, but its architecture was steadfastly European, with Doric columns, parapets on the roof, and an elaborate portico entrance. My office was in there, but I wasn't due at work for another couple of hours. My chosen breakfast venue, however, was on the opposite side of the street, about two hundred yards beyond Customs House. I slipped off the moving cart and patted the man on the back by way of thanks.

I paused before crossing the pavement and entering the café. The man I was hoping to dine with was a man of many moods and bewildering mood swings, and loyalties so mixed I could never figure out where he stood. He'd got word to me that we simply *had* to meet, urgently. The fact that he'd been in Berlin until recently made me wonder if I really wanted to hear what he had to say. Only a few years ago I got mixed up in geopolitics and was lucky to come out alive. I hoped against hope that his news was mundane, and wouldn't complicate my life, just when I'd got it running right.

Don't miss out!

Visit the website below and you can sign up to receive emails whenever Matthew Waite publishes a new book. There's no charge and no obligation.

https://books2read.com/r/B-A-IIWR-DTWYB

BOOKS 2 READ

Connecting independent readers to independent writers.

About the Author

I fell in love with China's people and history when I began teaching in Shandong Province some years ago. I'm an Australian man of no fixed address, teacher, writer, biker, sailor, with the hands of a surgeon and the body clock of a brothel owner.

Lightning Source UK Ltd.
Milton Keynes UK
UKHW012103020123
414739UK00008B/86